MONST

MIDWAY
1969
Sex, Drugs, Rock 'n' Roll, Viet Nam, Civil Rights, and Football
2d Edition
Jeff Rasley

Copyright 2016 Jeff Rasley (all rights reserved)
Published by Midsummer Books
Indianapolis, Indiana
http://www.jeffreyrasley.com

ISBN-13:
978-1540856210

ISBN-10:
1540856216

Original eBook publication of 1st edition by Midsummer
Books: April 10, 2012

Dedicated to the University of Chicago; my football coaches at UChicago, Walter Hass, Chet McGraw, Jesse Vail, Dan Tepke, and Bill Horgan; Maroons who played on the 1969-71 teams; my teammates on the 1974-75 teams; my wife Alicia, my parents, and the other loyal fans who braved the cold winds off Lake Michigan with only the comfort of hot peppermint schnapps and cheers of "Themistocles, Thucydides, the Peloponnesian War ..."

2010 Maroons, University Athletic Association champions

Acknowledgements and thanks for historical information and photos to Dave Hilbert and the University of Chicago Athletic Department, UChicago Archival Photographic Files, *University of Chicago Magazine* and *The Maroon* archives; members and supporters of the "resurrection era" football Maroons, especially Martin Northway, Dick Rubesch, Don Bingle, and Doug Richards; Al Gore for inventing the Internet; Wikipedia; and Alicia Rasley for helping to jog and/or confirm memories.

Those familiar with UChicago, Hyde Park, or Chicago during the 1960s and 70s might wish to read the Author's Note and Disclaimer at the end of the book prior to reading the text. For literary reasons and to save trees, historical and fictional events during the years and football seasons of 1969 through 1975 are compressed into three years, 1969-71.

Terminology sticklers please note that "U of C" is commonly used throughout this work, because that was the convention during the relevant time periods. "UChicago" has become the preferred shorthand for University of Chicago in more recent years. It is used when appropriate.

Chicago Football history, as I have learned it, is contained within these pages, particularly in Chapters 2, 26, and 30. However, this is also a work of fiction, romance, and comedy. Characters may be inspired by persons known to the author, but, except for actual historical persons named, all others are fictional.

-1-

Jack Blair ran all out toward the end zone. The opposing safety back pedaled for all he was worth. Jack cut left. It didn't work. The safety broke into a run shadowing him. Jack lowered his head and pumped his arms churning his long legs as hard as he could, but the safety stayed with him. Head fake right! The DB reacted shifting his shoulders. A tiny loss of momentum by his pursuer gave Jack the break he needed.

Jack launched his body into the air. The safety leaped after him. The ball was already air borne arcing toward the two opposing sets of hands. Jack stretched every fiber of muscles, tendons, and ligaments to the limit his fifteen-year old six-foot frame allowed. The tips of the fingers on his out-stretched left hand contacted the spiraling tip of the football. Jack opened his mouth and roared "Aahh!" He somehow elevated another inch before gravity and the weight of the safety on his back clawing at Jack's arms brought him crashing toward the ground.

As the ground rose up to meet him Jack pulled the ball into his body and extended the toes of his trailing right foot dragging his cleats across the back line of the end zone. Whump! He landed hard with the ball clutched to his chest. The face guard of his helmet smacked the ground bouncing his head against the pads inside his helmet.

Jack twisted away from the panting safety, pushed him off and rolled over onto his elbow. He looked up to see the back judge running toward him blowing his whistle with hands cupped together above his head in the sacred prayer-like symbol of touchdown.

That score sealed a victory for the fighting Owls of Seymour Indiana the last game of their 1965 season. The touchdown catch turned out to be the last play of Jack Blair's high school football career. But his high school football

experience did not quite end with that successful bang. It
ended with more of a whimper the following August.

Jack turned in his pads and practice uniform at the end
of the two weeks of preseason double-practices his junior
year in high school. He decided to quit the third day of
doubles. He waited to inform the coach until the two weeks
of grueling daily double-practices were over. He didn't want
to be accused by the coach or his teammates of quitting
because he wasn't tough enough. Sure, surviving the four
hours of football drills in the August humidity of Southern
Indiana was tough. But that was not the reason Jack quit the
football team.

One reason he quit was based on a cost-benefit analysis.
The cost of giving up every autumn to football was not worth
the benefit. He was already a three-sport letterman for the
Owls in football, swimming, and track. In what little spare
time he had, Jack loved to hike the hills and fish the streams
of the backwoods around his home in Jackson County,
Indiana. When he finished with summer chores, he also
loved to sit under the big oak tree in the front yard of the
Blairs' farmhouse reading a book. Solitude with Nature and
improving his mind through reading touched Jack Blair's
soul in a way that playing football did not.

Jack did love playing sports and he enjoyed being part of
a team. He recognized that his loner tendency, if given too
much rein, could be unhealthy and needed to be tempered
with a social life. In small-town Indiana playing on sports
teams was one of the few available social outlets. But, while
he liked playing football and being on a team with his high
school buddies, he considered most of the time spent in
practice an utter waste of time. It was not playing football. In
swimming, the team swam. During track season, the runners
ran. Preseason football practice was spent doing boring and,
in Jack's mind, needlessly painful drills. Bear crawls, push-
ups, barrel rolls, neck bridges, and jumping jacks consumed
large chunks of practice time.

Another reason Jack quit football was the result of serious self and social examination. He was sixteen, well read, and thoughtful. In the mid Sixties the country was beginning to turn against the war in Viet Nam. The civil rights movement was gaining momentum with increasing and escalating acts of civil disobedience. The United States was divided and people were choosing sides. Were you for or against equal rights for minorities and women; for or against the War in Viet Nam; for Elvis or the Beatles? Jack was beginning to feel ready to choose which side he wanted to be on. Continuing to play football seemed sort of contrary to the side he was drawn to. Counter-culture voices Jack had tuned into, like Timothy Leary, Allen Ginsberg , and Bob Dylan had turned him on to a zeitgeist much different from the small-town Midwestern traditional-values he'd grown up with. Jack heard those voices scorning football and rah-rah team spirit as uncool and a facet of the dominant military-industrial establishment.

He didn't actually hear any particular counter-cultural hero condemn the game of football, but that was his sense of it. He could feel the country and culture changing and he wanted to be part of where the future was going.

At the end of the afternoon practice on the third day of doubles, Jack's flat-topped ex-US Marines high-school coach lined up all the players. With spittle flying from his lips the coach stomped along the line of players growling and yelling. He punched each of the players in the stomach and shouted, "Tough as nails!" That did it for Jack. That was the moment he decided the cost wasn't worth the benefit. It wasn't the punch. It was the insufferable behavior of his coach. He decided he wasn't going to put up with that kind of Fascist shit anymore. After the last practice of the preseason he quit.

When he turned in his equipment to the team's manager, Jack expected that would be the last time he handled a football helmet. But the road of life has unexpected twists and turns. Flash forward to fall 1971.

Jack Blair did not attend any preseason practices the first two years he played football for the University of Chicago Maroons. "Doubles" were scheduled from nine to eleven in the morning and again from one to three in the afternoon. Just before the 1969 preseason-practices were to commence, Jack posted a letter to Coach Walter Hass informing him that Jack would be unable to attend doubles. The excuse given was that he had stepped on a nail causing a puncture wound. The following year, before the 1970 football season began, a letter from Jack informed Coach Hass that Jack had suffered a sprained foot and would be unable to participate in preseason practices. Foot problems seemed to be a common affliction of Jack's at the end of summer vacation. The day before preseason practices were to commence for the 1971 season, Jack's final year of college, Coach Hass received a letter advising him that Jack had fractured his big toe.

Jack's ailments coincidentally resolved just as double practices concluded the first two seasons he played for the Maroons. He reported to the team in prime condition ready to play in the first game of the 1969 and 70 seasons. The same pattern seemed to be playing out for the 1971 season with the letter from Jack to Coach Hass about a broken toe.

Jack's penchant for preseason issues relieving him of the necessity to attend the God-awful, dehydrating, exhausting, double practices in the humid September heat of Chicago would have earned him serious time on the bench or dismissal from the team at every other college football program. But Jack played for the University of Chicago Maroons. The U of C did not have a varsity football team for thirty years, from 1939 until 1969. Jack was a second-year (what other colleges call a sophomore) when football was resurrected in 1969.

During the previous school year, 1968-69, Jack's first year at U of C, the University's administration announced that football would be resumed as a varsity sport in the fall. Anyone interested in joining the team was requested to attend spring workouts, which would occur three times per week during spring quarter in May and June of 1969.

The Maroons needed bodies. That Jack had quit his high school football team was not a disqualification. Any body that was ambulatory and showed up for practice was welcomed onto the team.

Jack didn't mind spring workouts too much, since practice was optional and only three days per week for an hour. The players only suited up one of the three practices to hit each other. The other two practices were devoted to conditioning and learning plays on offense and formations on defense. On some Friday practices, just for fun, Coach Hass taught the team historic plays and formations from the Maroons' Big Ten era, when they were known as the Monsters of the Midway.

Jack was one of the best conditioned athletes on the team having lettered in swimming and track all four years in high school. He was used to hard physical labor. Like all Hoosier farm kids, Jack grew up helping his parents detassle corn, bale hay, feed livestock, and whatever else was required to keep the farm going. Playing sports was a welcome respite from farm work.

Jack's speed, strength, and coordination were superb. He excelled at every sport he tried. He liked the independence of swimming and running track. There was a spiritual feel to running and swimming. The isolation of the mind in a perfectly functioning body was a form of meditation. But Jack also enjoyed the comradery and teamwork of football. He appreciated how football combined strategic thinking in game planning and play selection as well as the necessity to react spontaneously to whatever situation developed after the ball was hiked.

All things considered, football was Jack's favorite sport, until it was spoiled by the sadism of his high school coach. When he first considered the possibility of joining the fledgling Maroons, Jack told himself that he had never lost the intrinsic joy of playing football. Rather, his introspective interpretation of what happened in high school was that, when his social consciousness was raised, he could no longer tolerate the authoritarian personality of his coach. Surely things would be different on a college team with a college coach.

As a child, Jack thought he was overly sensitive for a farm boy – which was regularly confirmed by his father. As he grew into adolescence, Jack knew he felt differently about a lot of things than his peers in Seymour. He was socially adept enough not to come off as weird – a terrible social stigma for a small-town Hoosier kid in the early 1960s. Athletic ability and good looks qualified him for membership within the in-crowd of Seymour Junior High and High School. Jack wanted and appreciated what little social advantage there was to be gained in Seymour from being one of the cool guys. But secretly, he knew he was different from the high school jocks, preppies, and greasers that comprised Seymour's teenage social-milieu. None of his buddies preferred reading or hiking by himself to hanging out at The Cherry Bomb, working on their pick-up trucks, whistling at girls, or drag-racing cars on County Road 19.

Jack thought most of the other kids looked at everything in very concrete-materialistic terms and in limited ways. He was careful not to come off as conceited, and didn't think any of his buddies would understand anyway. But Jack wanted to think in sophisticated ways and to comprehend great ideas. He sensed an effervescent realm of sublime intellect, which seemed out of reach in Seymour. He yearned to be part of a community that cared about ideals more than who was taking who to the next dance or who had the hottest car in the school parking lot. So he had applied and been admitted to the university that had pionee red the Great Books approach to education, required its college students to make it through the educational boot camp of the Common Core, and promoted the "life of the mind" as the highest form of human existence.

Jack assumed he'd never play football again after he quit his high school team, and he had no intention of playing any varsity sports at the University of Chicago when he applied for admission. He turned down scholarships in swimming at a couple second-rate Division I schools and a partial track scholarship at a D-II school. He wanted to leave organized sports behind and concentrate wholly on academics in college.

Jack's idealistic vision of college life, when he was dreaming about getting out of Seymour, was that it would be like living in the realm of Plato's higher reality of the Good, the True, and the Beautiful. There was no room in that universe for grunting, sweating, and crashing into other material bodies for the sole purpose of trying to move an inflated pigskin another yard. Football was too much like farming. It was hard and dirty, and not necessarily rewarding. Jack was determined that his life would be very different from his father's. He would not spend his life staring at, and grubbing in, dirt.

Jack was an honors student ranked third in his class of one-hundred sixty-six at Seymour High. He was recruited by the University of Chicago through its "grass roots intensive talent search" (GRITS); a program which sought out promising small town and rural students. He could have gone to Indiana University, Purdue, or Ball State, like the other twenty-five percent of his graduating class that went on to college. But the opportunity to attend a truly great academic institution in the third largest city in the nation fired Jack's imagination. He knew that U of C didn't have a football team when he applied for admission. He certainly did not imagine that, after a three year hiatus from the sport, come spring quarter of his first year in college he would be on a football team again.

Jack had learned through the materials sent to him by the University of Chicago that the University had a unique history and quirky attitude toward athletics. It had respectable Division III men's and women's basketball teams. Its track club, not the varsity team, but a club sponsored by the University, had world class runners on its roster. The track club and varsity team were coached by the renowned Ted Hayden who coached the US Olympics teams in 1968 and 1972. However, the most significant athletic activities on campus were intramurals. There was little interest in varsity sports.

But something which caught Jack's attention in the materials he received from the University Admissions Office was a rule of the Athletic Department that varsity athletes could not be disciplined for failure to attend practice or games due to academic conflicts. He reminded himself that he had no intention of playing sports at the U of C. But he filed the fact of that special rule in the back of his mind.

Jack recalled that rule when he decided to check out the possibility of joining the new football team spring quarter his first year at U of C. So, before the first practice Jack met privately with Coach Walter Hass. Jack asked, and Coach Hass affirmed, that the rule prohibiting disciplinary action against athletes who missed practice for academic reasons would apply to the new football team.

University of Chicago campus viewed from the Midway
Plaisance

-2-

John D. Rockefeller gave the money and Marshall Field gave the land to create the University of Chicago in 1890. Rockefeller considered the U of C "the best investment I ever made." Since its inception, Chicago has produced more college presidents than any other American university. 85 Nobel Prize winners have served on the illustrious faculty or studied at the University of Chicago. More "Nobels" have been granted to UChicago professors than any other university. Rockefeller, indeed, got his money's worth in his desire to create a great academic institution in the American Midwest.

In the first third of the 20th Century, however, U of C was as much, if not more, admired for the prowess of its football teams as its academics. Amos Alonzo Stagg was Director of Physical Culture and Athletics at the University. He quickly established football as the University's premier sports program. He was so successful that, as football coach, Stagg won more games than any other college football coach until Bear Bryant of Alabama eclipsed Stagg's record of 314 wins in 1982.

The "grand old man", Coach Amos Alonzo Stagg,
instructing his players

Stagg coached the University of Chicago Maroons from
1892 through 1932. During those 40 years he developed
innovations in the game of football still used by modern
teams, such as the lateral pass and the tackling dummy. He
coached legendary players like "mighty might" Walter
Eckersall, Clarence Herschberger, the first player to execute
the Statue of Liberty play, and Fritz Crisler, after whom
Michigan's Crisler Arena is named. Stagg's 1905 and 1913
teams were the declared national champions and he led the
Maroons to four undefeated seasons, the first in 1899. The
Maroons won seven Big Ten Conference titles during Coach
Stagg's tenure.

The team acquired its second nickname, "Monsters of
the Midway", because the University straddles the Midway
Plaisance. The Midway runs east-west through the UChicago
campus between 59th and 60th. It was created for the
Columbia Exposition World's Fair in 1893 to celebrate the

400th anniversary of the "discovery" of the New World by Christopher Columbus. Frederick Law Olmsted, the famous landscape architect, designed the Midway, as well as Jackson Park at the east end of the Midway and bordering Lake Michigan. Washington Park is at the west end of the Midway Plaisance in the neighborhood of Hyde Park on Chicago 's south side. The Barack Obama Presidential Center is planned to be located in Washington Park, not far from the Obama's Hyde Park home.

The Columbia Exposition had a second purpose, which was to show the world that Chicago had made a historical come-back from the Great Fire of 1871. That was the fire that Chicago school children learn was started by Mrs. O'Leary's cow kicking over a lantern. The story is apocryphal, but the tale continues to be told. The World Fair was a great success for the City of Chicago and brought international attention to the new university on the Midway. With the success of its athletic teams under Stagg's leadership and a first class faculty, the U of C came to represent a shining ideal in the Midwest by combining scholarship and athletics on a college campus.

In 1935 Jay Berwanger, a big powerful bruising halfback, won the first Heisman Trophy. The Trophy is given each year to "the best college football player in the country " by the New York Athletic Club. Contrary to American football lore, Berwanger did not serve as the model for the image on the trophy. But Berwanger was known for his punishing stiff arm, which is represented in the pose of the model for the trophy. Berwanger's trademark stiff-arm is still a favorite pose imitated by players after making a touchdown.

When a linebacker/center on the University of Michigan Wolverines team in 1934 tried to tackle Jay Berwanger, the Wolverine was introduced to the power of the Maroon's stiff arm and failed to make the tackle. Future President of the United States Gerald Ford bore a scar under his left eye the rest of his life as a result of his close encounter with Berwanger's stiff arm.

The great Berwanger in action utilizing the legendary stiff
arm replicated in the Heisman Trophy.

Jay Berwanger was the very first draft choice of the
inaugural National Football League draft in 1936. He turned
down a contract offer to play for the Chicago Bears, because
he thought he could make more money in business. He did.
George Halas, the longtime owner-coach of the Bears, tried
but failed to acquire Berwanger for a steal. He did, however,
steal the football-shaped 'C' logo of the Maroons for his
Chicago Bears.

Stagg Field, named for the legendary coach, seated
55,000 fans during the heydays of Maroons' football. It was
the largest college football stadium in the world when it
opened in 1913. The gargantuan stadium looked like a
medieval castle with battlements and turrets. Other than
lacking a moat, the stadium exhibited the masculine power
of a feudal lord. It was a coliseum worthy to be the
battleground for Monsters on the Midway.

[Gate 1 of Stagg Field in 1916; Archival Photographic Files, University of Chicago Library, Special Collections Research Center]

Maintaining the massive stadium and supporting a first class big-time football program came with a stiff price tag. Football had become important to the identity of the U of C, especially to alumni. Academic excellence, however, was of primary importance to the faculty and administration. Players were not routinely given scholarships nor were they to be given any slack in meeting academic requirements as they were, and are, in other Division I schools. When the University's reputation for high standards in teaching and research began to rival the Ivies by the 1930s, its recor d of success on the football field began to decline. The administration and Stagg were unyielding in requiring players to meet rigorous admissions standards and to meet all academic requirements for graduation. The consequence was that the Monsters were tamed and descended into mediocrity.

Robert Maynard Hutchins became president of the University of Chicago in 1929 at the age of thirty. He was considered a boy genius. He had neither love for football nor for Stagg. From the day of his inauguration as president, Hutchins was determined in his efforts to rid the University of varsity football. It took him ten years. His first step was to force Stagg into retirement at age seventy after the 1932 season.

After Coach Stagg left, Maroons' victories on the gridiron came less and less frequently. Attendance at the games fell off and the cost of maintaining the monstrous stadium became a drag on the University's budget. The halcyon days of raccoon-coat wearing fans waving "Go Chicago" pennants were coming to an end. Hutchins was gathering ammunition that even the most loyal alumni and students would be unable to ignore.

Stagg Field Stadium during the heydays of the Monsters of the Midway

"As for me, I am for exercise as long as I do not have to take any myself." "When I feel the urge to exercise, I lie down and wait for it to pass." These witticisms are ascribed to Robert Maynard Hutchins, fifth president of the University of Chicago. Hutchins and his academic sidekick Mortimer Adler brought a revolutionary approach to higher education, when they came to Chicago in 1929.

They developed "The Great Books" and "Common Core" curriculum for the College of the University. Hutchins and Adler had a vision for college education which threw to the winds many of the traditions which had evolved from Oxford and Cambridge dating back to the Twelfth and Thirteenth Centuries. Most Anglo-American universities had developed certain rules for admissions and graduation that were considered sacrosanct. Hutchins and Adler thought that age and even high school graduation were irrelevant to a student's readiness to commence college. So, U of C began admitting anyone able to pass its entrance exams no matter the student's age. As all knowledge required for college students to "enter the ranks of educated persons" was already contained in books, attending lectures and class es was not necessarily important. What was important was to "live" with the great books of (primarily Western) Civilization and for students to be able to demonstrate that they had acquired that knowledge. So, only end of term written exams should be required to demonstrate academic competence. Grades were irrelevant. Pass or fail was the only question, which should be answered by performance on a final exam.

Hutchins and Adler were unable to bring about all the changes they wanted to make to realize their vision for the College. But what they were able to accomplish was sweeping and impressive. Their legacy continues to challenge higher education. Some of their ideas were especially popular in the 1960s by providing intellectual support for the liberalization of grading systems and an emphasis on original sources on course reading-lists. The Hutchins-Adler philosophy of education has buttressed the charter schools movement to free educators from the strictures of state mandated curricula.

Given Hutchins' plan to revolutionize higher education by using the College of the University of Chicago as his laboratory, it is understandable he did not want to be bothered with big-time college football, or any sports for that matter. While he admitted that athletics were one of the building blocks of civilization, it was one of the bricks in the edifice that held little interest for him. Hutchins' vision for students and faculty at Chicago was that they should be completely engaged in "the life of the mind".

If scholars were to engage in competitions outside their academic exercises, Hutchins thought the annual Latke-Hamantash Debate a more appropriate sport. Established under the Hutchins regime in 1946 as an annual event, the debate over which of the two Jewish staple foods is superior draws huge crowds of cheering and jeering faculty and students each year. Eminent faculty members take to the floor to display their rhetorical skills, while ridiculed, praised, and lampooned by the crowd and then in the student press and university publications. Hutchins and his acolytes were determined in their efforts to deemphasize intercollegiate athletics and to introduce more intellectually high-brow events into campus life.

But Hutchins was not just an idealistic elitist-academic. He was a smart politician. The Maroons' 1939 season provided the leverage he needed to remove the distraction of football from his grand plan for the College.

In 1939 the diminished Monsters beat the Little Giants of Wabash College and the Oberlin Yeoman, but nobody else. They were outscored by the other six teams they played 306-0, including 61-0 defeats by Harvard and Ohio State and an 85-0 loss to Michigan. It was utter humiliation! Bad enough to be slaughtered by Ohio State and Michigan, but beaten by Harvard 61-0! Even the most devoted fans recognized the Monsters of the Midway had become the weenies of Big Ten football. Something had to change.

The start of World War II by Germany's invasion of Poland in September 1939 also contributed to a decrease in interest in football. Young men dying once again on European battlefields tended to fix the mind more on those fields than American football fields.

What was the U of C to do? Dropping down to play the cow colleges of the lesser conferences was unacceptable to the proud institution. Hutchins argued that killing off football at the University of Chicago was the logical solution. When the faculty approved Hutchins' proposal to terminate football with extreme prejudice, Hutchins reportedly said with little regret, "Football has the same relation to education that bullfighting has to agriculture." And it was done.

In 1939 Chicago dropped football. U of C remained a member of the Big Ten Conference in other sports until 1946. Then, by mutual agreement with the Conference , it withdrew and was replaced by Michigan State.

George Halas was free to poach the Chicago 'C' and the nickname for the Bears. The "Monsters of the Midway" no longer played in Stagg Field two blocks north of the Midway. The nickname and the football shaped C moved up Lake Shore Drive to Soldier Field.

Three years after the sun set on the Monsters of the Midway the first self-sustaining nuclear reaction occurred under the west grandstand of Stagg Field. A group of U of C scientists under the supervision of Enrico Fermi proved that nuclear fission was possible and controllable. That first twenty-eight minute long nuclear reaction would lead to the production of the atomic bomb which brought the Japanese to their knees and ended World War II.

["Nuclear Energy" is a bronze sculpture by Henry Moore located on the grounds of Regenstein Library at the site where, on Dec. 2, 1942 under the west stands of old Stagg Field, the first controlled nuclear chain reaction was achieved.]

"In many colleges, it is possible for a boy to win 12 letters without learning how to write one," Robert Maynard Hutchins opined in *The Saturday Evening Post*. Hutchins labeled college football an "infernal nuisance".

RELATIVE IMPORTANCE OF TWO ANNOUNCEMENTS

[This cartoon appeared in the *Chicago Tribune* shortly after President Hutchins abolished football at the University of Chicago. Photographic copy of drawing, Archival Photographic Files, Special Collections Research Center, University of Chicago Library]

Hutchins thought he had rid the University of Chicago of football for ever. But in 1969 the infernal nuisance was back.

-3-

Coach Walter Hass wanted to tell his players about this game tape he stored in his head. He replayed it regularly. It wasn't Super 8 film of any game he'd coached or played in. It was a mental talisman he pulled out and polished like a good luck charm from time to time. Well, he didn't exactly polish it, since it was in his head. But it did play like a movie in the private studio of his mind.

The voice over in the movie began, "When you are young, you look at life like it's this gigantic room with doors lining the walls – hundreds of doors." The scene in the movie is a room as big as the University's Henry Crown Field House, but filled with stout oak doors on all four walls. The narrator's voice resumes, "For whatever reason you choose one. And you enter a hallway." The scene shifts in the movie to a long corridor with walls painted off-white and a speckled white linoleum floor. It looks like a hallway in University Hospital, or maybe one of the classroom corridors in Cobb Hall. Anyway, it's a long hallway with doors lining both walls. The narrator says, "You choose one and enter another hallway. This hallway also has many doors, but not as many as the last one. You pick a door, walk through and find yourself in another hall with even fewer doors. And so on, until you find yourself in a hallway with no more doors. You look down the long hallway. There is only one way to go. You can't return. The door behind you is closed and locked. The question is, do you see light at the end of that last hallway or only darkness? You have to pick a door. That is the way of life, my son."

Wally wanted his football players to understand what life was really about. He wanted to call each one of them "son". And he wanted them to see that joining the football team was choosing a door into one of the hallways that had light in it, not darkness.

But times had changed and these kids might not appreciate being called 'son'. They might not appreciate being called 'kids'. At the U of C, it was customary to call students and professors alike, Mr. so and so, and Ms. so and so. It was a very strange place to coach. Calling a half-dressed player in the locker room, Mr. Northway --really!?

The kids he coached at U of C were a different breed of cat than his Korean War era players. His players back in the Fifties and early Sixties had crew cuts or flat tops and called him Sir or Coach. Wally couldn't remember the last time he was called Sir. None of the current players had called him Wally to his face, but he knew they did behind his back. The guys who came out for the team in Chicago had long hair and wore clothes that made them look like a bunch of raggedy hobos. If his players at Hibbing High or Carleton College wore blue jeans with holes in them it was because they were just off the farm and couldn't afford new pants. Back then, nobody wore bell bottom pants except sailors in uniform. But the times they were a changin' like it said in that song by that Dylan character the kids all listened to on the team bus.

But they were good kids in their own way. Most importantly, they were his kids. And these kids wanted to play football at a school that not only didn't give a damn about football but had resisted his efforts to resurrect varsity football from the ashes of Hutchins' fire.

Ha! It still amused Wally that the University's mascot was the Phoenix – the mythical bird that was born anew out of fire and arose from its own ashes. The Phoenix was chosen by Stagg himself as a symbol of the U niversity of Chicago arising from the ashes of the great Chicago fire of 1871. It had nothing to do with the resurrection of football in 1969, but it was appropriate.

Whenever Wally was confronted with administration or faculty resistance, as he fought the long fight to return varsity football to the U of C, he reminded himself and everyone who'd listen that football could be reborn just like the Phoenix Bird. He especially liked to reference the classical allusion of the Phoenix when high-brow faculty members with their pipes and elbow patches looked down on him and his appeal for support to resurrect football. Those tweedy souls had never known the joy of knocking another player on his ass with a perfectly executed crack-back block. No pipe-smoking philosophy professor would ever understand the aesthetics of football the way Wally understood the beauty of the game.

No matter, he had fought the good fight and after thirteen years of politicking had won authorization from the administration to resurrect football as a varsity sport at the U of C in 1969. His teams would not be the great Monsters of the Midway which had dominated the Big Ten under the legendary Stagg. Wally's Maroons would play Division III ball against small liberal arts colleges in the Midwest. But that was okay; whoever the Maroons played, it would be football!

[University of Chicago seal; the Phoenix rises from fire below the motto, "Crescat scientia, vita excolatur", translated from the Latin as "Let knowledge grow from more to more, and so be human life enriched." Exterior of Burton-Judson Courts, photo dated 1930-12-18, Archival Photographic Files, University of Chicago Library, Special Collections Research Center]

By the fall of 1971 Wally knew he was in that last hallway of his own movie. Retirement was just around the corner. He was sixty four and would reach the University's mandatory retirement age next September. Just one more academic year to survive and he'd qualify for a full pension. One last season as football coach, after sixteen years as Athletic Director, and it was the end of the line at the U of C.

Walter Hass had done the job he'd been hired to do. Football was again a varsity sport and all of the athletic programs had improved under his tenure as AD. The women's teams were gaining popularity with the recent requirements of the federal government's Title IX law. Intramural sports were more popular on campus than ever. The football team's losing record was the only painful thorn in his side. The Maroons had not won a game in the two seasons since football had arisen from the ashes.

Did he see light or darkness at the end of his own hallway? Sometimes it was light and sometimes dark. Wally had been so elated when he finally got the green light to restore football as a varsity sport. But the first two seasons were anything but gratifying. It was football, but my God! He hadn't thought it was possible to lose every game for two years running. As an assistant coach at the University of Minnesota, head coach for Hibbing High School, and head coach at Carleton College he'd not had a losing season. He had been the star halfback and captain of his team at University of Minnesota. Wally had known nothing but success in the game of football – until now.

Now, he coached a team that was arguably one of, if not the worst, team in the country. When Amos Alonzo Stagg came to Chicago to develop a football program, he was told by the administration that the school colors were yellow and white. Stagg wisely changed the dominant color from yellow to maroon. He didn't want to give opposing cheering sections the opportunity to call his players "yellow". The team became known as the Maroons and the nickname stuck for all U of C varsity teams. But the way the Maroons had played football the last two seasons, their own fans might justifiably call them yellow.

Despite all the losses on the field, Wally loved his players. He wished he could share the movie that played in his minds with these young men. They were in one of the first hallways and had just begun choosing doors that would open up into, and close off, the life that would define them. He wished they could see what he saw. Football could be a door that helped lead them to the light. It had everything in it that the philosophy professors at the University referred to as "the good life". Football was self discipline, comradeship, teamwork, and respect for authority as well as for a worthy opponent. It strengthened the mind, body, and spirit. To misquote the great Lombardi, football wasn't the only thing, but it offered everything to a young man who embraced it wholly.

Even more important to Wally than finding a way to win games was the challenge of imparting his love of the game and the understanding of how it helped to make a young man whole. Yes, the will to win and execution on the field was a big part of expressing love for and understanding of the game. He was convinced that would come, along with victories, if he could develop in his players a commitment to the sport. If only his players cared about football the way he did!

These young men were not playing for scholarship money. They weren't playing for the adulation of cheering fans. Only a few hundred hearty souls showed up to cheer on the team on cold Chicago afternoons with the Lake Michigan wind cutting through overcoats and blowing off the hats of shivering fans. Nobody was forcing or coercing the guys to play; they were on the team because they wanted to play football. It was pure and it was true. But most of the players put so many other priorities above the team and the sport.

Wally recognized that there were more distractions for players at the University of Chicago than at other colleges. A challenge unique to the U of C was that University Athletic Department rules prevented a coach from disciplining players who skipped practices for "any academic reason". Some of his players purposely scheduled classes to conflict with practice, so they only came to practice two or three times each week rather than the scheduled five. Others didn't show up for Saturday games when they had a term paper due on Monday or a major exam. In addition to the unique academic zeal of his players, Wally was well aware of the usual distractions of girls, parties, and the whole gamut of social and personal issues college athletes had to deal with.

The counter-culture movement had created another problem. In Wally's experience it had always been "hep" to be on a varsity team. But in the late 60s, just when football was resurrected at Chicago, some of the best athletes in the College wouldn't come out for varsity sports because it was no longer cool to be a jock.

Still, he loved coaching these kids. Despite the God awful music they liked and the slang terms they used, which Wally didn't understand, and their hair! Why would any man, especially a football player, want to wear his hair so long it hung outside his helmet? One of the fellas even had a pony tail. Lord! An opponent could grab that pony tail and yank the kid down if he was a ball carrier.

Wally never commented about hair length, style of dress, or any of that stuff to his players. They wouldn't have come out for the team if they didn't have a love of football in their own peculiar ways. They just weren't going all the way with the game. His players were dating football instead of marrying her.

Wally knew and appreciated that without the kids his dream of bringing back football to the U of C wouldn't have happened. These kids were the smartest and best students he'd ever coached. Jeez! The dumbest ones would go on to become doctors and lawyers. We have future nuclear physicists and classics scholars on our roster, he'd enthused to his staff. What other team in the country had a linebacker like Mancusa who was an expert on Italian Renaissance chamber music?

Wally had decided he wanted to make a life in football his senior year when he was elected captain of the University of Minnesota Gophers. He got his start in coaching the next fall. He was allowed to join the staff as a junior-assistant coach for the Gophers. He expected to make a career of coaching. If he was successful, he would move up within an athletic department at a university or college to become an Athletic Director. He had achieved his ambition, but, when he first started coaching, he never imagined he would end up at a school like the University of Chicago – not because it was such an elite institution, but because it didn't have a football team!

Chancellor Lawrence Kimpton, when he recruited Wally to become AD at the U of C in 1956, had promised to support the revival of football. The Chancellor told Wally that he thought "Coach Walter Hass was the right man to lead the charge."

And so, for thirteen years, he did. It often felt more like beating his head against a Gothic limestone wall than leading troops into battle. Lord! He hadn't expected it to take thirteen years of politicking within the University to achieve his dream of restoring football to the U of C. And then, losing every game for two seasons running; that was definitely not part of the dream.

The losses were tough, and any more would severely test Wally's tolerance to bear pain. But the challenge of relating

to the odd collection of characters that comprised the team –
well, nothing in his coaching experience with the Gophers or
at Hibbing High School or Carleton College had prepared
him to deal with the issues raised by an offensive guard like
Vandenberg.

During the 1970 season Heinz Vandenberg didn't report
to practice for a full week. He left a message with the
Athletic Department's secretary that he was "maxed out on
time" trying to finish a translation of The Epic of Gilgamesh
from Sumerian into English. The kid was trying to complete
PhD-level work as a third-year undergraduate! What was a
coach supposed to say to someone like Heinz? Football
practice is more important than a new translation of what
may be the first literary work in the history of written
language --?! Not likely. But football practice was important,
especially if the team was going to have any chance of
turning around its miserable record this last season of
Wally's coaching career.

It wasn't just selfishness to try to get that win that had
eluded him and his teams for two seasons. One more win
and Wally would have a lifetime record of one hundred wins
as a varsity football coach, because of all the wins he'd
racked up before he came to Chicago. It would be very
satisfying to cross that milestone. But his personal goals
aside, football practice was important for guys like Heinz.
The kid had a brilliant mind and would surely go on to
become a major scholar making significant contributions in
his field. But football would add meaning to his life too. If
Heinz experienced nothing more than scholarship, was that
really a good life? Football could help round out a young
man. Playing college football would give Heinz memories to
enjoy the rest of his life. Although, Wally grudgingly
admitted to himself that losing every game of his college
football career might not leave Heinz with the sweetest of
memories. Still, even playing on a losing team would give
Heinz, and guys like him, a more well-rounded college
experience.

When Ed Levi became president of the Univers ity in 1968, he informed the faculty that the University of Chicago should no longer be the university known for the slogan, "where fun comes to die". The new president urged faculty and staff to promote a more well-rounded experience for college students. President Levi had taken Wally aside after a luncheon at the Quad Club and told him that it was up to Wally as Athletic Director to promote a new emphasis on athletics. Ed Levi wanted the University to renew its commitment to athletics. He wasn't calling for a return to the Big Ten, mind you, but the University should take pride in and express appreciation for its scholar-athletes.

Wally liked the concept of "scholar-athlete". Advocating for scholar-athletes on campus was an initiative Wally believed in and would fight for. And he had the support of the administration, if only the tepid tolerance of the faculty.

Wally had done his best to understand and to integrate the "scholar-athlete" into his way of thinking about his players. He did look upon his football players as scholars and athletes. He just wished he could apply a little more weight in tipping the balance of the scales toward the athlete side.

But this was the challenge Wally had agreed to take on when he took the job of athletic director in 1956. Win or lose – he prayed every night for a win – he'd persevere. After two seasons of losses, a win was surely on the near horizon.

Coach Hass and players on the 1969 Chicago Maroons

-4-

Jack Blair knew he was at the right place the first day of
Orientation Week, September 30, 1968, at the University of
Chicago. Since fall term 1934 the University has held a week
of orientation activities for entering students. The Aims of
Education Address, which is given by a distinguished senior
scholar, is the traditional commencement of orientation for
incoming first-year students. Richard McKeon, former Dean
of Humanities and eminent philosopher, gave the address to
the students and their parents for Jack's entering class.
McKeon's speech in Mandel Hall was about how "the new
rhetoric must be universal, objective and must be focused on
the particular now". McKeon argued that, "The principles of
rhetoric formulated by Aristotle in the fourth century before
the Common Era maintain their power, even in 1968, for
effective persuasion."

The great scholar's address thrilled Jack. It was delivered
in a lofty intellectual tone with numerous historical,
philosophical, and literary references. Yes! This was exactly
the way professors were supposed to lecture at great
academic institutions. He desperately wanted to learn to talk
like that, to think like that.

Jack's parents sat through the lecture; his mother smiling
politely to hide her bewilderment; his father studying his
huge calloused hands. It was time for Mom and Dad to leave
after the "lunch with parents" in Hutchinson Commons.
Eleanor Blair teared up and hugged her son so long and
tight that Jack finally had to pry her hands loose and pull
away from her embrace.

Jack was the oldest of three siblings and the first member
of his family to enter college. He shook hands manfully with
his father. When Norman Blair took Jack's hand in his
strong farmer's grip, Jack noted that his father wouldn't meet
his gaze. Diffidence toward anything not involving agriculture
was Norman's ordinary mode. But was his father blinking

more rapidly than normal? Whatever. Norman kept his
feelings to himself, and so did Jack.

Everything else during the first day of O-Week went
pretty much as Jack expected. After his schedule for
placement exams was confirmed, he moseyed through the
student activities fair in Bartlett Gym. He didn't want to
commit his time to any activity except studies, but it was
interesting to check out all the clubs and student
organizations on campus. Coming from Seymour High
School he'd never been exposed to groups like the Gay
Liberation Alliance or even the Poetry Society. The
exhibition table of the Black Friars Theater Club caught his
interest mainly because a willowy dark-haired upper-class
woman was in charge of the table. She was wearing a black
beret with a Black Panthers pin, deep purple eye shadow, a
white blouse, and black chinos. He'd never seen a girl, er
woman, that looked like her. (The University's pre-
admissions materials stated that female students were to be
referred to as women and not girls or coeds.) Jack thought
she resembled Grace Slick like he'd seen on the cover of a
Jefferson Airplane album. Her name was Leyla. She said he
had a good voice for theater, because he spoke clearly and
had the flat accent of a rural Midwesterner.

Wow! Jack had never traveled outside of Indiana before
coming to Chicago. It had never occurred to him that he had
an accent. He moved on to check out the displays of other
organizations. He was exhilarated.

Jack wasn't put off by these firsts in his experience. It was
what he wanted. This was why he had chosen Chicago
instead of IU, Purdue, or Ball State. Not because of
intriguing, dark-haired older women, but because he wanted
to experience the world of cosmopolitan intellectuals and
the City.

Meeting his roommate for the first time was another
interesting experience. Steven Schwartz was more
intellectually precocious and culturally sophisticated than any

kid Jack had known in Seymour. Steven (he corrected Jack
when Jack called him Steve) was Jewish, but secular, and
lived in Manhattan. His father owned a business which
manufactured something called computer chips. Steven
intended to enroll in U of C's BS/MBA program. He hoped
to earn the dual degree within five years. He would then join
his father in the family business.

The first afternoon Steven and Jack spent together, their
conversation ranged from their personal backgrounds to
their mutual admiration of Jimi Hendrix's "Purple Haze"
and Plato's *Republic*. In the evening, Jack and Steven had
planned to take a walk around the Quadrangles to better
familiarize themselves with the campus layout . But they
never made it off the floor of Flint House in the Woodward
Court dormitory. Every student they talked with was
intellectually precocious and came from backgrounds unlike
Jack's.

Finnish architect Eero Saarinen was not entirely to
blame for the bleak basement-corridors, moist cinder-block
walls, and closet-sized rooms of Woodward Court
constructed in 1958. Saarinen's original design for the
dormitory called for Gothic architectural elements, including
arches and window canopies to match the elegant Gothic
stonework of the Main Quadrangle in the center of campus.
Budget constraints and several revisions resulte d in a final
"Modernist-Brutalist" design of three connected four-story
dorm buildings with a flat-roofed dining hall in the center
called the Common Unit. 330 students were stuffed two to
the closet-size rooms into the three buildings named
Wallace, Flint, and Rickert Houses. Wallace was exclusively
women, Rickert men, and Flint co-ed.

By fall of 1968 the drug culture was epidemic in
Woodward Court. The dorm was called "the
Pharmaceutical Society" by students. On the other hand, the
dorm was the host venue for the Woodward Court Lectures,
sponsored by Resident Masters Izaak and Pera Wirszup.
Lecturers were world class scholars such as physicist

Subrahmanyan Chandrasekhar, economist Milton
Friedman, and philosopher Mortimer Adler. After
delivering the lecture, the renowned guests would rub
shoulders with undergraduate residents of Woodward Court
in the Wirzup's apartment while enjoying wine and cheese.
Young minds were bent in all sorts of different directions
within the culture of Woodward Court in the 1960s and 70s.

While most of the rooms in Woodward were freezing or
boiling from ineffective control over the HVAC units, many
of the rooms also had views to the north of the elegant Robie
House designed by Frank Lloyd Wright. Students living in
the dorm the spring quarter before Jack and Steven moved
in were also privileged with a view to the south of riots after
the assassination of Martin Luther King Jr. on April 4, 1968.
From their dorm windows students watched the Blackstone
Rangers street-gang being surrounded by the National Guard
on the Midway Plaisance.

After Jack and Steven finished their first dinner in the
Common Unit, the roommates exited the cafeteria to
explore the Quads and study the Gothic grey-stone
architecture and gargoyles. In the hall just outside their dorm
room they struck up a conversation with one of the guys in
the next room. Seth Wilmer's father was the U.S.
Ambassador to Lichtenstein. Leaning against the wall
outside their rooms the three of them skipped over the
typical "get to know you" topics and got involved in a
conversation about German beer, the collapse of the
Weimar Republic, and the sexual practices of teenagers in
Lichtenstein.

Carol Rusinski came out of a room two doors down the
hall. She introduced herself as a second-year especially
interested in French cathedral architecture. She joined the
conversation and steered it into a course on the customs and
unique culture of Flint House. The three first-years knew
that Flint was the only co-ed dorm house with co-ed
bathrooms at the U of C. That was one of its attractions, or
distractions. Carol explained that a vote was taken by

residents at the first "house meeting" of each academic year to decide whether to keep the bathrooms coed or gender - separate. The meeting would be the first Tuesday after Orientation. Carol gave the three guys a pointed look when she said, "The vote each of the last two years was unanimous for coed bathrooms. We expect it to stay that way."

Carol confirmed that residents changed rooms and roommates at will, but never exposed themselves in the hallways or even in the bathrooms. Co-ed pair-offs and room sharing was not uncommon after first quarter. "If you smoke pot in your room, keep your door shut and turn a fan on to blow the smoke out the window," she advised. After finishing her tutorial on the culture of Flint House, Carol launched into a discourse about the architecture of Cologne Cathedral.

Jack was titillated thinking about sharing a bathroom with this girl, who had long white-blond hair, a lovely lithe figure, and the fairest complexion he'd ever seen. But, he was even more titillated by the breadth and depth of the conversation of his three new friends. A couple more students joined the discussion and so the six of them moved into the lounge down the hallway. Other students floated in and out of the discussion in the lounge. Topics ranged from the Pre-Socratic philosophers to the Heisenberg Uncertainty Principle and the civil rights movement.

Jack ate it up. He didn't sit back like a shy, slow-talking farm boy. Rather, he joined in expressing what he knew about the topics discussed and eagerly listened to what the other students had to say. Most of his dorm mates took a similar approach to the conversation. It grew heated at times. Carol accused a guy named Scribner of "sophistic invective". But Jack was pleased to observe that his hall mates seemed genuinely interested in learning from each other. There were arguments and disagreements. But, so long as the speaker was contributing interesting ideas or information, everyone listened and waited their turn to jump in. Only one guy, Stahler, who appeared to be a pretty serious pothead, was routinely interrupted. It took Stahler way too long to put whatever his thoughts were into words.

Jack and Steven's planned walk around the Quads would have to await another day. They finally retired to their own room around three in the morning. Jack drifted off to sleep in a state of happy contentment with his decision to come to the University of Chicago.

[Construction of Woodward Court was completed in 1958. The building was demolished in 2001 to be replaced by the University of Chicago Booth School of Business. Archival Photographic Files, Special Collections Research Center, University of Chicago Library.]

-5-

Fall quarter their first year in 1968 Jack and Steven were immersed in U of C's academic boot camp, the Common Core. The prevailing philosophy of education at the University of Chicago from its inception in 1891 was that college students should experience all of the traditional academic disciplines. Making it through "the Core" in the late 60s meant that students were required to take a full year of the primary disciplines of biological science, physical science, math, humanities, social science, history, and a language, i.e., two full years of general education requirements before being allowed to declare a major or to enroll in any elective courses. The U of C didn't actually have "majors". Students had "concentrations" in particular disciplines or courses of study.

One of Jack's attractions to the University of Chicago was the Common Core. When he applied for admission he didn't know what he wanted to study as a major concentration or what he might do after graduation from college. He did know that he wanted to learn as much as he could about as many subjects as possible. Jack was not alone. Typical of students in the College at the University of Chicago in the late 60s and early 70s was an openness and interest in generalist learning. Being career oriented or "teleological" in the pursuit of an undergraduate degree was uncool. Some students planning on pre-med or business were exceptions, but most of the students in the College took a renaissance approach to education. They truly wanted to live "the life of the mind" and scorned those who did not.

Fall Quarter 1968 exceeded Jack's expectations for what college should be like. He reveled in the life of the mind. Living in a coed dorm where precocious 18 to 20-year-olds were experimenting with free love, marijuana, and the hard rock coming out of San Francisco, created more learning opportunities for a farm boy from Seymour, Indiana, than he imagined possible. Still, Jack kept his primary focus on academics. He struggled to earn Bs in Calculus and Physics, but voraciously consumed every book and essay on the massive reading lists in his Humanities and Social Science sequences. Jack aced both those courses, as well as Bio Sci., and earned a 3.6 grade point for the fall term. He was looking forward to taking Ancient Greek for his language requirement next year.

In 1968 there was a force other than intellectual ferment raising the metaphorical temperature on campus. Like campuses all across the U.S. (and Europe), U of C was becoming embroiled in the anti-war, civil rights, women's liberation, students rights, and anti-establishment movements. Jack and Steven were interested in the movements and in general agreement with the leftist sentiments behind the increasingly angry forces gathering. They hung out at the back of a few anti-war demonstrations on campus. They stood across the street and watched other students carrying picket signs and marching around a Jewel Food Store in support of the United Farm Workers boycott of nonunion-picked grapes.

Jack and Steven both grew their hair longer than had been permitted by parents and high school dress codes. Steven's was black and curly, almost an Afro. Jack's was blond and wavy covering his ears and cascading down the back and sides of his neck.

Three weeks into Winter Quarter on January 29, 1969 twelve hundred students packed Mandel Hall without faculty or administration approval or supervision. The stated reason for the gathering, according to the student activists who organized the rally, was to show support for Marlene Dixon. Ms. Dixon was an assistant professor of Sociology whose contract had not been renewed. She was a well-known leftist within the faculty and popular with many students. There were allegations by less sanguine students that her lectures were not "objective". She confirmed that by telling a reporter for the student newspaper, *The Maroon*, "I increasingly realized that I couldn't stop being a radical in the classroom, and that furthermore I didn't believe in value-free sociology."

Several of the student radicals who organized the rally planned to expand the focus of the gathering beyond the issue of Ms. Dixon's contract termination. Campus activists had been engaged in a year-long campaign to raise the consciousness of students about the wider issues roiling across college campuses. They had little to show for their efforts. So, they intended to use the Marlene Dixon "firing" as the spark to set off an explosion at U of C. The goal of the radicals was to breach the barricades of Chicago's ivory tower and let in the barbarians of the anti-establishment culture war.

Organizers of the rally in Mandel Hall proposed that students should occupy the Administration Building. A vote was taken and the resolution narrowly passed. At noon the following day four hundred students tried to enter the Ad Building. At first, the protesters were blocked by twenty athletes. The jocks stood shoulder to shoulder in front of the doors. There was no violence, just a standoff. Eventually the athletes left because they were hungry and it was past lunch time. The 400 surged in.

After a week of occupation a counter movement began. On February seventh a group of three hundred students held a rally in opposition to the occupation of the Administration Building. Although classrooms had not been blocked by the protesters, university operations were compromised. Students were unable to pay their tuition bills at the Bursar's Office or obtain transcripts. *The Maroon* published a survey showing that a majority opposed the take-over of the Ad Building. Letters from well-known professors were also published in *The Maroon*. "To condone these tactics, explicitly or implicitly, is to cooperate willingly in the destruction of the very foundation of our University," wrote Milton Friedman. Bruno Bettelheim wrote that, "The historical parallels between what is happening here and what happened in the German universities before Hitler are unfortunately relevant."

In a strange twist of historical fate, the gatherings of students around campus for sit-ins, protests, and counter-demonstrations gave supporters of resurrecting football at U of C a rare opportunity. It became easier to obtain signatures on a petition requesting the return of football as a varsity sport. Players on a club team under coach Hass's guidance inserted themselves among the many other groups seeking signatures on the petitions supporting various issues and political factions. When they reached their goal of 1,500 signatures, the football players presented their document to the faculty, deans, and the Board of Trustees. Coach Hass later credited the success of the petition drive as key to his ultimate victory in convincing the Administration t hat football should rise again from the ashes.

Jack's politics had been moving steadily leftward since turning sixteen. He and Steven attended the rally in Mandel Hall, but they didn't join the occupation of the Administration Building. Steven was far more experienced with protests and the nuances of what was really brewing under the surface than Jack. Steven pointed out that neither he nor Jack had sufficient information to judge whether Ms. Dixon's contract should be renewed or not. He argued that taking over a building on campus would accomplish nothing to promote the greater struggle to stop the Viet Nam War , and it certainly wouldn't help gain equal rights for African-Americans or women. Lastly, if they joined the protest and were expelled from college, they would lose their student deferments from the Draft. That would mean they would be forced to join the imperialistic war machine which was bent on the destruction of Ho Chi Minh's fight for liberation of the Vietnamese people.

Jack was sympathetic with the greater goals of the protesters. In his view, what they ultimately stood for was a better and more compassionate world. But, he reluctantly agreed with the merits of Steven's arguments.

When the occupation of the Ad Building ended, other sit-ins, hunger strikes, and guerilla actions were taken by the radicals on campus. Classes were disrupted and faculty and administrators were assaulted in the Quad Club. The University responded by suspending or expelling ninety-nine students.

Jack participated in rallies supporting amnesty for student demonstrators in the sense that he stood among the student supporters. Otherwise, he remained on the sidelines. He did sign the petition to bring back football.

Despite the turmoil on campus, Jack maintained his personal discipline of physical conditioning. He was a regular in the weight room at Bartlett Gym and on the indoor track at Henry Crowne Field House during his first year on campus. Jack's high school regimen of swimming and track had turned him into an exercise addict. He simply had to work out. If he didn't exercise vigorously at least five days each week, he felt lethargic and unhealthy. Jack did not like feeling lethargic or unhealthy.

One of the other gym rats that had become a buddy of Jack's was a second-year student, Martin Westridge. Marty played linebacker on the club football team Coach Hass was running through the Phys Ed. Department. He told Jack that he planned to go out for the real thing when varsity football started with spring practices. Marty encouraged Jack to do the same. While spotting Jack on the bench press, Marty urged, "Come on man, with your ability and the shape you're in, spring practices won't even be a challenge. We'll show up for call outs together."

Jack was intrigued by the idea of playing football again for several reasons. He would actually be allowed to play football without attending all practices. It would be a distraction from the ferment on campus which was dividing the student body and breaking up friendships. More remotely, but maybe most important of all his reasons, Jack had looked into applying for the Rhodes scholarship. His thinking was that, if U of C was this great, studying at Oxford

University would be the ultimate academic experience. If he could win a Rhodes scholarship, he could pursue the equivalent of a Masters Degree at Oxford. And, he could get away from the roiling passions of campus politics and just concentrate on academics.

One of the requirements of the Rhodes was that the applicant had to participate in some form of athletics. Jack's research on Rhodes scholars indicated that most of the successful applicants were varsity college athletes. If he could put varsity football on his application, along with a stellar GPA from the U of C, he figured he'd have a pretty good shot at the scholarship to Oxford.

Imagining himself, a farm boy from Jackson County, Indiana, with a Masters Degree from Oxford, made Jack laugh. The idea also filled his chest with pride and his mind with possibility. Yeah, it might be worthwhile to give football another try.

[Anti-war activity has a long tradition among U of C students. Student members of the University of Chicago Youth Committee against the War are pictured here in a demonstration against U.S. entry into "another European war". Photograph date May 1939, Archival Photographic Files, Special Collections Research Center, University of Chicago Library]

-6-

Football did return to the University of Chicago in the fall of 1969 as an official varsity sport. It wasn't exactly a propitious start. Twenty students delayed the kickoff for the first game against Wheaton College's junior varsity team by running out onto the field carrying placards in English and Ancient Greek which read "Ban the Ball!" Counter protesters in the stands chanted "Football si, oddballs no!"

At the first Homecoming game of the "new era" of U of C football a refrigerator was proclaimed Homecoming Queen. The "Queen" was paraded around "new Stagg Field". Heated arguments broke out in the stands as to whether the refrigerator represented the frigidity of U of C women or the icy relations between the Soviet Union and U.S. during the Cold War. Most of the players for the Maroons enjoyed the spectacle and the attention it brought their fledgling team. The opposing players from Oberlin College stared in slack-jawed amazement at the refrigerator bedecked with crown and sash pulled in a cart by a riding lawn mower.

New traditions were started that first season, which were far different than those of the Big Ten era of raccoon coats and fans waving maroon C-pennants. Before the games a line of utility vehicles from the physical plant led a parade of kazoo-blowing students and little black-kids from the neighborhood. An anonymous steam calliope player rolled up outside the fence on 56th Street and piped away during games. The Kazoo Marching Band and members of Students for Violent Non-Action charged on to the field with the largest kazoo in the Western world, nicknamed Big Ed after U of C President Ed Levi, at halftime each game. Kazoos were handed out to fans who were invited to parade around the field behind Big Ed, which was pulled on a four-wheel wagon.

A halftime spectacle with the largest instrument in the Western world was consistent with tradition from Chicago's glory days in the Big Ten. In 1922 the University commissioned C.G. Conn Instruments to build a bass drum for the school's marching band. "Big Bertha" made its appearance in the 1922 game versus rival Princeton University. When football was dropped in 1939 Big Bertha was stored under the bleachers of "old Stagg Field". The drum became contaminated from exposure to radioactive materials used in Enrico Fermi's research for the Manhattan Project during the 1940s. Colonel D. Harold Byrd, a former member of the University of Texas Longhorn Band, bought the drum from the U of C in 1955 for one dollar plus the cost of having it decontaminated and restored. Big Bertha's Phoenix bird was plucked and she joined the Texas Longhorns.

The Worlds biggest drum
At the Princeton Game Oct. 28-1922

U of C had no marching band in the new era, but a group of eight college musicians formed "the Lower Brass Conspiracy", which served as the functional equivalent of both pep and marching band at Maroons' home games. When there was a break in the action of the game, the musicians would run around the field in different directions randomly tooting and thumping their instruments. They called their formation Brownian Motion. Nineteenth Century botanist Robert Brown observed that pollen particles move randomly when suspended in water. Einstein tipped his hat to botanist Brown by adopting the term "Brownian motion" in his particle theory of quantum physics. So, the Lower Brass Conspiracy tipped their proverbial hats to Albert by demonstrating the random movement of atoms described in Einstein's particle theory by running chaotically around the field.

Only a few hundred fans regularly attended the Maroons' home games that first year, except when the visiting team bused in their own fans. As the weather turned colder and fall turned to winter, icy winds off Lake Michigan blasted fans huddled on the exposed aluminum stands of new Stagg Field. The only comfort for the spectators from the brutal weather and another loss by the Maroons were thermoses of hot chocolate laced with peppermint schnapps passed around the stands. By the end of the last game of the resurrected Maroons' first season, only a few girlfriends, visiting parents of players, old men who belonged to the Order of the C and had supported Chicago athletics since the Big Ten era, and members of the Sociology Department studying "the culture of college sports", remained on the cold metal seats of new Stagg Field.

Two fans who did stoically and proudly endure the lashings of lake winds and sleet to attend every game of the Maroons' inaugural season of 1969 were Bernard DelGiorno and "General" Lawrence Whiting. Bernie DelGiorno was a Maroons letterman in gymnastics and earned three degrees from the University in the mid 1950s. He remained in Hyde Park after graduation and became the super fan of Maroons' athletics as well as a very successful stock broker. Bernie endowed facilities for the Athletic Department and residence halls for the College. He was especially beloved by the football team for opening his Hyde Park mansion to the team for post-game receptions.

General Whiting, one of Stagg's star players from the Class of 1912, promised Stagg, when the old coach was dying, that he would be in the stands to represent the coach if the university ever brought football back. Whiting was a decorated soldier serving in both great wars of the Twentieth Century. He was not really a general, but he did become a prominent Chicago industrialist. Whiting was true to the promise he made to his old coach and mentor. The General attended every home game of the 1969 season. He sat in the stands of the much reduced Stagg Field bundled up in his C-blanket and a fur hat.

The old General's presence failed to recall the winning spirit of Stagg for the resurrected Maroons. Perhaps the ghosts of Stagg and Hutchins were still locked in metaphysical combat over the fate of football for the University. Doleful fans wondered whether Fermi's specter had irradiated the team and reduced the Monsters to the lab mice of the Midway.

An article in *People Magazine* labeled the Maroons "the worst team in college ball". The article portrayed the team as under-sized egg heads who went out for football as a diversion from the rigors of U of C's academics. The fans were described as "funny". The article noted that the entire budget for the football program in 1969 was $6,500.

The publisher of *People* offered to fly the Chicago team out to the Rose Bowl to play Cal Tech. The Cal Tech team supposedly claimed that the average IQ of its players was a number greater than their average weight. *People* proposed to call the game "The Toilet Bowl". Coach Hass declined the offer on the grounds that it would do irreparable psychological harm to his players to participate in The Toilet Bowl. He didn't relent when the magazine offered to change the name to "The Brain Bowl".

The players to a man clamored for the free trip to sunny Southern California regardless of what name was applied to the game. But Coach Hass dug in his heels on the grounds that the magazine had taken a derisive attitude toward the team's efforts to re-establish football. And by God, he wouldn't have it!

News of the article spread slowly around campus and within the faculty. No faculty member would readily admit to reading such a low-brow rag as *People*. Wally grumbled defensively to anyone who brought up the subject that his team was not the worst team in college football. A team should not be judged solely on its won/loss record , he argued. The Maroons were scholar-athletes and the team was in a rebuilding mode. In time, he was confident (at least, that's what he said publicly) a winning team would emerge from the ashes as the team's mascot, the Phoenix, implied.

Coach Hass let his old buddy and assistant coach, Mick McVale, have the honor of leading the twenty-six members of the Chicago Maroons football team onto the field for the first game of that first season on October 4, 1969. Mick had been at Wally's side lobbying for the return of football from the beginning. Wally wanted to watch the team take the field for the first time. He stood outside the gate of new Stagg Field watching in satisfaction as the team jogged onto the field. Wally wore his customary Chicago Athletics maroon-windbreaker and maroon skally-cap. Sentiment welled in his chest as he watched his team begin their warm up calisthenics and drills.

He accepted congratulations from two elderly members of the Order of the C and then started to walk through the gate. A long-haired student in a jeans jacket sat on a metal folding chair behind a card table just inside the gate. His job was to collect a one-dollar admission fee from non-students. As Wally started to walk past the ticket collector, the young man called out, "Uh, sorry sir, it's one dollar admission!" Wally chuckled, assuming the youngster was joking, and took another step forward. The student stood up quickly saying, "Really, admission is one dollar, unless you're a student." Wally glanced meaningfully down at the Phoenix emblem and "University of Chicago Athletics Department" logo on his maroon windbreaker. The student held his ground with his hand out. Wally reached into his back pocket, pulled out his wallet, gave the ticket taker a dollar and said, "Good to see football is already a revenue sport."

As Wally walked across the running track toward the Home Team's sideline, he heard one of the old C-Men upbraiding the student, "Don't you know who that is!?" Wally could hear the gulping sound of embarrassment and contrition in the voice of the first-year student as he spluttered that he hadn't realized he had just charged admission to the coach and Athletic Director, i.e., the man who signed the kid's paycheck.

The referee blew his whistle to call the captains of the teams to the center of the field for the coin flip. Students with the signs of "Ban the Ball" had been hanging around the entrance gate. When the whistle blew they rushed through the gate and onto the field. The protesters milled around just downfield from the flummoxed referee. They raised their cardboard signs and shouted, "Ban the ball! Ban fascist imperialism on campus!"

Marty Westridge and Charlie Ozman, co-captains of the Maroons, looked horror stricken. They turned toward the sideline for instructions from the coaches. Mick McVale stood with his hands on his hips muttering and shaking his head. Wally was looking skyward as if asking for divine intervention. The referee started blowing his whistle maniacally and moving his arms in a shooing motion as if he could sweep the demonstrators off the field. Marty and Charlie started laughing and then shook hands with their counterparts from Wheaton. The three captains of the Wheaton Thunder Junior Varsity team looked like they wanted to scream and run away.

The demonstration only delayed the kickoff by fifteen minutes. Dean of Students Warren Wick left the stands and confronted the protesters. He informed them that they would be subject to disciplinary action for disrupting a sanctioned University event if they did not immediately leave the field. Allen Schmidt, leader of the demonstrators, argued with the Dean about whether a football game qualified as an event. The argument became more heated as issues of judicial procedure and notice were introduced. Dean Wick suggested they continue the argument on the sidelines.

The fans in the stands started the chant of "football si, idiots no!" and were stomping their feet. After their initial surprise and amusement wore off, some of the players began muttering amongst themselves about running the kickoff return team like mounted Cossacks through the milling protestors.

Jack watched the events unfold with ambivalence. He was amused – only at the University of Chicago, he thought – and irritated. The protesters could have found another venue to vent their disapproval of the resumption of football as a varsity sport. It was disrespectful to the players. It was especially disrespectful to Coaches Hass and McVale, who had worked so long and hard to bring back the sport. On the other hand, he could imagine himself among the demonstrators if he wasn't on the team. His interest became more personal though, when he noticed Alice Novak among the crowd of demonstrators. He stood up taller.

Alice and Jack had met for coffee and bagels at the Blue Gargoyle after Western Civ class just the day before. He was impressed with her ability to answer hectoring questions posed by Professor Karl Weintraub to the class. Weintraub was one of the College's most famous, respected, and intimidating professors. Students camped out the night before registration to put in their bid for one of Weintraub's classes.

As the protestors straggled off the playing field, Alice's eyes met Jack's. He lifted his hands, palm upwards in a questioning gesture. She shouted, "Football is a manifestation of the rapacious male-dominant culture! First it's oppression, next subjugation, then rape!" She shook her small fist and yelled, "Violence solves nothing!"

Jack shook his head and then mouthed, "I'll call you." He strapped on his helmet and snapped the chin guard. The first game of the resurrected Monsters of the Midway would finally begin.

The first half ended with the Maroons leading the Wheaton Thunder JV squad 6-0. Since there were no locker rooms in new Stagg Field, the teams gathered in the end zones at opposite ends of the field.

It was a beautiful fall day. The air was crisp. Trees were colorful with leaves just beginning to prepare their departure for the year. The Lake wind was only a slight breeze. The coaches talked strategy and laid out a game plan for the second half.

Jack's number-84 uniform was satisfactorily dirty. He had played both ways. He hadn't contributed much on offense, catching one pass for a five-yard gain. But he'd made a couple key blocks to help set up the Maroons' first touchdown. The score came on a straight buck up the gut by halfback Bob Lovavich. On defense Jack had tipped a pass which was intercepted by safety Larry Woodcock, which ended Wheaton's only serious scoring threat.

Jack lay in the grass with his elbow resting on his helmet. It felt good to inhale the earthy smell of the field. His mind wandered from the coaches' excited description of how the Maroons would hold their lead and pressure the Thunder with a more aggressive passing offense. He was really looking forward to a second after-class meeting with Alice Novak.

The triumph of the first half of a varsity-football game played at the University of Chicago in thirty years was short-lived. The Wheaton JV-team held Chicago scoreless the second half and won 16 to 6.

Given Jack's ambivalence about playing football again, he invested little thought about the momentous return of the Monsters of the Midway. He did, however, invest thought into pursuing Alice Novak.

When they met after class the following Monday at the Frog and Peach in Ida Noyes Hall, Alice was still worked up about opposing the return of football. She was a Slovak

Catholic who had grown up in a working class Westside neighborhood, the daughter of school teachers who subscribed to *The Catholic Worker* newspaper. Alice imbibed the Catholic-Marxist influence of Dorothy Day with her mother's milk. As a first-year at U of C she joined a feminist consciousness-raising group which met in Ida Noyes Hall. She was emerging as a campus leader of the women 's liberation movement and an influential member of the U of C's chapter of Women's Radical Action Project (WRAP).

While Alice lectured Jack over herbal tea about the historical subjugation of women by the dominant patriarchal culture, he was digging her tight little ass. She wore ripped and patched hip-hugger blue jeans, a halter top revealing the shape of very perky tits, a blue-jean jacket, and a painter's cap. Her jet black hair was parted behind bangs down the center of her head and was ironed so it fell perfectly straight just below her shoulders. Jack eventually interrupted Alice and made an offer. Instead of arguing about football now, how about she agree to meet some of Jack's football buddies at Jimmy's, a favorite neighborhood bar. In return, he would attend a feminist consciousness-raising meeting in Ida Noyes sponsored by WRAP. Alice accepted and they shook on it.

Maroons name MVP

Jim McGraw of Hastings, Minn., the University of Chicago football team's Most Valuable Player for 1969, examines school mementos with Jay Berwanger, who was the first Heisman Trophy winner in 1935. McGraw, the Maroons' leading scorer, is the first MVP at Chicago since the school dropped football before World War II. (Sun-Times Photo by Jim Klepitsch)

The Chicago Sun-Times
Wed., Nov. 26, 1969

Archival Photographic Files, University of Chicago Library, Special Collections Research Center

-7-

Jack and two of his teammates squeezed into a window table at Jimmy's Woodlawn Tap. Smoke hung so heavy scissors couldn't cut through it. Steppenwolf's "Born to be Wild" was blasting on the juke box. On the TV set above the bar Brent Musburger, the CBS Channel Two sportscaster, was yakking about the Bears getting whipped by the Minnesota Vikings. Saul Bellow held court at a corner table in the back room surrounded by acolyte grad-students smoking pipes or Gauloises cigarettes. Jack tried to listen in to their conversation, but all he could make out was Bellow bellowing about some "hideous barbarism" committed by Nelson Algren. Cracker barrel philosophers from the Hyde Park neighborhood bloviated amidst frat boys, old beatniks, young hippies, and student radicals. The three football players were surrounded by animated jaw flapping about local politics in which the names of Da Mayor (Richard J. Daly), Saul Alinsky, and Leon Despres were praised or taken in vain. The noise level was close to 90 decibels.

Jack tapped on the window and waved at Alice when he saw her walking up 55th Street with a friend. Tank Stevens and Mike Kovatch each grabbed another chair and made room for Alice and Jan McKay at the table.

Introductions were made and Kovatch poured glasses of PBR from a pitcher for the women. Tank called for another pitcher and then Alice launched into her argument. "I'm not condemning any individual for playing football. My opposition to it as a varsity sport at U of C is contextual."

"Go on," Jack encouraged.

Alice hesitated. She looked at Tank, the Maroons' big bruising two hundred five pound fullback. He had a mess of curly light-brown hair, a small silver-ring in his right ear lobe, a prominent dimple in his right cheek, bright blue amused eyes, and a friendly grin inside a droopy mustache on his broad face. She looked across the table at Kovatch, a compact two hundred pound linebacker and wrestler. His neck was bigger than her thigh. He had a prominent brow ridge running below a wide forehead, which would have made him look Neanderthal, except that a serious look of interest and black chin beard gave him the appearance of intense intelligence. His eyes were dark and brooding under heavy lids below a shock of unruly black hair. She went on. "The context at U of C is that we haven't had a football team for what, twenty years or so?"

"Thirty," Kovatch interjected.

"Okay, thirty. My question is, what has the University community lost by not having a football team?"

"We hadn't lost a game in thirty years, until last Saturday," Tank said with a laugh.

Alice and Jan exchanged smiles. "The point is, a culture has developed at U of C, since it left the Big Ten, that all the rah-rah nonsense of college sports is absent here."

"Yeah," Jack agreed.

"And that's why most of the students who come here—"

"Wait a minute," Jack interrupted. "I seriously doubt that any students chose U of C because it does not have a football team."

"No, I don't mean that. I mean that the whole essence of the college experience here is about intellectual endeavor. You know, 'the life of the mind', as everyone around here calls it."

"I don't see how football is necessarily antithetical to intellectual endeavor," Kovatch said.

Jan, who had squeezed in between Tank and Kovatch, looked from one to the other, smiled and giggled. "Alice, you didn't tell me football players were so cute. And these guys are much cooler than the nerds we usually meet at Jimmy's."

"Jan!" Alice gasped.

"Yeah, and just imagine, we can do calculus and push-ups," Tank said with a wry grin.

Alice straightened her back and said, "I think we're getting off the subject."

"Not really. Tank's little witticism makes the point I started to bring up the other day," Jack said.

"Yeah, sorry. I was a little worked up, you know, the demonstration and all."

"Not a problem. Here's my point. Athletics have been an integral part of Western culture at least since the ancient Greeks and probably before that."

Jan offered, "Sure, the Olympics—"

"But consider it even more deeply," Kovatch said. "The cave art in Chauvet in France is thirty-five-thousand-years old."

"I've heard of that!" Jan gushed.

Kovatch gave Jan a quizzical once over, then went on, "From our earliest origins as a species, physical capabilities were important to survival. We had to hunt to survive. Physical prowess of the hunter was important. It meant survival or death for the community."

"But with the development of agriculture, hunting became unnecessary, obsolete." Alice protested.

Jack jumped in, "Alice, the point is that physical expression has always been part of culture. Through sports, war is sublimated."

"The Greeks had a truce during the Olympics, right?" Jan asked.

"Yeah, but I don't mean just to equate athletics with war," Jack said.

"But you did, and that's my problem with it!" Alice erupted.

"Look, sport combines body, mind, and spirit. And yes, football is a form of controlled violence or combat. But that is part of our culture, like it or not." Jack retorted.

"I don't," Alice replied.

"Would you prefer that *The Iliad*, *War and Peace*, and *For Whom the Bell Tolls* all be dropped from the canon?" Kovatch asked.

"As something to study, no; as something to do, yes," Alice said firmly.

"Hey, everyone at this table is against the War in Viet Nam. Football players aren't lusting for war," Jack said.

Jan, who had drunk two glasses of Pabst beer, put her arms through the adjacent arms of Tank and Kovatch. "You guys really do have muscles and brains." She giggled.

Alice and Jack exchanged smiles. "Alice, Socrates was a soldier. His most famous student, Alcibiades, was a general and the most significant actor in Thucydides' *Peloponnesian War*."

"Correction Eighty-Four, Aristotle was Socrates' most famous student." Tank interjected.

"Tanker, stick with calculus. Aristotle was Plato's most famous student. But there's another example – who was Aristotle's most famous student?"

"I know, I know!" Jan waved her hand like she was in grade school.

Jack ignored her. "Alexander the Great was tutored by Aristotle. He was probably the greatest military commander of all time."

"He had brains and brawn just like you guys," Jan sighed and leaned her head against Tank's broad shoulder.

"Well, I've read *The Iliad* and parts of Thucydides' *Peloponnesian War*," Alice continued trying to ignore her friend. "The Greeks were damn bloody minded. If football replaced that kind of violence in the culture, I'd be all for it - - shaking poms-poms and waving pennants, the whole bit. But war hasn't been abolished. We've just gotten more efficient at killing."

Her argument quieted the players. Kovatch got up and brought another pitcher of PBR from the bar. Finally, Jack said, "You're right. Football and other sports haven't and probably never will replace war. But, at least athletes aren't engaged in war. What we do is supposed to be for fun."

"It doesn't look like fun to me! Is smashing into other people fun!?" Alice expostulated.

"Uh, yeah," Tank replied.

"Yup," Kovatch said and gulped his beer.

Jack smiled at his teammates, chuckled, and nodded his head. "Yeah, it may seem kind of weird, but yes, it is fun to run into other people -- at least, if you're wearing a helmet and shoulder pads."

Jan appeared to be comfortably numb or pleasantly buzzed with her head against Tank's shoulder. All of a sudden her eyes fluttered open and she said drowsily, "I like the idea of running into guys, but I don't wear pads."

The three guys and Alice snickered. Jan sighed and let her head loll back against Tank's shoulder.

"We don't wear pads in Rugby -- which reminds me, Blair, Kovatch, you guys really ought to come out for the UC Rugby Club in the spring," Tank lifted his glass and drained it.

"Off the subject again, Tankman, but let's definitely talk about Rugby in the spring," Jack said then took a long draught of beer.

"What about spring football practice?" Kovatch asked looking at Jack.

"Oh yeah, that. Guess you'll have to hold up the hooker without Vatch and me, Tank."

"Whatever. But rugby's a really cool game. No pads, lots of wrestling around in the mud, and great parties."

"Well, looks like you'll be engaged in sublimated combat both fall and spring," Alice said cattily, then sipped her beer.

"I'll drink to that!" Tank lifted his glass. Jack and Kovatch clinked their glasses against Tank's.

"Explain to me what is so fun about running into other people," Alice demanded.

"Just is," Tank said.

"Is what it is," Kovatch said. They clinked glasses and drained their glasses of beer.

"Okay, I'm going to change the subject slightly," Jack said. "And this actually has been bothering me about football at U of C."

"What? The ultimately cool Jack Blair is bothered about something?" Tank slapped his friend on the shoulder.

"Go on," Kovatch encouraged.

"Back to Thucydides, U of C culture is Athenian in the sense of being open, liberal, interested in the arts, inclined to democracy, critical, questioning of authority. If you've read *The Peloponnesian War*, you know what I mean."

"Yeah, yeah, go ahead," Kovatch urged.

"Well, football is very Spartan."

"In what sense?" Alice asked

"I know what you're thinking," Kovatch butted in. "Football is highly authoritarian--"

"It requires discipline, practice, submission to command," Jack added.

"Each player has to subsume his individuality into the greater order of the team and the authority of the coach," Kovatch finished.

"Exactly," Jack concluded.

"So, does it belong here?" Alice asked.

Tank drained his glass slammed it down on the table, "Hell yes!"

The following Thursday Tank and Jack walked up the magnificent walnut-railed staircase in Ida Noyes Hall passing below the portrait of Ida Noyes. They peered into the third floor theater through the glass panes of the closed doors. Jack realized he must have misunderstood Alice's instructions on the time the feminist consciousness-raising meeting of WRAP was supposed to begin. It was obviously well underway as he noticed in a glance that the theater was packed and someone was speaking from a lectern. Jack grabbed Tank's arm and pulled him away from the door.

A queasy feeling in his gut confirmed Jack's fear that two football players attending a women's consciousness-raising session wasn't such a great idea after all. To try to quell his nervousness he shifted his gaze to the mural on the wall outside the theater and quickly read the attached plaque.

"The Masque of Youth is a celebration of the 1916 opening of Ida Noyes Hall, which is to serve as a building for women's activities on campus. During the opening celebration three hundred students, alumni, and schoolchildren participated in a dramatic pageant recreated in the mural painting. The style of artist Jesse Arms Botke is early Italian Renaissance. The painting depicts the procession of costumed figures that paraded around the Gothic buildings of the university campus. 'Youth', crowned with spring flowers, is followed by children dressed in blue representing Lake Michigan...."

Tank broke Jack's nervous concentration by placing a big hand behind his neck and propelling Jack forward through the theater doors. Erika Fromm, a Psychology professor famous for her research on hypnosis and altered states of consciousness, stood at the lectern. She paused a moment as the two men entered. Jack noticed Alice sitting at the speakers' table to the right of Ms. Fromm. Alice caught Jack's eye and motioned toward Jan McKay standing in the back corner of the room. Jan rushed over, squeezed Tank's arm, and bustled the only two men in the theater into empty seats Jan had saved for them.

Twenty minutes later Erika Fromm finished her talk on "Feminism and a Higher State of Political Consciousness ". Questions from women in the audience first centered on the psychology of feminism, but then moved to the history of women at U of C. Ms. Fromm reminded the students that women had been admitted to the U of C from its beginning. The University's 1892 Articles of Incorporation state that it will "provide, impart, and furnish opportunities for all departments of higher education to persons of both sexes on equal terms." Ms. Fromm went on, "This very building, Ida Noyes Hall, was the result of a $300,000 gift in 1913 from industrialist La Verne Noyes for a women's clubhouse in memory of his late wife, Ida."

Jan whispered to Tank and Jack that they had missed the part of Professor Fromm's talk about women's athletics. "She said Gertrude Dudley was the first women 's Athletic Director and she was as famous as Amos Alonzo Stagg, because she pioneered women's sports and intramural competitions. I think Alice especially wanted you to hear that, Jack."

Ms. Fromm mentioned several rising stars in the current faculty; Suzanne Rudolph in Political Science and Janel Mueller in the English Department, both of whom were on the way to becoming department chairs, according to Ms. Fromm. She even predicted optimistically that the University would have a woman president in the foreseeable future.

When the meeting was just about to wrap up, Tank raised his hand and asked whether men were allowed to join WRAP. Erika Fromm raised an eyebrow and looked to her left where Jane Goldberg, the fourth-year president of WRAP, was seated. Jane stood up. She gave Tank a withering look and said, "This is a women's organization, for women only. Are you asking in jest?"

Tank had a jovial personality to begin with and was even happier when he'd smoked a doobie or two -- which he had while he and Jack were walking across campus to Ida Noyes Hall. "No way! I wanna join. This is a great place to meet chicks and you need to integrate. Look around, Jack and I are the only guys here."

There was stunned silence for a moment. Jack hung his head. Jan burst out laughing. Alice stood up and announced, "I think we better call this meeting adjourned."

A harsh buzzing sound started in the front row and was moving menacingly toward Tank and Jack. Jack heard Jane Goldberg remonstrating with Alice, "What do you think you're doing, inviting men here! They're just ripping off our energy!"

Jan took the two men by the arms and hustled them out of the theater before the animus against the football players boiled over into a lynching.

Ida Noyes Hall, Photograph Date unknown, Archival
Photographic Files, Special Collections Research Center,
University of Chicago Library

-8-

All of the comedy and drama surrounding the football team that Fall Quarter of 1969 paled in comparison to the abolition of the student deferment and institution of a lottery system for the military draft. The evening of December 1, 1969 half the members of the football team, including Jack, gathered at the Phi Gamma Delta fraternity house around a twenty-four inch black and white Zenith TV-set. Two joints circulated counter clockwise.

The lottery for the first military draft following abolition of the student deferment was televised from the Selective Service National Headquarters in Washington, D.C. The Viet Nam War was at its bloody peak. The Tet Offensive of the previous year proved that the North Vietnamese and Viet Cong were anything but beaten. President Johnson's bombing campaign of the North had not succeeded in smashing the spirit or crippling the military capability of the North Vietnamese Army. But it had crippled Johnson's presidency and Richard Nixon was to be sworn in as President in January. The exemption from the Draft and the security that college students would not be sent to Viet Nam was history. The cost of the war paid by the blood and sacrifice of working-class kids was now going to be shared by children of the more privileged.

Creedence Clearwater Revival's "Fortunate Son" played on the turn table of a high-fidelity stereo in the Phi Gam House. That choice of a tune for background music was not unintentional as the young men turned their attention to the Draft Lottery drawing on the TV set.

Some folks are born, made to wave the flag
Ooh, they're red, white and blue
And when the band plays, "Hail to the Chief"
Ooh, they point the cannon at you, Lord ...
Yeah, some folks inherit star-spangled eyes
Ooh, they send you down to war, Lord

And when you ask them, "How much should we give?"
Ooh, they only answer, "More, more, more" yoh
It ain't me, it ain't me
I ain't no military son, son ...

The Lottery determined the order of "call up" for involuntary induction into service in the U.S. military during calendar year 1970. It applied to all male-citizens born between January 1, 1944 and December 31, 1950, ages 18 to 26. That cohort included every member of the Maroons football team watching the Zenith TV-set. 366 blue plastic capsules containing birth dates were placed in a large glass jar and drawn by hand to assign "order-of-call numbers" as specified by the Selective Service law.

The first capsule was drawn by Congressman Alexander Pirnie, a Republican from New York serving on the House Armed Services Committee. The capsule drawn contained the date September 14. All men born on September 14 in any year between 1944 and 1950 were assigned Lottery Number-1.

Opey O'Byrne shouted, "Thank you Jesus, Joseph, and Mary! I'm still a fortunate son!" All the other guys let out a sigh of relief. Dickey Roudebush muttered, "T'ain't over yet."

The drawing continued until all days of the year had been matched to lottery numbers. Mike Cripe's birth date was drawn number-22 and Big Ed Hanson's was 34. The party no longer felt like a party, as the reality of what those numbers meant for those two teammates. Rumor had it that, if your number was under 40, you were definitely going to be called up.

Their teammates slapped "Cripples" and Big Ed on the back and tried to buck them up with words of encouragement and offers of more beer. But the two 19-year-olds left the Fiji House with their heads hung low.

Jack's heart was split in two as he walked along University Avenue. It was a tremendous relief that his birth date was drawn 248, so there was almost no chance he would be drafted. But, for Hanson and Cripe, he felt terrible. On the other hand, he agreed with the sentiment of Creedence's "Fortunate Son". It was wrong that PhD students who stayed in school until they were twenty six didn't get drafted. College kids got deferred and anyone whose parents had political influence didn't get sent to Viet Nam. Jack was very glad that he'd benefited from his student deferment from the Draft. But he knew it wasn't fair that his high school buddies who hadn't enrolled in college either had to join the military or face the Draft. Well, it was fair now, he thought. But he still felt awful for Cripples and Big Ed.

Jack developed his own opposition to the Viet Nam War, when he learned about the roots of the conflict researching a term paper for World History his junior year in high school. His research led him to the conclusion that, if the U.S. was to be involved at all, we should have supported Ho Chi Minh when he appealed to the U.S. for help to gain independence from the French. Instead, Eisenhower, Kennedy, and Johnson had chosen to support regimes in the South, despite strong evidence that the Vietnamese people, even in South Viet Nam, wanted a united country. It seemed clear to Jack that the Vietnamese did not want their destiny to be determined by the U .S. military. This conclusion was one of the factors that tipped the balance of Jack's political consciousness toward the anti-establishment Left and away from his traditional Midwestern-Republican roots.

Before Jack registered with the Selective Service on his eighteenth birthday, he agonized over whether to apply for Conscientious Objector status. Eventually, he concluded that he didn't qualify, because he could support a war he considered just, like World War II. But, he couldn't justify supporting the Viet Nam War and wasn't sure what he would do if drafted into the military. Two older guys from Seymour Jack knew took radical, but different, routes to oppose the War and refuse the Draft. Willis Miller, a Mennonite who was eligible for CO status, refused to register for the Draft in 1966. He was sent to federal prison for three years. Jeb Stewart, a high school hippie-radical a year ahead of Jack, bolted for Canada. Neither of those options was the least bit attractive to Jack. He was very glad it looked like he wouldn't have to make such a life-changing decision.

But man! He felt bad for Cripe, Hanson, and all the other guys who got low numbers. It felt like he was dragging a lead anvil behind him as he walked back to Woodward Court.

[Congressman Alexander Pirnie (R-NY) drawing the first capsule for the Selective Service draft, Dec 1, 1969]

Two years later in the Fall of 1971 the Maroons and Jack were beginning a third season of varsity college football. They had not won a game in either the 1969 or 70 seasons.

Jack's resurrected career as a football player was near its end. He was a fourth-year on track to graduate in the spring.

It was also the final season of coaching before retirement for Coach Walter Hass. Bringing varsity football back to the U of C was a personal crusade for Coach Hass. He was hired as the Athletic Director of the University of Chicago in 1956. Wally dreamed of resurrecting the Monsters of the Midway from the moment he heard of the job opening for AD. His dream was finally realized thirteen years later, just three years before his planned retirement.

Thirteen years of patient wheedling and quiet diplomacy with the administration and key faculty members by Wally eventually paid off. The administration granted approval for the Athletic Department to re-institute football as an unaligned non-scholarship NCAA Division III varsity sport. In other words, the team would not be a member of a conference and could not give athletic scholarships to players. The Maroons' schedule the first two years even included playing some junior varsity teams. But, after thirty years with no football on campus, it was a start. The crack of pads, the smack of hands on pigskin, and "Hut! Hut!" were heard again at a new and smaller Stagg Field on the campus of the University of Chicago.

However, after losing every game the first two seasons, Wally could not help but question whether his long and sometimes lonely fight was worth it. He had one last season before retirement to pull the Maroons up from the very bottom of college football's standings.

Walter Hass at dedication of new Stagg Field; photograph date 1968-09-21, Archival Photographic Files, Special Collections Research Center, University of Chicago Library

-9-

Near the end of the summer of 1971 Coach Hass sat in his office in Bartlett Gym studying the upcoming season's schedule for the hundredth time. As usual, he was scratching his thinning hair pondering how to find a way to win a game. Wally's mind often turned to one particular player. Jack Blair, a kid from a little farm town in Southern Indiana, posed a most interesting challenge. Jack was the best natural athlete on the Maroons' roster. In high school the kid had lettered in football, track, and swimming. The kid was 6-foot 3-inches tall and weighed 190 pounds. Jack had all the physical tools to be a truly outstanding receiver or defensive back, tall, fast, strong, good hands, and tough.

But, swimming! Wally had never had a swimmer on any of the football teams he'd coached until coming to Chicago. Swimmers didn't play football. It wasn't natural. In Wally's day, any football player who admitted doing the breast stroke would either be laughed at or envied by his teammates. And any football player seen in a public place wearing one of those little skin-tight swimsuits would suffer a ribbing from his fellows in the locker room. But at U of C he had three swimmers on the roster – indeed, the times they are a changin'.

Wally knew that Jack had quit football for some inscrutable reason his junior year in high school. But, with the kid's combination of speed, agility, and strength, that he hadn't played four full years of high school ball was of little consequence. Jack's coverage technique on defense wasn't perfect, and he didn't immediately grasp some of the offensive schemes, the Xs and Os, but the kid's natural ability was well beyond what Division III coaches expected to see on their rosters.

Yet, Jack was one of the players who intentionally scheduled classes to conflict with football practice! And Jack had not deigned to show up for preseason doubles for the

69 or 70 seasons. He'd attend spring workouts, but then he'd disappear until classes started in the fall just days before the first game.

Wally had tried talking to him, had tried benching him, had tried to motivate Jack in every creative way permitted to a U of C coach the two years Jack had played for the Maroons. As yet, nothing Wally tried had worked. Jack was always polite and never made excuses for missing practices other than to explain that he liked playing football, but academics had to come first. As to why he didn't come to campus early for preseason doubles, each year Jack seemed to develop some injury that fortuitously healed just as doubles ended. Wally knew what it was like to grow up on a farm. Perhaps Jack's folks needed him to help out on the farm through the end of the summer. If that was the case, why didn't Jack just say so? Wally could more easily accept that a kid needed to help out his family as an excuse to miss practice than a broken toe or he had an English paper due.

On the other hand, there might be more to the mystery than farm work. Coach Dubka had overheard Jack talking with a group of players in the locker room last spring about a summer job. How could Jack work a summer job if he had to work on the farm? Wally suspected there was more to Jack's refusal to participate in preseason practices than foot problems. On the other hand, maybe it was no more complicated than Jack liked playing football, but he just didn't like practicing.

If so, that struck at the very heart of the challenge Wally faced. How could he get his players to commit fully to becoming the best players they could be, if they only liked football and didn't love it? If a kid with Jack Blair's talent, potential, and leadership qualities didn't care enough to come to practice, what was the likelihood Wally would be able to convince other players to make a true and full commitment to the team?

If it wasn't for that damn rule which allowed athletes to miss practices "for any academic reason!" Wally fumed to himself. Of course Wally knew that, if he could and did punish his players for missing practices, they would probably just quit the team. His hands were tied. Getting the most out of these "scholar-athletes" was like trying to make an open-field tackle wearing handcuffs. Still, he had to try.

The University Administration granted Wally's request for a budget increase and permission to upgrade the coaching staff for the 1971 season. He was allowed to hire two additional assistant coaches.

Donny Dubka was a good-looking youngster with blond hair and blue eyes just two years out of college. He'd been a killer on the field as the middle linebacker and captain of the defense for the Illinois Illini. Donny joined the staff for spring workouts and was already popular with the players. He not only coached, but got out on the field and mixed it up with the players. Donny sported one of those Beatle-type haircuts, but his hair wasn't as long and unkempt as most of the guys' on the team. Any player who dared to show up at practice with long hair back in Wally's playing days would have been the butt of cracks like, "Hey Thelma, do you squat to piss?" But, since Donny had just graduated two years ago in 1969, Wally figured it would be helpful to have an assistant coach who understood the styles and slang of the players. He chuckled to himself thinking the players might be fooled into expecting Coach Dubka would accept a laid back attitude on the field. If the players thought Donny was some kind of "let it be" Beach Boy, they'd get quite a surprise when they saw the fire in those baby blue eyes of Donny's on game day. Donny was an All Big-Ten linebacker. You don't perform at that level, unless you have a fire burning hot in your belly when the whistle blows.

Wally's other hire as an assistant coach was Tom Rogan. Tom came with a higher risk but possibly a higher reward. Wally hoped to groom Coach Rogan to succeed him as head coach of the Maroons. Coach Rogan was a highly successful high school coach in Wheaton, Illinois. In five years as head coach at Wheaton High, he'd taken a team that had won only two games and lost six the year before

Rogan took over, and immediately turned the team around. The Wheaton Knights won five games and lost three Rogan's first year at the helm. Two years later they were conference champs.

The risk was that it just might not be in Rogan's tool kit to understand the culture of the players at U of C. His approach was more like that of a drill sergeant than counselor or diplomat. Wally hoped Rogan could help instill a greater commitment to discipline and a winning attitude within the Maroons. But he had reservations as to how well his new assistant would relate to the players.

Wally carefully explained the unique challenges of coaching at the U of C to Coach Rogan during the interview process. Rogan said all the right things during the series of interviews. He came out to Stagg Field to observe the team for three games during the 1970 season and was well aware of the Maroons' abysmal record their first two seasons. Wally could tell that Rogan understood on a conceptual level that players could not be disciplined for missing practices and that academics came first for most Chicago athletes. But Rogan's bearing was as stiff and military as the U.S. Marines captain he'd been. Well, it would be interesting to see how the kids adapted to Coach Rogan and how he adapted to them.

Donny had been hired as defensive coordinator and Rogan as offensive coordinator. Wally's oldest friend on the faculty, Mick McVale, remained on staff as the senior assistant-coach. Mick was senior-faculty member of the Physical Education Department at U of C. He'd been with the PE Department for 40 years and was 68 years old. Mick received a special dispensation from the president of the University to continue teaching and coaching beyond the mandatory retirement age of 65. Mick had been invaluable in the campaign to convince faculty and alumni t o support the return of football. Because Mick had been around so long, he knew everybody. He was "Marshall" of the most popular faculty club, the Quad Club. Mick had been the Phys. Ed. instructor of some of the University's most eminent professors when they were undergrads. He was not above reminding those faculty members of boners they pulled in PE class, if need be, when asking for their support.

Wally had co-signed the petition to President Levi to keep Mick on staff through the 1971 season. Since it was granted, he and Mick would both be able to retire at the end of the year. The two old war horses wanted to go out together. They'd had each other's back all these years, through the long struggle to resurrect football and the two painful losing seasons after their mutual dream was realized. Wally wanted to win one for Mick almost as much as he wanted a win for the team and, of course, for himself. Wally had even prayed in church, "God, if I don't deserve it, and the team doesn't deserve it, Mick deserves to win before he retires. Please God."

Mick bled Maroon. He attended just about every major sports event on campus, basketball, baseball, and track, along with coaching the football team. As head of the Physical Education Department, and with his many connections throughout the University, Mick helped every athlete that needed a job to find one. Mick and Wally were both loved and respected by all the men who played sports for the U of C.

Together, Wally and Mick would break in the two new coaches. Maybe with the vigor of youth and the wisdom of age the four coaches together would figure out how to find that elusive victory. Wally couldn't help but feel optimistic despite the pain and frustration of the last two seasons. He leaned back in his office chair with his hands behind his head. It was a new season and football was back at the U of C. He thought he could see light at the end of his tunnel.

Coach Amos Alonzo Stagg of the University of Chicago
Maroons directing a practice session

-10-

Jack hugged his Mom, and then shook hands with his father. Jack's younger brother Jim tossed an Army-surplus duffel bag full of Jack's clothes into the trunk and slammed the lid. Jack tousled Jim's hair and Jim playfully punched his older brother on the shoulder. Jack's 10-year-old sister Josie shoved the last box of books into the back seat which was already crammed with stuff Jack was taking back to Chicago for his last year of college. Josie threw her arms around Jack's neck. He lifted her off the ground and hugged her. She squealed with delight and he let her drop back to her feet. Jack chucked his little sister under the chin and then tweaked her nose. Josie's freckled face squinched into a silly grin.

Jack slid into the seat behind the wheel of his 1962 Rambler Ambassador. He rolled down the window so his mother could give him one last kiss. Jack released the parking brake and then glanced in the rearview mirror for once last peek at his family. The rusty black Rambler puttered down the dirt lane leading out of the farm onto County Road 36. Eleanor Blair was waving her white hankie. Norman Blair stood silently studying the rich Indiana dirt between his size-fourteen chukka boots. Jack's siblings had already run off.

Jack drove the rutted county road until he came to Hangman Crossing. He waved at Ike who owned and operated the Texaco station at the Crossing, then gunned the engine and cranked it up to 60 miles per hour before he had to slow down for town. He turned right on Tipton Street which turns into US-50 east of Seymour. He continued on US-50 until he came to the entrance ramp for I-65 North. Onto the Interstate and now it was just a four hour cruise north to the Indiana Toll Road, then the Skyway into Chicago, get off on Stony Island Avenue to Hyde Park, and he'd be back on campus for his last year in college at the U of C.

As he nursed his old rust-bucket north on I-65, the image of his parents flickered alternately with the painting "American Gothic" in Jack's mind. Norman Blair didn't really look at all like the farmer-husband in American Gothic. Norman was big and strong with a full head of dark hair. His father had been dressed, as usual, in Oshkosh overalls with a Pioneer Seed cap on his head. He was six foot three, same height and lanky build as Jack, with a high forehead, wide-set blue eyes, strong jaw, and leathery face. Jack was his father's spitting image, except for the older man's dark hair, aged face, and perpetually glum look. His father's gaze always seemed to be focused on something other than the people around him. He'd study his hands, the ground, or something in the distance, but he rarely looked Jack in the eye. He was a laconic hard-working Hoosier farmer.

Norman Blair seemed to expect everybody else to be as devoted to working hard as he was. That's just who he was. And that was who Jack absolutely did not want to be.

Jack knew his dad loved the land. He worked the fields every day dawn to dusk to keep the farm going. They'd had tough times. In drought years and flood years they went without anything but necessities. Somehow they hung on year after year and the old man always made enough from the farm to keep food on the table. Jack respected his father for his work ethic and providing for the family. He just wished his dad would show a little love for Mom, for Jim and Josie, for Jack.

Jack's Mom, on the other hand, bubbled with affection and concern, like a brood hen with her three chicks. Eleanor lived for her children. She didn't look at all like the severe and gaunt farm wife in American Gothic. She was only five foot two, a little dumpling of a figure with straw-blond hair, like Jack's, but with just a tint of light red mixed in with some grey strands.

Her life wasn't easy as a farm wife. She had round the clock chores. Eleanor pretty much ran the poultry operation solo. She cooked every meal, which meant she was always the first one up. A hot breakfast was ready and waiting for Norman and the kids every day of every week. Living the hard life of a farm wife hadn't dampened Eleanor's spirit one bit. Norman had become as hard and silent as a rocky field that needed clearing. Eleanor was as cheerful as the song birds that flitted around the front yard on a spr ing morning.

Jack tuned his AM radio to Ft. Wayne's WOWO at 1190 on the dial to catch Bob Sievers Top-40 show. He would have preferred listening to Larry Lujack on Chicago's WLS, but his antenna was broken and the reception on the Rambler's radio was so weak it couldn't pick up a Chicago station until he was in Lake County, Indiana. Jack was grooving to Rod Stewart's "Maggie May" and then Carole King's "It's Too Late", but switched the radio off when the DJ announced "Knock Three Times" by Tony Orlando and Dawn. He needed to concentrate anyway. He had things to think through.

He'd employed his annual tactic to avoid preseason football practice. The two previous years he sent a letter informing Coach Hass he wouldn't be able to make practice and then showed up the week classes started. No problem. This time Coach Hass sent a reply. Wally's letter informed Jack that his name was being put forward as a co-captain and asked if Jack could come up to Chicago for at least the last day of preseason practice to be there when the team voted on captains. Jack hadn't replied. He wasn't sure what to say.

For the previous two seasons Jack had successfully maintained the tight rope walk with Coach Hass and the football team the way he had planned. Put as little time into football as he could get away with, but, be able to claim the varsity sport on his resume and, most important, qualify as a college athlete for the Rhodes Scholarship. Wally had tried unsuccessfully to suck Jack in deeper, but Jack resisted the carrots and the sticks. Jack knew the rules. And he had Wally's personal promise that no disciplinary action would be taken for missed practices, so long as there was an academic or medical reason. Wally had not asked for a doctor's note to prove Jack's annual preseason ailments, and Jack had not proffered one.

This new tactic of Wally's did get Jack's attention. Being able to put captain down on his resume might really impress the Rhodes Selection Committee. Leadership was one of the criteria. Jack had been on the student council in high school, but there wasn't really anything he could put on the application showing leadership in college. If he became a co-captain on the football team that would definitely be a point in his favor on the leadership quotient.

Jack scheduled a Monday, Wednesday, and Friday class to conflict with practice the first season in 1969, and a Tuesday and Thursday class during the 1970 season. He'd planned to go back to the Monday, Wednesday, Friday conflict schedule for his final season in 71. His football stats did improve significantly going to practice three times per week last year over his two practices per week schedule in 69. On defense he knocked down two balls, had four interceptions and led the Maroons in tackles for two games last season. On offense he caught at least two passes every game and scored more touchdowns than any of the other receivers on the team. During the 69 season he only ranked third on the team's depth chart for receivers. In 1970 he was the top receiver and usually the team's most potent offensive scoring threat. His improvement was considerable and noticed. He was named to the NCAA's list for top-ten receivers for total yardage among Division III players.

Jack felt a swell of pride thinking about his accomplishments during the last season. That warm feeling, however, was soon displaced with sourness – the sour taste of defeat. The team's failure to win a single game in two years always spoiled any joy or satisfaction Jack momentarily felt about his own achievements on the field. But so what!?

He wasn't going anywhere with football. It was a dead end. You couldn't play football after college. Sports like basketball and tennis at least had adult recreational leagues. He could swim and run into old age, if he wanted to. But Football? Nada. After college, it was over and done with for ever. He certainly wouldn't be playing football at Oxford in England! Not American football, anyway. He reminded himself that he just wanted to enjoy the games and have fun with the guys on the team that he liked. And, of course, be able to claim he qualified as a varsity athlete – and maybe team captain -- for the Rhodes application.

So why did Coach Hass keep trying to pressure him into giving more? Everyone knew Wally was retiring at the end of the year. Just like Jack, this was the end of the line for Coach Hass. Why not be satisfied to cruise into retirement and be done with it. Take the wife to Hilton Head and play golf. Wally had confided to Jack last season that having a condo on Hilton Head in South Carolina and playing golf every day was his dream retirement.

Jesus! Jack slapped the stiff plastic steering wheel. We haven't won a game since football came back to U of C, and we probably won't. The other teams have more players, bigger linemen, faster backs, and they can afford to put in more time on sports and less on academics. But w ho the hell really cares whether we win or lose a football game – other than the coaches? And, well, some of the players who are really committed, like Mancusa, Kovatch, and Cauley. Hmm, all three of them are fourth-years too. They surely deserve to be made captains. What was Coach Hass really up to writing the letter about coming to preseason practice for election of team captains? Wally must have something up his sleeve.

The Rambler rolled up to a toll booth. Jack took the ticket for the Indiana Toll Road. He eased into the on-lane. Jack resumed his interior monologue.

So at this point, I've made the cut for the Rhodes as one of the University's candidates. With George and Muriel Beadle's support, I'm pretty well assured of being passed on for regional consideration. Jack's mind drifted back to the pleasantly rewarding evening he'd spent with the Beadles.

George and Muriel Beadle were pillars of the University community. George was a Nobel winner and former president of the University, now retired. The Beadles had Jack to dinner at their home in Hyde Park to help prepare him for the Rhodes application process. Muriel was in charge of assisting all U of C applicants for the Rhodes and she was chairwoman of the candidate selection committee for Illinois. Her support virtually guaranteed Jack being chosen for the regional competition.

The dinner had gone exceedingly well. When George discovered that Jack grew up on a farm, the conversation turned to genetics and agriculture. Jack had done his homework and knew that George Beadle had won the Nobel for his "one gene one enzyme" hypothesis.

Norman Blair had been interested in genetics and it was one of the few topics he cared to discuss at the dinner table. Jack had absorbed his father's practical knowledge about hybrid plants. And Jack had aced Bio Sci first year with a paper on Gregor Mendel's early experiments in plant genetics. He wasn't stupid enough to try to match wits with a Nobel Prize winner. But he was able to engage with the old prof by asking intelligent questions and not coming off like a suck-up or an idiot in their conversation about genetics and plant pathology. When George started to discourse on the surprisingly diverse flora around Hyde Park , Muriel interrupted by insisting they each have a slice of her walnut pie for dessert.

Muriel hugged Jack on the steps of the Beadles' Hyde Park brownstone as he departed. He knew then the Rhodes scholarship was a real possibility. If he made it through the Midwest regional, it was on to Oxford.

His old beater Rambler coughed and wheezed its way up 55th Street past Pierce Tower. Jack turned right on Greenwood Avenue. He lucked into a street parking spot opposite the four flat in which he and Steven Schwartz had rented an apartment. The two friends had roomed together since their first year in Flint House in Woodward Court. They planned to finish their undergraduate careers at U of C as fourth-years and still roommates.

Botany Pond was designed by the Olmsted Brothers as part of the greater plan for the Quadrangles. Analysis and protection of its ecosystem became Nobel-Prize winner George Beadle's pet project.

-11-

On September 25, 1971 the Maroons football team assembled on the east bleachers of Crowne Field House beside the indoor basketball court. It was the last day of preseason practice. First game was scheduled for Saturday, October 2d.

One of the difficulties the University of Chicago faced in developing a football program was that classes didn't start at U of C until the first of October. While the Maroons were holding preseason practices the two weeks before the players' classes started, their opponents had already played two or three games. The Maroons first opponent would have completed preseason practices a month before the Maroons held their first "summer practice".

Wally and Mick told the players who joined the team the first season in 1969 that the schedule was not really a disadvantage. Players on opposing teams would have suffered injuries and would be feeling tired from playing and practicing for six weeks before they had to take on the fresh Maroons. And, because the Maroons' season started so late, the schedule only included seven games instead of the eight to ten game schedules of their opponents. The coaches didn't bother trying to make that hopeful point after two losing seasons.

The assembled players were dressed in full uniform s ready for practice. The team meeting had just started when Jack Blair walked across the hardwood floor of the basketball court with a slight limp. His penny loafers clacked on the wood flooring. Unlike his uniformed teammates, Jack was dressed in a grey Chicago Bears t-shirt and jeans.

Coach Hass had just finished explaining the new coaches' duties and was just starting to describe the strategy for the first game. Several players hooted at Jack and called out good-natured jibes. "Unbelievable! Classes don't start for a week – it must be a hallucination!" yelled Tim Shooks, the team's center. "That can't be Jack Blair, we've got a day of doubles left!" bellowed Rick Douglas, who went both ways at end. Coach Hass nodded benignly at Jack and waited for him to take a seat with his teammates.

Wally resumed his description of the game plan for the first game of the season against Lake Forest College. He reminded the team that they'd played well against Lake Forest last year. He didn't mention the 0 to 54 drubbing they'd taken in 1969. Nor did he remind the team of the final score in 1970, which was 26 to 6. What he did say was, "We held them scoreless in the second half and we scored a touchdown." Wally nodded at Jack, "Thanks to Number-84."

It had been one of Jack's best games. With less than five minutes left in the fourth quarter Jack intercepted a pass on the Maroons' 15-yard line. The Lake Forest receiver Jack was covering slipped and fell down when he broke stride to cut inside on a crossing route. The Forester's QB threw the timed pass to hit his wide-out as he made the inside cut. Jack's coverage of his man was so tight that when the receiver went down the ball was thrown right into the 84 on Jack's jersey. Jack returned the ball to the forty five. Three series of downs later, Bob Cauley, the Maroons QB, hit Jack on a post route just across the goal line for a touchdown.

It was a sort of moral victory. Chicago scored a touchdown at the end of their last game of the season and held their opponent scoreless for a half. A team that lost every game for two seasons had to find victories in ways other than the final score.

Wally's strategy against Lake Forest this year was based on the assumption that the Maroons would be quicker than the Foresters. Chicago had two behemoths, Heinz Vandenberg at just under 300 pounds and Kevin (Moose) Harris at 265. They both, however, started each season pathetically out of shape, essentially fat guys who had hoped, but so far failed, to use football as a weight loss program. The next heaviest players on the Maroons roster all weighed less than 225 pounds. Other than Moose and Heinz, the

Maroons linemen were no bigger than the guys on Jack's high school team.

While Coach Hass talked excitedly about speed beating size, Jack thought cynically that Wally assumed the Maroons would be faster than the Foresters because we're smaller. Unfortunately, small didn't necessarily mean faster. Jack recalled the 275-pound nose tackle on Oberlin's team last year that was so quick off the line he knocked Shooksie on his ass the moment he hiked the ball. That monster in a football uniform was on top of QB Cauley before he could back pedal or hand the ball off.

Chicago's nose tackle was quick, and small. Jerry Mansueto was a five foot six inch 135- pound wrestler Coach McVale had talked into joining the football team. Yes, Jerry was quick, but he'd never played football before joining the Maroons. He was routinely outweighed 100 pounds by the offensive lineman assigned to block him. As a wrestler, Jerry was used to having his face ground into a sweat-stained mat, his ears almost ripped off, and his nose bloodied. He was tough as nails, but always the smallest player on the field. The coaches told him to use his quickness and grappling moves to try to squirm past blockers and get to the quarterback or ball carrier. It sounded good in theory, but rarely worked. Jerry usually ended up compacted at the bottom of a pile of linemen on running plays or blown off the line by a blocker twice his size on pass plays. On rare occasion Jerry did worm his way past a slow-footed guard to wrap himself around the ball carrier's ankle. He would get dragged a few yards like a rag doll until another Maroon defender brought down the runner.

The Maroons' two big men, Moose and Heinz, did outweigh most of the linemen on teams the Maroons played. The coaches at first used them as blocking guards. As much room as the two big guys took up, Wally figured they'd create an unbreachable wall to protect the quarterback. Unfortunately, they were so slow defenders just ran around them. He tried them on defense, but battering their huge bodies against tougher, quicker blockers tired them out and they were exhausted before the first half ended. Coach Hass put them back on "guard duty" on the offensive line.

Wally wrapped up the skull session for the first game with his usual, "Gentlemen, any questions or comments?"

Unlike Jack's high school coach, when he finished his prepared remarks, Wally actually meant it when he asked the players for input. A couple guys raised their hands and a discussion about defensive formations and coverages ensued. Coach Dubka planned to institute a 3-4 Monster Defense in passing situations against spread offenses. There was still some confusion about the roving "monster" linebacker's responsibilities. Dubka scratched out the different coverage options on a chalkboard.

While the colloquy over the new defense continued, Wally and Jack caught each other's eye. Jack returned Wally's smile and nod with genuine affection. Despite Wally's ploys to suck Jack more deeply into football, Jack was very fond of the old guy. Unlike his high school coach, Jack knew that Wally respected his players and seemed to care about each one of them as a person. Jack could not imagine Coach Hass lining the team up to punch each of them in the gut. When Wally was most disgusted with the team's incompetent performance he would raise his clipboard as if he was going to dash it down on the ground. Then, he would breathe slowly -- he was probably counting to ten -- would shake his head and calmly ask the offensive unit or defense, whichever screwed up, to try it again.

After Coach Dubka finished clarifying the defensive changes, Wally called the team to attention. He declared that it was now time to elect captains for the season. He explained that only fourth-years were eligible. He went on to say that of the nine seniors on the team five had joined the team at its inception, spring of 1969. It was the coaches' recommendation that these five lettermen be nominated and elected co-captains.

Jack shot a startled look at Coach Hass. If all five were to be elected, what was the big deal about Jack needing to be here for the team meeting?

Wally went on, "This is a team decision. The coaches have made a recommendation, but we established the tradition our first year that captains are chosen by the team. So, your coaches will go downstairs and wait in the locker room. Make your decision in fifteen minutes, please. You know that's about as long as Coach McVale can stand the smell of your sweaty locker room." Wally chuckled at his own joke and there were sympathetic sniggers from the players. Mick McVale's jowly cheeks shook with amusement and Danny Dubka laughed out loud. Coach Rogan smiled not and looked impassively at the seated players.

As the coaches filed out, Wally called over his shoulder, "Mr. Blair, since you're the only one in street clothes, you should take charge. Don't forget to follow Robert's Rules of Order." Wally chuckled again as he started down the stairs.

Jack was surprised a second time. He furrowed his brow thinking, the old rascal! But, he stood up, walked out in front of the bleachers, and faced his teammates.

"All right, you heard Coach Hass. Anyone want to move for nomination of, let's see, I guess it would be Cauley, Shooksie, Mancusa, Kovatch, and me."

Moose Harris bellowed, "Jack, if you're a captain does that mean you'll come to practice at least three times a week this year!?"

"Sorry Moose, you're out of order," Jack shot back. "I've called for nominations, is there a motion?"

The team followed Roberts Rules of Order and Wally's recommendation. The five graduating fourth-years who had endured losing fourteen games in a row since the resurrection of football at U of C were elected co-captains.

Construction of Henry Crown Field House was completed in1932. The "new era" football team's locker room was in the basement of the Field House. Archival Photographic Files, Special Collections Research Center, University of Chicago Library.

-12-

Thirty-two pairs of cleated shoes click-clacked on the concrete sidewalk along 56th Street. Jack fell into step with the coaching staff following the team to Stagg Field after the team meeting.

"Jack, I'd like you to meet Coach Rogan," Wally said. "You know he'll be taking over as offensive coordinator, so the two of you are going to be spending a lot of time together. You'll still play in the secondary, but I'm hoping to work this new kid, a first-year, Greg Vendel in there too. I don't want you playing both ways the whole game anymore. Let's see what you can do if you concentrate mostly on catching the ball."

"Whatever you say, Coach. Any way to get out of the clutches of Donny, I mean, Coach Dubka."

"Watch it buddy!" Donny Dubka said with a laugh.

Jack turned, extended his hand and said, "Nice to meet you, Coach Rogan." Rogan gripped Jack's hand with a knuckle crunching grip, nodded curtly, and walked on.

Jack hoped he didn't show it, but Rogan's grip was such a bone crusher it actually hurt. He'd heard that Rogan had been in the Marines. Jack wondered if it was a Marines thing, or was the new coach so insecure he has to prove his manhood by trying to intimidate every guy he meets with a phalanges-crushing handshake.

The team formed up on the practice field in three rows of ten. The four new captains, Cauley, Shooksie, Mancusa, and Kovatch took their places facing their teammates. Jack stood off to the side with the coaches. This was the first time he'd attended a preseason practice. He was curious to see if it differed much from the way practice was run during the season.

Cauley shouted, "Jumping jacks, let's go, count 'em out!"

"Wait! Wait a minute," Mancusa growled in his distinctive "da Region" accent. "We got another captain here. You ain't a coach or a manager, Eighty-Four. Get up here!"

Mancusa grew up a steel-mill worker's son in East Chicago. He weighed 195 pounds and stood 5-foot-10, had a scar on his chin, and looked and sounded like a tough mill worker himself. And, in fact, he worked summers as a millwright apprentice since he'd been in college. His scholastic interests were, however, rather unusual for a tough steel mill worker from da Region. Xavier Mancusa had three loves, the Roman Catholic Church, Italian Renaissance chamber music, and football, in that order. He planned to enter a Franciscan seminary after graduation, was a DJ on the University's WHPK radio station hosting an Italian Renaissance chamber music program, and played linebacker for the Maroons. He also swam butterfly on the college swim team and carried a 3.8 GPA at a school which had not given in to grade inflation like the Ivies.

Jack glanced over at Wally. The coach arched his eyebrows in a question and inclined his head toward the line of captains. A sly grin sneaked across Wally's face when Jack yelled, "All right Mancusa! Then you better keep up with me!" Jack pulled an American flag bandana out of his back pocket and slipped it over his head to keep his long blond-hair out of his eyes. Jack kicked off his penny loafers from his sock-less feet revealing a white bandage around his left big toe. He jogged up beside Shooksie and stood in a ready position. Cauley gave him the thumbs up then bellowed, "Maroons! Count off one two, one! One two, two!"

After twenty minutes of exercises and stretching Mick McVale shouted out as loud as he could in his ancient raspy voice, "Take a lap gentlemen, then we'll work some position drills." The players broke into a run, backs and ends sprinting to the front, linebackers in the middle , and linemen lumbering behind. Heinz and Moose trailed the pack breathing hard at a pace that barely qualified as a jog. After they finished the run, Wally broke the team up into different units for drills. Coach McVale took the offensive linemen. He shook his head in disgust waiting for Heinz and Moose who walked the last hundred yards of the half -mile run. Coach Dubka took the defensive linemen and linebackers, Rogan the offensive and defensive backs and receivers, and Wally the kickers.

Jack wasn't sure what to do, so he followed Wally and the kickers. Wally told him to go down field and catch and retrieve kicks and punts.

Jack liked the feel of running barefoot on the grass of the neatly trimmed field. He'd spent many Saturday and Sunday afternoons as a child running shoeless through the hills and along the streams of Jackson County, gigging frogs, fishing, and catching turtles and crawdads. The clipped turf of Stagg Field was easy on the bottoms of his feet compared to the rocky creek beds and limestone studded hills around the family farm.

Jack sailed easily around the field, forward, then back pedaling, cutting and diving. He caught every ball that was kicked within ten yards of his outstretched hands. It was fun for awhile, but it wasn't much of a workout. Despite having already violated his principle of not participating in preseason practices and feeling kind of suckered by Wally, Jack wished he was in pads. Too late for that, but he could at least run some routes with the other receivers before they started hitting.

Whump! Mike Chefski, the Maroons' kicker launched the ball trying for a thirty yard field goal. Short again. Jack ran the ball down. Before he threw the pigskin back to Mike, he called up field to Wally, "Hey Coach, okay if I run some patterns with the receivers?"

Wally motioned for Jack to "bring it in". Jack jogged over to where Wally, Mike, and Dennis Maroni, the team's punter, were gathered. "Mr. Blair, since you're now a captain, perhaps you can help settle the debate our two scholar-athlete kickers have been carrying on while you've been shagging balls."

"Sure, Coach."

"Well, Mr. Chefski claims that a kickoff is more aesthetically pleasing than a punt, but Mr. Maroni here disagrees."

Mike Chefski earnestly stated his case, "It's really quite obvious. The arc of the parabola formed by a kick is more elegant than a punt. On the point-after or a field goal, when the ball's parabolic arc bisects the imaginary lines formed by the uprights of the goalposts, it's especially aesthetically pleasing."

Dennis Maroni was shaking his head vigorously while Chefski exposed his theory of kicking aesthetics. But before he could respond, Jack cut in, "Coach, I've actually heard this argument before. On the bus to Valparaiso last year Maroni and Chefski held a point/counterpoint debate, like on the Sixty-Minutes TV show--"

"But—"

Wally cut Dennis off, "Well, I wish you hadn't reminded us of the Valpo game. Jeez Louise! A forty four to zero thrashing! Had Mr. Chefski actually put his theory into practice and bisected the real, and not his imaginary goalposts, we'd have had at least six points and been spared the indignity of a white wash." Wally shook his head disgustedly. Mike Chefski hung his head.

"But—"

Wally held his hand up to silence Dennis again. "And Mr. Maroni, how many times did you get to practice your punting parabola?"

"Let's see, the Valpo game, we punted eight times in the first half, but only five in the second," Dennis said helpfully.

Wally muttered, "Probably a new record -- but can't cry over spilled milk." Then, with a sharp look at his punter, "If Mr. Maroni was as good with his leg as he is with statistics, and had put the ball in the coffin corner a few times – well, just maybe we would have had the field position to score a touchdown." Wally huffed, "Instead, we started deep in our own end of the field every time!"

The old coach was working himself up to the point of threatening to dash his clipboard to the ground, so Jack thought this would be a good time to extricate himself as arbitrator of the debate. "Uh, sorry, but my own aesthetic judgment is way too crude to resolve such a sublime issue. Coach, would it be okay if I joined the receivers and ran some routes?"

Wally waved his hand dismissively. He was obviously still reliving the painful loss to the Valparaiso Crusaders JV team. "See what Coach Rogan wants you to do."

Jack trotted down to the opposite end of the field, where the QBs, backs, and ends were running pass patterns and hand-offs under Rogan's direction. Jack stood off to the side waiting respectfully for Coach Rogan to recognize him. Rogan stood with his hands behind his back, his jaw thrust out at a parade-rest yet aggressive sort of posture. He barked crisp orders of instruction at the players. Rogan didn't acknowledge Jack's presence.

Jack's patience began to wear thin after a few minutes of silent waiting. He cleared his throat and said, "Coach, can I work in with the guys and run some patterns?"

Without looking at Jack, Rogan put his whistle in his mouth and gave a sharp blast. "Gentlemen, take a knee." Coach Rogan strode over to Jack, stopped right in front of him, looked him up and down and then said in a voice purposefully loud enough for the other players to hear, "Mr. Blair, you are not in uniform. Correct?"

"Uh, yeah."

"Football players wear uniforms when they practice or play, do they not, Mr. Blair?"

"Uh, usually."

"So where's your uniform, Mr. Blair?"

"Well, I turned it in after spring practice and haven't got one—"

"Mr. Blair, I am well aware of your proclivity for missing practices. And I am also aware of the rule that coaches cannot discipline players, if there is a medical or academic excuse for missing practice. You, however, have no such excuse. You have shown your teammates and coaches that your toe injury does not prevent you from practicing. So, as far as I am concerned, Mr. Blair, you are either not here as a member of this team. Or, if you are here, then you should be in uniform. Your choice, Mr. Blair, go get your uniform or get off my field."

"But Coach, how can I get a uniform—"

Rogan turned and blew another blast on his whistle. He waved at Reb Cratchet signaling the student manager to come. Cratch looked up from the equipment box he was organizing on the sidelines. "Cratchet! On the double!" Rogan yelled. As Cratchet jogged toward them, Rogan turned back to Jack and said in a lowered voice, "You're going to learn that things will be different while I'm in charge, Mr. Blair. No exceptions."

Cratch stopped beside Jack, and said with an innocent grin, "Hey Jack. What's up, Coach?"

"Mr. Blair hasn't been issued a uniform yet. Escort him back to the equipment room, fit him out, and then it's up to him to decide whether he is part of this team or not." Rogan turned his back on Jack and Cratchet, blew his whistle, then shouted, "Let's go, back in formation! Cauley, ten-yard curls! We're behind schedule!"

Cratch looked at Jack. The muscles in Jack's jaw tightened and he pressed a thumb hard into his other palm. He glared at Rogan's retreating back. Cratchet touched Jack lightly on the shoulder, "You okay, Jack?"

"Yeah, I'm okay, Cratch. Let's get my uniform. You saved '84' for me, didn't you?"

With Cratch's help, Jack picked out and tried on equipment until he was fitted with helmet, shoulder pads, hip pads, practice pants and game pants with thigh and knee pads, low cut hard-rubber cleated shoes, two practice jerseys, a white game-jersey and maroon game-jersey with number-84. Jack stripped off the uniform and packed all his newly issued gear into the locker Cratch assigned him. Jack slammed the metal door shut and spun the combination lock.

"Uh, Jack, aren't you going to suit up for practice?" Cratch asked.

"Nope." Jack walked out of the locker room in his street clothes.

[Assistant Coach Chet McGraw at team practice the first year of the "resurrection" of football at U of C; undated photo 1968-69, Archival Photographic Files, Special Collections Research Center, University of Chicago Library.]

-13-

It was the Sunday before classes were to commence Fall Quarter 1971, when Steven Schwartz arrived at the apartment on Greenwood Avenue he and Jack had rented. Jack helped unload Steven's stereo, record collection, books, clothes, and personal effects from the little U-Haul truck Steven had driven from New York. While they unloaded and organized Steven's stuff in the apartment, Jack laid out his dilemma.

"So I signed up to take Literary Criticism with Herman Sinaiko Monday, Wednesday, and Friday at four o'clock, you know, to conflict with practice—"

"I know! Jack, we talked through this last spring. You said you wanted to go back to practicing only two days a week. What's the problem? Classes start tomorrow, and you got the schedule you wanted."

"Yeah, I know, but I'm thinking that maybe I could stick with a Tuesday-Thursday schedule and practice three times a week, like last year. Getting elected co-captain is making me feel guilty about showing up for practice less than any of the other captains."

"A little late for that, isn't it? How're you going to change your class schedule with classes starting tomorrow?"

Steven and Jack roomed together each year since their first year in Woodward Court. They had become best friends and confidantes, despite a wide gulf in backgrounds and interests. Steven was from a wealthy New York Jewish family. His parents met at U of C, and so, Steven was a "legacy". Like many outstanding Jewish students and faculty, Steven's parent came to Chicago after being snubbed back East by the Ivies.

Steven was a complete klutz at sports. The most physical activity he'd tried was ballet to fulfill his Phys Ed requirement first year. He not only sucked at ballet, with short legs and a long torso, he looked ridiculous in tights. A fact which Jack pointed out every time Steven suited up for ballet.

Steven's interest in football had begun and ended one day at recess when he was in grade school. He related the incident to Jack, when Jack informed Steven he was considering going out for the new football team. Steven explained that he had no idea how the game was played. But he was forced into a sandlot game by the teacher supervising recess. When the ball was hiked, the next thing he knew another kid knocked him down. He left the playground in tears and never played another down. Nevertheless, he was a regular at all the Maroons' home games. Whenever Jack or the team did something that Steven could discern was worth cheering about, he was out of his seat yelling with the few hundred other hearty souls who came out to cheer for the Home Team. He even wrote a cheer during the 1969 season which had become a fan favorite:

Themistocles, Thucydides
The Peloponnesian War
X-squared, Y-squared
H2SO4
Who for? What for?
Who we gonna yell for?
Chicago! Chicago! Chicago!

Steven's actual knowledge about football had changed little in the three years he'd roomed with Jack. But he was a deeply loyal friend to his roommate. So, he not only attended every home game but had become the unofficial cheerleader of the hand full of students who came out to watch the Maroons play. And, he discovered that he had a gift for producing clever cheers which appealed to the intellectually snobbery of his fellow U of C fans.

"Okay, so let's think through the issue," Steven said in a stentorian tone. "The facts are: One, you've received what you wanted from playing on the football team, i.e., qualification for the Rhodes. Two, getting elected captain is icing on the cake, but you're a captain now whether you go to practice two or three times per week. Three, this new coach Rogan is a dick. You've already butted heads with him. Why would you want to spend anymore time with that asshole than you have to?"

"Not a bad brief, Perry Mason--"

"Clarence Darrow, if you please—"

"Right! Anyway, I agree with the facts as stated, but you left out three: One, the team; two, Wally Hass; and three, Coach McVale."

"I assume you'll elaborate."

"Thank you Clarence, I will. The team elected me captain. I owe it to them to show some leadership. This is the last season before Coach Hass and Coach McVale retire. My stats improved fifty percent by going to practice three times instead of two times a week. If I can kick it up another notch, I can help the team break through to get a win for Mick and Wally before they retire."

"Well then, Hamilton Burger—"

"Hey, I'd rather be Paul Drake; he's the handsome guy on the winning side."

"You can have Drake; I'll take Della Reese—"

"Yeah, you look like her in your tights."

"Only in your dreams, roomie. Now, back to the subject at hand. Given your arguments, it would seem to follow that you should commit to going to practice every day, not just three times each week. No?"'

"Yes, but no."

"No, how so?"

"Your number-three."

"Which was?"

"Coach Rogan is a dick."

-14-

Before his first class on Monday morning Jack popped into Enid Rieser's office in Harper Commons. As Assistant Dean of Students, Ms. Rieser was in charge of the rural scholarship program. She had corresponded with Jack during the admission process and had taken him under her wing his first quarter on campus. She reminded Jack of his mom. Not in looks, because, although she was short like his mom, the assistant dean had elegantly coifed black hair, always wore pearls around her neck, and Jack was sure she'd never plucked a chicken. But she seemed so genuinely concerned with helping Jack, her tone and attitude of tender care always reminded him of his mom.

With Dean Rieser's help, Jack was able to switch out of the Literary Criticism class and into a Tuesday-Thursday seminar class on Plato's *Symposium*. The Plato class was taught by James Blackford, who was Jack's favorite professor. Jack was satisfied he'd made the right decision to change his class schedule.

As he stood up to leave Dean Rieser's office, she asked, "So when are the Maroons going to get that first elusive victory, Jack?" When she met privately with students, Dean Rieser dispensed with the University's custom of addressing students as 'Mr.' or 'Ms'.

Jack stopped, looked down and shook his head dolefully. But he brightened when he looked into the dean's sparkling green eyes, and replied, "Soon, I hope. We've gotta send Coach Hass into retirement with at least one win. Dean Rieser, did you know that Coach's career victories are ninety nine?"

"No, I didn't know that."

"Yeah, wouldn't it be cool for him to get number 100 before he retires?"

"Yes it would, Jack. No one deserves an honor like that more than Walter Hass. You know he worked like a dog for over ten years to bring football back to the University."

"Yeah, I've heard about that. Huh! As rough as it's been though, losing every game for two seasons, I'm not sure Wally, er, Coach Hass still thinks it's worth it."

"Oh yes he does! I was at the table next to his for lunch at the Quad Club the other day. He and Coach McVale were talking excitedly about the upcoming season and the two new coaches on staff. I heard them mention your name too."

Jack gulped self consciously.

"Mr. Hass said something along the lines of, 'Of the players I've coached, Jack Blair is as talented as any who played for Stagg's Monsters of the Midway.'"

Jack's cheeks flushed. He felt both pride and embarrassment. He stammered, "Uh, okay, well, thanks again, Dean Rieser." He turned and hurried out of her office.

It was a grey Chicago rainy-afternoon when the team gathered for practice at three-thirty that same Monday afternoon. There were only five more practices to get ready for the first game against Lake Forest on Saturday. The coaches decided the team would start practice in the weight room in Bartlett Gymnasium and then shift to the outfield of the softball diamond between Crowne Field House and Pierce Tower, if the rain let up.

The players clambered up the creaking stairway in Bartlett Gymnasium in stocking feet. Every time Jack used these steps he hesitated to admire the panoramic frieze mounted above the massive oak doorways into the gym. "Athletic Games in the Middle Ages" was painted, Jack had learned, by the artist Frederic Clay Bartlett in 1904 in blended Gothic and English Arts and Crafts style. Bartlett Gymnasium was built with funds donated by the artist's father in memory of another son. At the center of the painting is a shield bearing the dedication: "To the advancement of Physical Education and the Glory of Manly Sports this gymnasium is dedicated to the memory of Frank Dickinson Bartlett, 1880-1900." Another inscription reads,

"How happy is he born and taught that serveth not another's will; whose armor is his honest thought and simple truth his utmost skill." The gym was designed to Amos Alonzo Stagg's specifications to inspire "athletic culture" at the U of C.

The team halted in the upper level of the gym in a corner beside the running track. Jack surveyed the equipment scattered around the area which served as the team's workout room. The condition of the facilities was in stark contrast to the elevated sentiments expressed in the frieze above the entrance to the gym.

When the team used the weight room for its very first practice, spring in 1969, Jack thought the coaches were playing a joke on their new recruits. Barbells were made of Hills Brothers coffee cans filled with cement and stuck on the ends of iron bars. Wooden "Indian clubs" were stacked in racks against the wall. They looked like the implements Teddy Roosevelt worked out with in pictures Jack had seen in his high-school history text-book. The weight bench was a wooden contraption painted with black pine tar. It had "arms" notched for barbells at different levels. The weight room looked like a museum preserved in tact since the University dropped out of the Big Ten. It smelled musty and there was a layer of dust covering the equipment. Jack imagined legendary players during the Maroons' glory years, like George Gipp, Bronko Nagurski, or Red Grange stopping by to take turns with Jay Berwanger on the ancient bench-press. The physical remains of the athletic culture Stagg had inspired in the 1920s had declined from disuse into rusted, moldy bric-a-brac.

But, like the coaching staff, the weight room had finally been upgraded for the 1971 season. The old pine-tar painted weight-bench was replaced with two padded steel-benches for the bench press. Two Universal machines had been installed. Bar bells and weights of varying sizes we re stacked in iron racks. Jack wondered if the better equipment meant the Administration finally and fully accepted that football was once again part of the University's unique culture. Maybe the powers that be were embarrassed by the Maroons' dismal record.

Jack scanned the new equipment with only mild gratitude. It was a pretty paltry financial commitment by the University Administration to help the team become competitive. He considered that improved workout facilities and an expanded coaching staff were important first steps. Yet the quality of facilities in Bartlett Gym was below what Seymour High School provided for its varsity teams. While Coaches Hass and McVale were more humane than Jack's high school coaches, whether the quality of coaching was any better, given the addition of Dubka and Rogan, well, the jury was out on that.

It was clear to the team and coaches that the level of commitment of the University Administration to the football program remained fairly tepid in 1971. The players had seen the sparkling new athletic centers at some of the colleges the Maroons played. These small Midwestern liberal-arts colleges took more pride in their athletics than the greatest university in the Midwest.

Jack had often debated in his own mind, with Steve n, and with guys on the team: Which made more sense, for a college to binge spend on its sports programs or for sports to be a low priority in a school's budget? Despite his disappointment in the quality of facilities, Jack remained convinced the U of C had the better side of the argument. Academics are the purpose of a college and sports are a mere adjunct to that purpose. He didn't understand how schools justified spending millions of dollars on sports programs and paying their coaches salaries comparable to those of movie stars. The outrageous amounts paid to coaches at major state universities seemed especially unjust, considering that taxpayers might have to foot the bill, while players receive nothing more than a scholarship. If a player was injured or his grades declined, the scholarship could be rescinded. If a coach got fired or retired, he'd probably walk away with a hefty contract settlement and a pension. Not fair and not right in Jack's opinion.

And yet, when he wandered into the Bartlett Trophy Room and gazed through the glass cases at the Big Ten Championship plaques, the old footballs commemorating victories over Notre Dame and Michigan, and Berwanger's Heisman Trophy, Jack felt a pang of regret. He could imagine what it was like playing in the monstrous gothic stadium against the best teams in the country with tens of thousands of cheering fans. To develop a team that could play at that level required a commitment from a university, as well as the coaches and players, that would never happen again at the U of C. Still, it would have been amazing to play with the Monsters of the Midway under the great Amos Alonzo Stagg and to compete for a national championship.

That idea was filed in the folder for fantasies in Jack's mind. He was happy to be playing for Wally Hass on a Division III team which gave no scholarships. It was pure. Athletics was one of the many disciplines offered by the University. As a scholar-athlete Jack could develop his athletic self under the guidance of Coach Hass just as he was improving his skill and knowledge of Attic Greek and philosophy under the guidance of Professor Blackford. He just wished his efforts on the football field would be rewarded with a win like his efforts in the classroom had been recognized with a 3.7 GPA.

[Bartlett Gym was designed to Stagg's specifications to promote "athletic culture". Undated photo, Archival Photographic Files, University of Chicago Library, Special Collections Research Center]

-15-

Before taking to the field for the first game of the 1 971
Season the Maroons gathered in the maintenance shed at
the south end of Stagg Field. They sat on and among
lawnmowers, wheel barrows, and motorized carts. The Lake
Forest Foresters held their pre-game meeting in their team
bus. Wally stood with his back to the door of the shed
flanked by the other coaches. The tension among the
players was palpable. Guys stared at the coaches with wall-
eyed blank looks or had their heads bowed chanting good
luck mantras. Jack felt an uncomfortable buzzing inside his
head and weakness in his stomach. Pre-game jitters were a
familiar, although unwelcome, companion. He knew they
would depart once he got into the flow of the game. The
entire team had a case of the nervous Nellie 's waiting for
Coach Hass's pregame pep talk.

Wally took his time. He glanced around gravely at his
players. His once chiseled halfback's upper body had
devolved into elderly softness. His round face was tanned
from supervising practices outdoors. Wally looked like a
cute and cuddly grandpa, but his blue eyes were clear and
focused. Finally, Coach Hass waved his clipboard for
attention.

"We've worked hard for this moment. Each of you are
prepared. You know your assignments. I don't need to tell
you how important it is to get off on the right foot this
season. This will be the last season for eleven of us – the 9
fourth-years, Coach McVale, and me. I said all I need to say
at the last team meeting. I know you'll each do your best.
Coach McVale?"

Mick shook his jowls and growled, "Leave it all on the
field."

"Coach Rogan?" Rogan shook his head.

Wally turned to Coach Dubka, who let out a whoop,
"Maroons! Bring it in!"

The players jumped off the utility vehicles to form a tight circle in front of the coaches. With their arms up and hands clasped into a united knot the players roared, "Go Maroons!"

The team burst out of the maintenance shed and ran onto the playing field. Dubka and Rogan jogged after the team to form up the players into lines for jumping jacks and warm-up drills. Wally and Mick followed slowly.

"First of the last," Wally said quietly.

"I'm ready. Are you?" Mick grunted.

Wally squeezed Mick on the arm, smiled, and then pretended to swing a golf club. "Next year, this time, Hilton Head."

The Foresters won the coin flip and elected to receive. Chefski, kicking with the wind, lofted a beautiful parabolic kick into the air. But the ball only sailed thirty-five yards down field. Coach McVale growled into Coach Hass's ear, "Damn it Walter, have Karchuk kick off! It's not pretty, but at least he's got the power to send it down to the twenty! " Wally shook his head regretfully.

The short kick gave the Foresters good field position and they took advantage. In a succession of running plays up the middle and short slants and button hook passes they scored the first touchdown of the game. Less than four minutes after the kickoff the Maroons were down six to zero.

On the point after, Opey O'Byrne and Dickey Roudebush ran a stunt they'd practiced to perfection. Opey lined up across from the tight end but threw himself into the shoulder pad of the Forester's left tackle. The end fell forward trying to block Opey. Dickey had lined up behind Opey and blasted through the gap. Dickey got his fingertips on the ball just as it left the foot of the kicker. The ball was slightly deflected, but it hit the right upright and bounced through. The score was seven nothing.

The Maroons' little speedster, Denny Murphy, fielded the Forester's kick on the fifteen and scooted up the field dodging the first two tackles before he was brought down on the Maroons' 34-yard line. The Lower Brass Conspiracy tootled and thumped "Wave the Flag of Old Chicago". Old alumni from the Big Ten era and current students stood and sang:

Wave the flag of old Chicago,
Maroon the color grand.
Ever shall her team be victors
Known throughout the land.
With the grand old man to lead them,
Without a peer they'll stand.
Wave again the dear old banner,
For they're heroes every man.

The fans settled back in their seats to watch the Maroons' first offensive series of the 1971 season. Coach Rogan hoped to surprise the Foresters on the first play from scrimmage. Jack was used as a decoy. He split wide right and ran a post pattern to draw the left cornerback with him, and hopefully, the left safety too. Johnny Jones, the only player faster than Jack in a forty-yard dash, shot out of the backfield in a fly pattern up the right side. The corner bumped and ran with Jack. Unfortunately, the safety wasn't fooled and hit Jones just as Cauley's pass reached him. Incomplete.

A groan went up from the stands. On the sideline, Wally shook his head. "So close," he muttered to Mick. Coach Rogan looked on impassively, and then spoke firmly into the ear hole of Denny Murphy's helmet, "Spread option shovel pass." Rogan swatted Denny on the butt to send him in with the play.

Cauley took the snap and sprinted left, waited for the tackler to close and just as he was hit executed a perfect shovel pass to Denny. The five foot eight scat-back scampered for a first down.

Boisterous students leaped to their feet. Steven Schwartz led the cheer:

Logarithm, biorhythm,
Entropy, kinetics,
MPC, GNP, bioenergetics!
Maximize and integrate,

Titrate and Equilibrate--
Go, Maroons!

Unfortunately, the Maroons failed to advance the ball
on any of the next three plays. Maroni came in to punt from
the Foresters' 48-yard line and kicked the ball neatly out of
bounds at the fourteen. After that, the game settled into a
back and forth defensive struggle. The Foresters were clearly
the bigger and stronger team. They were able to push the
Maroons defenders off the line for short yardage gains.
However, the Maroons did prove to be the quicker team.
The Foresters passing attack was stymied by Chicago 's
speedy secondary. Although most of the half was played at
the Maroons' end of the field, the Visitors were unable to
put together a successful string of plays to score again. The
Maroons offense, utilizing Coach Rogan's strategy of
sophisticated pass plays with simple run plays mixed in,
however, failed to move the ball closer than the Foresters'
40-yard line. The half ended, Maroons-0, Lake Forest-7.

The teams retired to opposite ends of the field. Big Ed,
the largest Kazoo in the world, was wheeled onto the field by
members of Students for Violent Non-Action. The Lower
Brass Conspiracy Band struck up a bizarre but jaunty tune.
Students and kids from the neighborhood screeched and
honked on kazoos. At first, they paraded around the field in
a quasi formation simulating the performance of a marching
band. Then, the ragtag troupe broke out into the fan favorite
Brownian Motion. Kids ran all over the field blowing on
kazoos, colliding with each other, falling down and getting up
to dash about randomly.

The halftime fun was brought to an end when the
announcer boomed over the crackling loudspeaker a
warning to leave the field. Before play resumed, Jim Capps,
the student announcer, informed the fans of hypothetical
and absurd scores like "Harvard ten, Princeton; Yale sixty
nine, with whom?"

[Photo provided by Don Bingle, UChicago Class of 1976,
leader of the Fez Faction and caretaker of Big Ed.]

The second half began as the first half ended. Lake
Forest moved the ball, but couldn't punch it in for a score.
Chicago's offense continued to splutter, but its defense
stiffened whenever the Foresters pushed very deep into the
Home Team's territory. But then, on the first series the
Maroons had the ball in the fourth quarter, Rogan's strategy
finally worked. He sent in Murphy with instructions to call a
double reverse flea flicker.

Bob Cauley bootlegged left, disguised his hand-off to
Murphy who was running the opposite direction from his
slot position. Johnny Jones had started right as the lone back
in an I-Formation, but then cut back left to take the hand-off

from Murphy. Cauley was tackled by the confused defensive end, but had popped up and was now standing alone on the left side of a scrum of players. The defenders were unsure who had the ball. Jones pitched the ball to Cauley. Bob threw a beautiful arcing cross-field pass to Jack who was waiting alone in the deep right corner of the end zone. The Field Judge brought his hands up in the air signaling touchdown.

Pandemonium broke out in the stands. The Lower Brass Conspiracy struck up "Ode to Joy" while a hundred kazoos bleated and tooted. White haired alumni in maroon-colored sweaters rose shakily to their feet, shook their fists, and croaked out a joyful "Go Maroons!"

The Lake Forest coach ran onto the field waving his arms and shouting. The referee was blasting away on his whistle. Maroons jumped in the air and hugged each other. Donny Dubka threw his hat in the air, ran over to Coach McVale and started to lift him up, but was dissuaded by a low guttural sound emanating from the old coach's viscera. Rogan stood stock still staring intently at the ref. Wally also watched the ref intently while rocking nervously back and forth from one foot to the other.

The ref blew a final shrill tweet on his whistle and waved his hand beckoning Wally onto the field. Coach Hass trudged slowly toward the center of the playing field. Players crowded excitedly around the ref. He blew two sharp blasts on his whistle and ordered all the players on both teams to their respective sidelines. The referee, two head coaches, the umpire, and field judge were left alone in the center of the field.

The Maroons stood on their sideline anxiously awaiting the outcome of the conversation of the authorities on the field. QB Bob, Denny Murphy, Johnny Jones, and Jack linked arms. Mancusa crossed himself. Shooksie, Heinz, and Moose, who had just been high fiving, stood quietly holding their helmets behind their backs. The tumult of the several hundred joyous spectators died to a hushed silence.

Even the loquacious announcer, Jim Capps, remained silent awaiting a final judgment by the referees.

Lake Forest's coach continued waving his arms like a busted windmill in a storm. The head ref looked to the field judge who nodded and again signaled a catch. But the umpire was shaking his head and slicing downward with his left hand. What any of them were saying was indistinguishable to Jack and his teammates on the sideline. Wally had added little to the colloquy, apparently content to let the others have their say and await the head ref's decision.

Jack was able to make out the referee's barely audible "... two forward passes ..." at which point Wally lifted his clipboard high above his head and then threw it to the ground. With their helmets off Jack and his comrades started to run onto the field howling in despair. Mick McVale barked out a warning and Coach Dubka ran out and started pushing players back toward the sideline. Wally bent over slowly and picked up his clipboard.

The dispirited Maroons gave up a field goal near the end of the game.

Final score: Lake Forest-10, Chicago-0.

[The resurrected Maroons' first season in 1969; photo undated, Archival Photographic Files, University of Chicago Library, Special Collections Research Center]

-16-

Jack, Moose Harris, and Mike Kovatch met for lunch at the C-Shop beside Hutchinson Commons Monday after the season opening loss to Lake Forest. They settled into a window booth with their milkshakes, hamburgers , and French fries. The three players were silent for a moment staring out the window at pigeons gathered on the edge of the fountain in the middle of Hutch Quad. The grey limestone of the buildings of the quadrangle reflected the melancholy mood of the three players.

After awhile, Moose and Jack began pissing and moaning about the ref's call which took away Jack's touchdown catch. "God damn it! I saw Bob step back from the line of scrimmage before Denny pitched him the ball," Moose grumped.

"But that wasn't the issue, Moose," Jack said in an irritable tone. "The penalty wasn't a forward pass beyond the line of scrimmage. It was for a second forward pass behind the line. Bob was supposed to back pedal before Jonesy pitched him be ball, so the pitch wouldn't be a forward pass."

"Yeah, I know. But Cauley probably got his bell rung hard enough when he got tackled on the bootleg he forgot to back pedal," Moose said morosely.

Jack turned to Kovatch, who was staring silently and distractedly out the window. "Why so quiet, Vatch?"

Kovatch remained silent. Jack and Moose exchanged curious glances. "Come on, Mike, what's up?" Moose elbowed Kovatch in the ribs.

A crease furrowed Mike Kovatch's wide forehead. He cast a worried look around the C-Shop. Students at other tables munched on burgers or Vienna Beef hotdogs. Most were engaged in animated discussions about their classes, a new TV-show called Soul Train, or the opening performance of T. S. Eliot's "Murder in the Cathedral" in

Rockefeller Chapel. No one paid any attention to the three football players in their midst.

Kovatch sighed and gave his two friends a long look. "My brother's in the psych ward in University Hospital."

"Your younger brother, Paul?" Jack asked in a shocked tone.

"Yeah, he's on suicide watch," Kovatch said glumly.

"Wait a minute," Moose said in a loud whisper. "Paul, the second-year who's going through Rush with the Fijis?'

"Yeah, that's my little brother. He was gonna go out for the wrestling team too."

"Yeah, I met him at our Rush party," Moose said looking incredulous.

Moose and ten other football players belonged to the Fiji House. It was known as the jock frat at U of C. A few of the players belonged to the Psi U House and a couple joined the Alpha Delts. However, half the team had not joined fraternities. Some were vociferously opposed to the Greek system, like many other students in the late 60s and early 70s at U of C. These students considered fraternities and sororities a manifestation of a colonialist-imperialistic-hegemonistic world view which expressed itself in discriminatory exclusivist-enclaves hostile to women and minorities.

U of C had no sororities in 1971. There were no sororities on campus at UChicago from the founding of the University until 1985 with the charter of Alpha Omicron Pi. The urban legend passed down through generations of UChicago students to explain why there were no sororities was that Ida Noyes had killed herself by drowning in Lake Michigan after she was rejected by every campus sorority. Her rich father donated Ida Noyes Hall on the condition that the University never allow sororities on campus. A supplemental edition of the legend was that the College's requirement that all students pass a swimming test before graduation came about after Ida's drowning. According to that version of the story, after she threw herself disconsolately into the lake, Ida tried to save herself but couldn't because she didn't know how to swim.

There was no truth to either version of the legend. Ida was the wife, not daughter, of the inventor and industrialist La Verne Noyes, who donated the funds to build Ida Noyes Hall without any conditions imposed on the University. Sororities simply never germinated at U of C, because there were many other organizations for women. Also, many U of C women, especially Jewish students, disapproved of the exclusionary and anti-intellectual aspects of Greek societies.

Jack considered joining one of the fraternities, but decided he didn't want to make the commitment. He figured that the initiation fee and dues would severely dent, or exhaust, his summer earnings. Plus, he liked rooming with Steven. Since he wasn't a member of any fraternity, he was free to hang out with friends at any of the frat houses.

He and Steven joked that the frat boys who played sports at U of C belonged to a radical minority. "Those guys want to have a normal college experience -- you know, fraternity beer parties, varsity sports, and pinning their girlfriends. At U of C, man, that's radical," Steven opined.

In defense of his frat boy jock-friends, Jack pointed out that they tended not to be intellectually pretentious. An irritating quality, Steven agreed, which was quite common among U of C students. And, the best weed and beer parties on campus were at the Psi U House. Their parties got wild enough students regularly jumped out the second -story windows high on pot or LSD. Jack quoted Robby Robertson, an English Lit concentrator, poet, football player, and member of Psi U. "All these pseudo intellectuals at U of C don't know a thing about real life. They've lived with their noses stuck inside a book from the time they could read. You have to look around man, see the country. Feel life!"

Steven's rejoinder was that it is all well and good to feel life, but you probably won't know what to make of your feelings if you're unable to analyze them thoughtfully. "And, if you don't have your nose in a book now and then, your analysis will not be very well informed." He went on, "It was

your Jesus who said, 'know the truth and the truth will set
you free', right? Knowing requires learning, which requires
study." Steven concluded by folding his arms across his
chest. A self-satisfied smile spread across his narrow face.

Jack's rejoinder, "Yeah, but at the U of C I think
Flannery O'Connor might have gotten it as right as Jesus,
'Seek the truth and the truth will make you odd.'"

Kovatch let the story about his younger brother dribble
out as Jack and Moose sucked noisily through straws to get
the last drops of their milkshakes. The teammates tried to
console their friend, as well as self-absorbed 21-year-olds do
that sort of thing.

It seemed that Paul was living a kind of double life. He
was being torn between two opposing forces. His roommate
in Vincent House at Burton-Judson Courts dorm was a
third-year and serious methamphetamines user who was into
French nihilism. Mike Kovatch thought that Drake Soltan
had a sinister influence over Paul. "Paul was always a
bookworm, but who isn't at U of C?" Mike asked
rhetorically. During Paul's senior year in high school his
literary interests had turned darkly philosophical. He was
especially taken with Dostoevsky and developed an interest
in Nietzsche's philosophy. He also listened to a lot of
Wagnerian opera. Mike surmised that rooming with Drake
had pushed Paul further into a dark and depressing outlook.

Mike explained that, when Paul entered U of C last year
Mike had introduced his brother to his jock friends and had
encouraged Paul to go through fraternity Rush and join the
wrestling team. "Before his senior year in high school, Paul
was a popular kid and he won the sectional tournament in
wrestling. So, I hoped he'd pull out of the dark place he'd
gotten into his last year in high school. Get back to the
happy little brother I used to have. Instead, he seemed to
withdraw even further his first year here. Like, he'd only
leave his room in Burton-Judson to go to class. You know
BJ can be kind of depressing, especially on cold, grey winter-
days. He and Drake just holed up in their cave, smoked pot,

popped pills, and talked about the meaninglessness of life,"
Mike said shaking his head.

"He seemed fine when I met him at the Rush party,"
Moose said in a sympathetic tone.

"I know. I spent time with him over summer break. He
was going to join a frat. He planned to go out for wrestling. I
thought he'd finally come out of his depression. But then
school started and he was rooming with Drake again in
Vincent House. I shouldn't have let him—"

"Come on Vatch, it's not your fault, man," Jack
interrupted. "You couldn't tell him where to live."

"So why exactly is he in the psych ward?" Moose asked.

Mike explained that Paul had attempted suicide Saturday
night. He smoked a lot of pot, drank some whiskey , and
then jumped off the roof of BJ. Students on Paul and
Drake's floor reported that the roommates had been talking
about a suicide pact. But no one had taken them seriously.

According to Burton-Judson Courts lore, a decade
earlier several students had made and carried out a suicide
pact by jumping off the roof of the dorm. Two Vincent
House student-residents, who gave statements about Paul's
jump to the investigator for the University Police, each said
that Drake seemed obsessed with the legend of a suicide
pact. They told the investigator that Drake often retold and
embellished the story with his own sick fantasies.

Kovatch concluded his description of Paul's condition by
telling his friends that Paul was hospitalized in the psych
ward with fractures in both feet and his right wrist, along with
a dislocated shoulder, broken front teeth, and a concussion.
Drake had disappeared.

To Jack, Paul's injuries were shocking and disturbing;
but that a U of C student had attempted suicide was not.
During his first year in Woodward Court, two residents had
attempted suicide. Dan Stahler, the Flint House pothead,
and Jennifer Kraeger, a little waif who lived in Wallace
House, had each failed in their attempts. It seemed like
every quarter there was a new rumor of someone attempting

suicide. It also seemed like, despite the regularity of attempts, the success rate was nil. Kind of like our football team, Jack thought. He respectfully kept that thought to himself.

Jack wondered if students at other colleges attempted suicide at rates similar to U of C students. He theorized that brutal Chicago winters, the grey Medieval Gothic architecture, and the high octane academics at U of C might exert a dialectic of stress and melancholy to a point that suicide might seem to be the appropriate Hegelian synthesis. On the other hand, any prospective student who did due diligence in the application process would know that U of C is ranked at the very bottom of surveys to determine the "best party schools". It's not like a big surprise that U of C can be a tough place for sensitive 18-year-olds. The campus gift shop sells t-shirts with the logo, "University of Chicago -- where fun goes to die", for God's sake.

Jack stood up to depart and patted Kovatch on his shoulder, after Mike finished describing Paul's situation . Jack knew it sounded conventionally trivial, but couldn 't come up with a parting remark other than, "Let me know if there's anything I can do."

Whap! Moose slammed his big ham-hock of a fist down on the table. "Shit, Kovatch!"

Jack stopped in his tracks. Kovatch looked at Moose sourly, but said nothing.

"He needs to play football!" Moose slapped the table again, this time with the palm of his hand. Plates and utensils jumped and clattered.

"Moose, what are you saying? Paul is in the hospital," Jack said querulously.

Moose looked imploringly from Jack to Kovatch, then said, "I've never told you guys this. Only Coach Hass knows."

"Knows what?" Jack asked.

"Spring quarter my first year I slit my wrists."

Jack's eyes widened. He didn't know what to say. Kovatch didn't look at Moose, but he squeezed his forearm and said, "It's alright. You can tell us. It'll stay at this table. Right, Jack?"

Jack sat back down in the booth across from Moose. "Yeah, of course. It stays here."

Moose told his friends that his weight problem began to develop in high school. His parents went through a nasty divorce. They fought over custody of his sister and him, as well as every pot and pan. Moose was always the biggest kid in his class, but not really fat. He was popular. He played on the football team and was a shot putter on the track team. But he felt like shit while the divorce was pending. His mom and dad used the kids as tools to vent their fury at each other. He began to eat as soon as he got home from school. "It was the only thing that made me feel better," he explained.

Moose said his weight went from 225 to 275 pounds during his junior year in high school. He was so ashamed of his body he didn't go out for football or track senior year. He hoped getting away from home in Winnetka and coming to U of C, his weight would come down and he could concentrate on studies. "But I mainly just needed to get away from giving depositions and being evaluated by court-appointed counselors. Unfortunately, things went from bad to worse first year on campus."

Moose's roommate was an orthodox Jewish kid from Miami who cooked the most god-awful smelling gefilte fish in their room. Moose was interested in philosophy and theology. Aaron was a pre-med. They had nothing in common and increasingly got on each other's nerves. Moose liked to play his hi-fi stereo when studying. Aaron liked quiet. One day, after Moose dropped King Crimson on the turn table and turned up the volume, Aaron walked over and picked up the needle. During the ensuing argument, Aaron called Moose "fat" and "stinky".

Jack said, "At least he was honest." Moose grinned and Kovatch chuckled.

"Yeah, I suppose he was that. But he also got a bloody nose and cracked rib when I was done beating the shit out of him."

"Jesus, Moose. I never heard of that. We were both in BJ first year. I'm surprised that wasn't all over the dorm," Kovatch said. Mike had finally perked up and was showing a little life for the first time since the three friends had arrived at the C-Shop.

"Yeah, that's another story. Suffice it to say the resident heads handled it. Anyway, it didn't help my self esteem and I was in this downward spiral that just got worse. I found myself reading Camus' *The Stranger* over and over. I felt like I was going to have to kill somebody or myself. But I felt guilty enough about beating up Aaron -- I didn't think I had it in me to kill somebody else."

"Glad you didn't go the Loeb and Leopold route," Kovatch muttered.

"Jeez Moose, I wish I'd known—"

"Jack, we didn't even know each other then. But actually, Vatch, I thought about it."

"You thought about imitating Loeb and Leopold and trying to commit the perfect murder? Really?" Kovatch eyed Moose carefully.

"Yup. I researched the 1924 murder case. I figured since they went to U of C they could serve as my imaginary mentors. I also read Richard Wright's *Native Son.* Do you know the story?"

"I read it first-year Humanities sequence," Jack answered. "Bigger Thomas murders a little girl in Kenwood, just north of here. He is sort of inspired by the Loeb and Leopold murder of the kid -- what's his name?"

"Bobby Franks. He was fourteen when they killed him," Moose said. He scowled and went on, "Anyway, that's how crazy I was when I slit my wrists. I sat down in the shower in Chamberlin House."

"Damn, Moose." Jack shook his head. Kovatch continued studying Moose intently.

"Well, long story short, I survived. The shrink assigned to me in the psych ward new Wally somehow. I think he played for him at Carleton College. For some reason we talked a lot about football. I realized during therapy the last time I'd been really happy was playing on my high school football team. Anyway, he set up a meeting with Wally and me. I came out for the team that next fall term. I met you guys and I haven't seriously thought about killing myself or anybody else since."

"I wish you would have thought about killing some of those assholes from Lake Forest Saturday. Those dirty bastards punched me in the ribs every time there was a pile up on a loose ball," Kovatch bitched.

"Or the refs," Jack grumped.

Moose snorted and continued, "When I had that meeting with Wally he talked about how playing on a team, especially a football team, meant being part of something bigger than yourself. It meant commitment to others and to a higher ideal."

"What ideal is that, to finally win a freakin' game so Wally can get his hundredth victory?" Jack asked with a touch of sarcasm.

"Maybe, but that's not what we talked about. We actually talked about how the team is like a family, or a company. He even likened it to a theater company. Everyone on a team has a part to play."

"I hadn't realized our coach was a Shakespeare scholar," Jack scoffed.

"Well anyway, it worked for me. I still have a long way to go to lose as much weight as I'd like, but I have lost ten pounds. And, at least I'm not suicidal anymore."

"Roger that," Jack said.

"You know, Wally can be very philosophical about football," Moose said.

"No shit," Kovatch muttered. "My first season I got to a point where I didn't think I could handle everything. I was elected our house representative to Student Government. With that responsibility, school, and football, it felt like I didn't have any time for myself. I started to feel a little crazy."

"You too?" Moose questioned.

"Not to the point of killing anyone, but definitely stressed."

"So what'd you do?" Jack asked.

"I decided to quit football. You know, being a Poli Sci major I wanted to stick with Student Government , and I have to keep the grades up for law school. Anyway, I went in and talked with Wally. We got into this long discussion about the meaning of being on a team, basically the same thing you said, Moose. As we were talking, I realized that playing on a team is exactly like the Marxian prescription for the perfect communist society."

"You mean, 'from each according to his ability, to each according to his need', like in the *Communist Manifesto*," Moose said with a preening air.

"Close, but no cigar," Kovatch retorted. "It's from Marx's *1875 Critique of the Gotha Program*."

"Huh?" Moose grunted

"You know Marx took that dictum out of the *New Testament*. Read *Acts*, Chapter Four, verses thirty-two to thirty-seven," Jack said.

"Christ, you would bring up the Bible—"

"All right, let's leave religion out of it for now," Kovatch interrupted Moose. "You can settle that next time we play the Valpo Crusaders." Kovatch resumed, "I told Wally I had a paper due on Marx. He goes on this riff about how, when we run a play, if everyone contributes exactly what's needed, it works. Then, it hit me -- a team should function like Marxist communism, but we often play for our own egotistical reasons--"

"What hit you, Wally's copy of Adam Smith's *Wealth of Nations*? Wally is a sweet old guy, but he's no Marxist. I'm pretty sure he voted for Nixon, and he told me not to miss Milton Friedman's talk at the Woodward Court lecture series," Jack said acidly.

"No Jack off, it hit me that, if I stayed on the football team, I could do an analysis of the socio-political dynamics of the team. I got interested to the point that I did that first paper on it, and I've been keeping a journal since then as a longitudinal study. Suzanne Rudolph approved the topic for my B.A. paper. It's going to be titled, The Political Dynamics of Maroons Football 1969 to 71 Utilizing Marxist and Machiavellian Critiques." Kovatch finally smiled.

"With a title like that, it's gonna climb to the top of the bestseller list, no doubt about it!" Jack cracked.

"You bastard! You've been spying on us! Recording our private conversations and secret rituals!" Moose roared in mock indignation.

"Is that really what kept you on the team?" Jack asked with genuine interest.

"Well, one other thing Wally said that got to me -- ready for this, Jack?" Kovatch gave Jack a meaningful look.

"Yes?"

"He said something like, 'Take Jack Blair, if he made a commitment to the team like you have, and came to every practice, imagine what he could do for this team -- if he would give according to his ability.'" Kovatch stopped and looked away. Jack squirmed uncomfortably in the seat across the table from his friends.

Moose broke the strained silence. "So it's another beautiful day in Chicago. Kovatch's little brother is in the hospital, I'm still a fat tub of shit, and Jack Blair -- well, what is your problem Blair?"

"My problem? My problem is I've got this chocolate milk shake sitting in the pit of my stomach like a bowling ball and I've got Greek Justice in Harper in ten minutes. " Jack stood up to leave. Kovatch and Moose did likewise.

"So Moose, how about bringing some of that murderous desire back on Saturday when we go up to Lawrence College and whip on them Vikings," Kovatch suggested.

Moose put his huge hands on the shoulders of his teammates. "Come on guys, group hug."

"For Christ sakes Harris, you haven't turned queer on us have you?" Kovatch kidded.

"No, Carl's got that covered," Moose said with a laugh. Kovatch and Jack each slapped Moose on his massive shoulders.

"So how about we get this one for Wally on Saturday," Kovatch said as the teammates walked through Hutchinson Commons.

"Yeah, sure," Jack muttered as they dodged other students coming out of Mandel Hall and exited Hutch into the sunlit Quads.

Moose stopped and called after his faster moving friends, "Hey Jack, you coming to practice this afternoon?"

Jack broke into a run. He sprinted past Kovatch and hurdled the steps by the Hutchinson Court fountain with his long legs leaving his two friends behind. Without breaking stride he called over his shoulder, "It's Monday!"

Burton-Judson Courts on the south side of the Midway Plaisance; *Wikipedia* entry for "Burton-Judson Courts"

-17-

It's a three and a half hour bus ride to Appleton, Wisconsin from Hyde Park. The University of Chicago only shelled out enough money to rent a yellow Blue Bird school bus with bench seats to transport the team to Lawrence College. The team made the ride to their second game of the 1971 season in relative discomfort. No toilet in the bus meant the driver had to stop three times for pee breaks. The stops weren't needed by the players as much as the two elder coaches. Mick McVale's aged bladder could only handle an hour before he required relief. Drinking coffee nonstop and chain smoking Lucky Strikes didn't help Mick's endurance.

The team bus followed northbound Saturday morning traffic out of Chicago on the Dan Ryan and then chugged up Interstate-43 tracking the west side of Lake Michigan. Players sitting on the thinly padded bench-seats were getting irritable. The team dressed out before they boarded the bus, so the players sat uncomfortably in girdle and thigh pads. Leg room for the athletes was minimal, because they had to stash helmets and shoulder pads under the seats. Guys bitched about classes, girlfriends, and all the other subjects 18 to 22-year-olds with high IQs, some level of athletic talent, and a pain in their asses, bitch about on a long bus ride.

Across the aisle from Jack and Mancusa, Chuck Dalrymple and Zack Stubblefield, both of whom played safety, were trading jokes. Mancusa had lapsed into morose silence looking out the window watching the skyscrapers and warehouses recede into the distance. Jack turned away from his friend to listen to Chuck's joke.

"So three guys are arrested in a porno shop an d appear before the judge. He asks the first guy to stand. 'What's your name?' the judge says. 'John,' the guy answers. 'And why were you arrested?' the judge asks. 'I was by the magazine rack holding a big fat cigar and blowing smoke.' The judge doesn't see anything wrong with that, so he dismisses the case and calls up the next one. 'What's your name?' he asks. 'John,' the guy answers. 'Why were you arrested?' the Judge asks. 'I was by the magazine rack holding a big fat cigar and blowing smoke,' he answers. The judge says, 'This so-called porno shop is beginning to sound more like a smoking club!' He dismissed the charge and called up the next defendent. 'What's your name? No wait, let me guess. John,' he says. 'No,' the guy says, 'my name is Smoke.'"

Jack, Zack, and the other guys sitting nearby started laughing, thankful to have something to take their minds off the discomfort of their cramped quarters in the bus. But Carl Lipscomb and Dave Waters, sitting in the seat behind Chuck and Zack didn't laugh. Carl turned away and looked out the window.

"Real sensitive!" Dave said angrily.

"What, we can't even joke about blowjobs and queers now, because we've got one on the team!?" Chuck replied belligerently.

Dave started to stand up with his fist drawn back. Jack leaned across the aisle and grabbed Dave by the shoulder, "Whoa buddy! Not here." He looked at Carl, who was still staring out the window. Chuck started to stand up, but Mancusa, who had stepped into the aisle behind Jack, pushed Chuck back down into his seat. Chuck opened his mouth to protest, but Mancusa put a finger to his own lips and shook his head. Chuck weighed 20 pounds less than Mancusa and wisely closed his mouth and looked away.

"Come on, Carl, Dave," Jack indicated they should follow him down the aisle.

Carl said, "It's okay. Really, it's okay."

"I know it is, but come on," Jack urged. Mancusa flicked his long brown bangs toward the back of the bus and patted Waters on the shoulder indicating he should come too. The four of them made their way to the bench seat a t the very back of the bus. Carl and Dave sat between Jack and Mancusa.

Dave and Carl were both second-years. It was Dave's second year on the team, but Carl's first. They were roommates in Snell House first year and got an apartment together second year. Carl revealed he was gay the first week they were roommates. Dave was straight. His parents were both family counselors. Dave was brought up in a very liberal and tolerant household in the wealthy tree-lined Village of Kenilworth north of Chicago. He not only had no problem with having a homosexual roommate, he was happy for the opportunity to learn more about homosexuality. Dave wanted to become a clinical psychologist. Dave and Carl had become good friends, despite Dave's clinical interest in Carl's sexual preference.

Carl was from Centerville, Ohio. His father was the town drunk. His mother was abused by his father. She worked herself to death supporting and protecting her five children. Carl was the youngest. His mother died when he was twelve. He was shuffled around among different aunts and uncles through middle school and high school. He spent a lot of time alone, and he spent a lot of time reading. He graduated second in his class from Centerville High.

Dave was a talented football player, but, like Jack, he skipped practice regularly. He was 6-feet tall, weighed 180 pounds, and could play multiple positions. He rotated into the backfield at running back or slot, came off the bench to relieve the starting DBs, and returned punts and kicks.

Carl was 6-foot-2, a lean 175 pounds. He'd played two seasons on his high school tennis team, but the sport he enjoyed the most was volleyball. Centerville High School didn't have a volleyball team. Very few high schools had volleyball teams in the 1960s or 70s, either boys or girls. Of course, very few high schools in the Midwest had any varsity sports teams for girls prior to the passage of Title IX in 1972. Carl's only outlet for his enjoyment of volleyball was playing in church leagues. So, he played in three of them and helped coach and referee. He especially liked playing setter.

Carl had never played any contact sport before joining the Maroons. He went to the home games his first year to watch his roommate play. He discovered that he very much enjoyed watching the games. He liked watching the players hit each other, but then form up to execute the next play. Violence contained by strict rules appealed to him. He also discovered that he envied Dave's easy way with the guys on the team and their comradery. Before the 1970 season was over, Carl confided to Dave that he wished he could be included in the fellowship of the team.

Dave encouraged Carl to join the team, and so he did for the 1971 season. Dave told Carl it would be good for Carl's self esteem to engage in a manly sport. Dave's ulterior motive was that he wanted to observe the interaction of a gay man among heterosexuals in the macho environment of a football team. Dave discovered that his intention to maintain the objective perspective of a neutral observer of behavior was undermined by his subjective attachment to the subject of the experiment. Carl was his best friend, not a lab rat.

Carl had naturally good hands from spending many hours passing and setting volleyballs, so the coaches thought he'd make an excellent pass receiver. But, it was apparent from the first time the ball was thrown to him in a live scrimmage that Carl was afraid to take a hit. He'd flub the catch if a tackler was anywhere near him. He was pretty hopeless at any defensive position, because his tackling technique could best be described as extremely tentative. Unlike his more talented roommate, Carl never missed practice unless he was sick. He was accepted by the team on the surface, insofar as no one openly hassled him for being gay. Guys did make jokes behind his back, like, "Jonesy, saw you getting up kind of slowly after Carl tackled you from behind." Or, "Tank, what were you and Lipscomb doing at the bottom of that pile?" But the jokes were always made outside of Carl's hearing. His sexuality seemed to be forgotten when the whistle blew and the hitting started during practice.

Mancusa felt protective of Carl. Xavier Mancusa planned to go to Catholic seminary after college graduation and then join the Franciscan Order. Carl was Lutheran and planned to go to seminary and then into the Lutheran ministry. Their mutual interest in ministry and the Church had created a bond between the two players.

After the four were seated, Mancusa spoke first, "Look, we all know Chuckles is a dick." The other three laughed. "I don't know whether he was trying to embarrass you or not --"

"I think he was!" Waters interrupted.

"Let Mancusa finish," Jack said calmly.

Carl looked at Mancusa expectantly. The older player went on, "Anyway, the point is, Carl, if you're gonna be on a football team, you've gotta accept that guys are gonna make jokes about queers and faggots."

"It may be 1971, not the 50s, and these guys are Chicago students, but they're still football players," Jack added.

"I know," Carl said quietly. Waters started to interject again, but Jack slapped him lightly on the knee.

"Thing is," Mancusa went on, "Dalrymple wasn't looking at you when he was telling the joke. If he meant to start something with you, he would've said it to your face. Chuck's not subtle enough to engage in subterfuge. If he was trying to give you shit, he would've thrown it right at you."

"Not with me sitting beside him!" Dave said through clenched teeth.

Mancusa ignored Waters. "Carl, everybody accepts you as part of this team, and most of us are glad you 're a Maroon. But, you're the only gay guy on the team--"

"As far as we know," Jack put in. They all smiled at that; then paused for a few seconds to speculate in the privacy of their own thoughts which of their teammates might be gay but in the closet.

"Well, I just wanted to let you know that the captains aren't gonna let some dip shit like Dalrymple hassle you. But you can't take jokes about homos personal. Okay?" Mancusa looked at Carl questioningly.

"Thanks, Xavier. I understand. I wouldn't have said anything."

"And Waters," Jack said, "You gotta be cool, dude."

"Yeah, okay. I guess I over reacted. Chuckles just gets on my nerves sometimes. He's so full of shit."

"And you're not," Jack said with a laugh and slapped Waters on the knee again. They all laughed.

Then Mancusa looked serious again and said, "But Carl, I gotta say it, the way you hit--"

"You mean, the way I don't hit," Carl said smiling sheepishly.

"Uh, yeah," Mancusa said nodding. "You know it kind of plays into the stereotype guys have about homosexuals."

"Hey, come on Mancusa," Dave complained, "I'm working on it with him."

"Well, work harder," Mancusa said sternly.

Jack added, "But Mancusa's right. You know, Carl, in a way you're like Jackie Robinson for most of the guys -- me included. We've never had a gay teammate before."

Carl nodded seriously, but Waters said, "Right, like let's not put any more pressure on the guy."

"Dave, I'm not trying to put anymore pressure on him. I'm just telling it like it is," Jack replied.

Carl looked from one to the other of his teammates, but then screwed up his face and said, "Do you guys smell something weird? I'm starting to feel a little nauseous, and--"

"Me too," Dave said furrowing his brow. Is somebody smoking a joint?"

"Tanker!" Jack called to his friend who was sitting with Jonesy three seats in front of them. "You tokin' up there?"

Tank turned around with a quizzical look on his face. "What of it?"

Mancusa cut in, "Guys, that's not it. It ain't weed. Look!" He pointed at a half dollar-size hole in the floor board under the seat immediately in front of them.

"So?" Waters asked.

"Shit!" Jack cursed. "Guys, come on! Move up to the front of the bus!" They started forward. "Tank, Jonesy, move up to the front," Jack encouraged.

"What the fuck, dude?" Tank asked irritably while shielding his roach behind the back of the seat in front of him.

"Maroons, everybody move forward! Come on! Off your asses, pick 'em up!" Mancusa ordered.

Mancusa and Jack herded their teammates forward to the front of the bus. The players packed the door well and aisle and crammed themselves three and four in seats designed for school children. Jack and Mancusa pushed their way back through the scrum of tightly packed players and trotted down the aisle to the back of the bus. They opened the four windows nearest the back.

Players were crowded so close to the bus driver that he protested he couldn't see out his side view mirrors. Mick McVale growled at him to shut up and drive the "damn bag of rusted bolts" faster.

-18-

Players poured out of the bus coughing and hacking. A few of the Maroons muttered curses and insults at th e bus driver and Blue Bird Bus Company. Several weaved unsteadily in the wrong direction and had to be directed toward the entrance into the Lawrence Bowl football stadium. Heinz tripped on the curb and had to be helped back up to his feet. Donny Dubka pounded the palm of his right hand on the hood of the bus, shook his left index finger at the bus driver and shouted, "You better be back here with another bus!" Mick followed the players into the stadium grousing and grumbling. He ordered the student usher at the gate to point him toward the Men's restroom. Wally walked carefully toward the Visitors' side of the field shaking his head and clutching his clipboard. Rogan didn't say anything. As soon as the players were inside the Lawrence Bowl, Coach Rogan was all business shouting instructions at the team to line up for warm ups on the field.

As they coaxed and herded their teammates to the front of the bus, Jack and Mancusa had shouted that there was a hole in the floor board near the back. It was over the exhaust pipe, which also had a hole in it. The cheapskates who controlled the football team's travel budget were indirectly responsible for delivering the team to Appleton, Wisconsin suffering the first symptoms of carbon monoxide poisoning.

Understandably, the Maroons played slow, sluggish, and confused the first quarter. Lawrence leapt out to a fourteen point lead. Cauley fumbled a hike from Shooksie. Johnny Jones dropped a hand-off and Murphy fumbled after catching a five-yard quick-out pass. Chicago managed positive yardage on only play the entire quarter.

On first down of the Maroons' last possession of the quarter, Cauley hit Jack on a curl pattern for eleven yards and a first down. Except for that play, the Maroons line was a sieve. Hans and Moose were even slower than usual at their guard positions. Lawrence's defensive tackles and linebackers blew past the Maroons' linemen before the blockers could get up out of their stances. Cauley was repeatedly hurried on pass plays. The pocket collapsed before the QB could scan the field and set his feet to throw. The Maroons didn't even penetrate Vikings territory until the second quarter.

Chicago's defense wasn't much better. Linemen were knocked on their asses by quicker, stronger blockers. The secondary was slow to react to obvious pass plays and confused by simple pass patterns. The only surprise of the first quarter, given how poorly the Maroons defended, was that the Vikings only scored two touchdowns.

The second quarter began with Lawrence working the ball methodically down the field for another touchdown. After a successful point after, the ball landed right in front of Carl Lipscomb on the following kickoff.

Carl hadn't played a down on offense or defense, but the coaches wanted to find some place for him on the team. So Coach McVale assigned him the up-back position on the kickoff return team with the hope that the ball would never come to him. "Just get in the way of the first blue jersey you see," Mick told him as he sent him on to the field with a butt slap.

But nothing went as planned, or hoped for, by the Maroons' coaches the first half. The Vikings kicker squibed the ball on the kickoff. It bounced erratically toward Carl. He did the right thing. He fell on the ball in a fetal position. Instead of touching Carl's helmet to down him where he lay, the Vikings' gunner rocketed down field and nailed Carl in the ribs with his helmet. The ref threw a flag for unnecessary roughness. Carl had to be helped off the field by two teammates. The fifteen-yard penalty gave the team its best field position of the half. Carl suffered several whacks to the helmet, shoulder pads and butt by grateful teammates as he staggered to the safety of the Chicago bench.

His sacrifice was for naught. The Maroons failed to advance the ball on their next series for a three and out.

Shooksie hiked the ball over Maroni's head on the punt. Maroni managed to chase the ball down and heave it out of bounds just before he was blasted by two Lawrence Vikings.

Chicago players standing on the sideline parted like the Red Sea for the Israelites, as the punt team stalked off the field. Shooksie threw his helmet. It bounced through the gap in the line of players, smacked Carl in the shin, and came to rest under the Visitors' bench. Whenever Shooksie blew a hike, he would storm off the field and throw his helmet at the sidelines. Veteran players knew his routine and rookies learned quickly or took a flying helmet to the shin or knee. A new U of C record was set in the first half of the Lawrence game. Shooksie's helmet came flying off the field bouncing past his teammates on the side line and into the Visitors ' bench three times. Shooksie had only blown two snaps in an entire game the two previous seasons.

Mick McVale was nearly apoplectic at halftime. The team had never seen the old assistant coach so worked up. Maybe his swollen bladder was bothering him more than usual or the carbon monoxide affected his temper. The Maroons were behind twenty-eight to zero. It was the worst performance of the team in the "modern era". They had never been down by four touchdowns at the half. While the team sprawled around on benches and the floor of the Visitors' locker room, Mick lit into them.

"Do you know why the Russians will never beat us!?" he demanded in his gravelly smoker's voice. Players looked at Mick and each other through dull eyes with slack jaws. "Because they don't play football!" he thundered. "We're tougher than the god damn Ruskies because we play football! But I haven't seen one of you playing football today. You look like a bunch of pansies out there! I don't give a god damn if the floor of the bus had a hole in it! Do you think those American boys fighting the Commies over in North Viet Nam give up because they get a little poison gas thrown at 'em? Huh, do you?" he demanded.

By this time the players were sitting up straight staring with gimlet eyes at Coach McVale. Mick was a crotchety old fart, but they'd never seen steam coming out of his ears like this. Wally was looking down studying his clipboard and shaking his head. Dubka was hopping from one foot to another looking like he dearly wanted to throw on a uniform to take on the whole Lawrence team himself. Rogan remained silent, his steely gaze boring a hole in the wall above Jack's head.

The team responded to Mick's rant with incredulous silence. There would be many jokes back in Chicago at practices the rest of the season about why the Russians would never beat America: "Because we play football!"

But in the Visitors' locker room of the Lawrence Bowl something transformative did happen. After a moment of strained silence, Wally asked the team to stand. Players and coaches stood with their heads bowed. Then Wally said softly, "We can leave this field today with our heads down. We can ride back to Chicago embarrassed and humiliated because we gave up. Or, we can go out there and play a second half of football with our hearts and minds committed to play the best game we've ever played. You have to decide now. Who are you? Do you want to quit and walk off the field feeling the same way you do now? Or do you want to finish this game knowing you gave everything you have to this team? I don't care what the score is at the end of the game. But I do care about who you are as young men. So, gentlemen, it's up to you. What do you say?"

With one voice the Maroons yelled and roared until their lungs hurt. Coach Dubka led the team on the run out of the locker room bellowing like a banshee.

Dave Waters fielded the kickoff to start the second half on the Maroons' 10-yard line. He scampered up the left sideline juking and dodging until he was finally pushed out of bounds at the Maroons' 42-yard line. Rogan's first called play was a play action with fake hand-off to Jonesy and then a screen pass to Tank coming out of the fullback position. Dax Brockton and John Kimson, blasted out of their offensive tackle positions and mowed down the Lawrence linebackers. Murphy cut the safety down by taking him out at the knees. Jack leveled his opposing number at cornerback with a perfectly executed roll block. Tank rumbled for a twenty-yard gain before he was brought down by the weak-side safety from behind.

The next play Jack lined up wide right and Jonesy was at slot four yards to Jack's left. Shooksie hiked the ball to Cauley in the shot gun. The two fastest Maroons on the roster streaked down field in a parallel line. At the Lawrence twenty they executed a superbly timed crossing pattern. The cornerback covering Jack fell a step behind when Jack cut left. But the safety shadowing Jonesy lost his footing and went down when Jones cut right. Cauley rolled right and this time Heinz, Moose, Brock, and Kimson held the line giving their QB plenty of time to get the pass off. Cauley could have thrown to either receiver but picked the wide open Jonesy. He made the catch and loped into the end zone for a score.

The Maroons did not go on to win the game. They scored another touchdown early in the fourth quarter on a play action screen pass to Tank. They only gave up a field goal to Lawrence in the second half. But the game proved to be another moral victory of sorts, or at least an uplifting loss.

On the final play of the game the Vikings had the ball on the Chicago 41-yard line. The Vikings had taken a whipping the second half on their home field by "the worst team in college football". This was their last chance for pay back. Apparently the Lawrence coach wanted to try to catch the Visitors off guard and send them home with another score in the Vikings' column. Instead of just letting the clock expire, they tried a Hail Mary.

Jack and Greg Vendel were in at cornerbacks. They chased their respective wide outs into the end zone where Chuck Dalrymple and Zack Stubblefield, the Maroon safeties, had shadowed the tight end and slot receiver. The pass was a wobbly duck. Jack saw it was going to fall short.

He left his man and bolted forward. Leaping above the outstretched hands of Dalrymple and the Vikings tight end, Jack grabbed the ball and took off running up field.

By God, he thought, we'll teach those sons of bitches! The Lawrence running-back came streaking at Jack head on. They met at the Chicago 10-yard line. As Number-32 drove his helmet at Jack's gut, Number-84 swiveled his torso to the side and jammed his left hand as hard as he could down on the opponent's helmet. 32's face mask dug turf as he flailed at Jack's legs which were flying past the sprawled defender. Jack cut to his right and saw a Lawrence tackler angling toward him. Out of the corner of his left eye he also saw Rick Douglas closing on the tackler. But the Viking's 72 didn't see Rick who blasted into his side. Jack heard his teammate's triumphant bellow as Jack's legs churned up field. Over the puffing noise of his own breath and air whistling through the ear-holes of his helmet, Jack heard the faint call of Greg Vendel's voice, "With you!" Jack swung his head left to look for Greg. That was a mistake. Just as his eyes refocused up field the Viking's center closed on him. Jack leaped hurdling over the would-be tackler. Jack's lead leg made it over the shorter player's helmet but the front cleats on the shoe of Jack's trailing foot clipped the Viking's face mask. It was enough to knock Jack off balance. As his feet contacted the ground Jack stumbled and was yawing to his left out of control. He glimpsed Greg a few feet behind. Jack lurched and flicked the ball out of his right hand just before he crashed to the ground. Greg scooped the ball up just inches above the grass. Jack raised his chin to see Vendel motoring down field, then jumped up and chased after him.

Only the Vikings' QB was between Vendel and the goal. Greg cut to his left angling toward the left corner of the end zone. The quarterback adjusted his approach and it was a foot race. They met at the 5-yard line. Running full speed his spikes flying, Jack trailed the pair by eight yards. He yelled, "Greg! Greg! With you!" Vendel went down with the Viking's QB on top of him. he tried to pitch the ball to Jack.

But Greg's arms were pinned to his sides in the grasp of the tackler. He limp-wristed the ball as best he could before crashing onto his side under the weight of the Viking tackler. The ball dribbled off the hip of the Viking QB. But, as the Viking hit the dirt he instinctively kicked out. His foot contacted the ball to slow its descent. Jack made a diving lunge for the ball and shoveled it in with his left hand as the pig skin grazed the tips of the grass. Jack drove his right hand palm-down to keep his balance and threw his weight forward. He thrust the ball out as far as he could reach just as he landed in the grass his chin strap skidding in the turf.

Jack opened his eyes, looked at the ball. Its tip was over the line. He heard a whistle blowing and looked up. The field judge was running toward him signaling touchdown.

Final score: Chicago–21, Lawrence-31.

-19-

The next issue of the U of C student paper, *The Maroon*, featured a photo of Jack stretched out on the field with the nose of the ball on the goal line. Reese Davis, a fourth-year who was a friend of Jack's and *The Maroon's* sportswriter, titled his article on the Lawrence game, "Maroons Lose on Bus, Win on Field". Reese's article lacerated Chicago's administration for hiring a carbon-monoxide leaking school bus to transport the team to Appleton.

"Stagg's ghost should haunt President Levi's office until this Administration gives the football team the support it deserves. The team's losing record aside, if the athletes fighting to resurrect the legacy of Stagg, Berwanger, and 'the men who stopped Red Grange' on the gridiron don't deserve a bus with individual seats and a toilet, then the University should admit its mistake and drop football again. But, any fan who witnessed the gutsy play of the Maroons in the second half of the Lawrence game would gnash his teeth and tear his hair at that prospect. This reporter predicts that, if the Maroons maintain the level of play they demonstrated against the Vikings in the second half of Saturday's game, they will win out the rest of the season."

Jack and Tank were reading *The Maroon* together. They sat at their favorite reading table by the north-bay window on the first floor of Regenstein Library. "The Reg" is a behemoth 577,085 square-foot building finished in 1970 and situated across the street from the Gothic buildings forming the U of C's famed Quads. Its exterior walls are grooved limestone, the same material as the original 19th Century buildings forming the Quads. But the stone is a lighter color and the massive modern-looking structure contrasts with the smooth dark-grey limestone of the Medieval Oxbridge design of the Quads. The Reg sits on the site of the original Stagg Field, which was finally torn down in 1967. Henry Moore's bronze sculpture, "Nuclear Energy", memorializes the spot on the west side of the library's grounds where Enrico Fermi's team of scientists achieved the first controlled, self-sustaining, nuclear chain reaction on December 2, 1942. Tradition at UChicago holds that the four gargoyles on Cobb Gate across 57th Street from The Reg represent the classes, first-year in the lowest position and-fourth year perched atop the Gate. Students in the early 70s, after the massive Regenstein Library was completed , revised the tradition to claim that the gargoyles were looking across the street in dismay at the modern monstrosity which had replaced the fortress that Stagg built.

But Tank and Jack weren't thinking about gargoyles or architecture. They were still feeling a joyful buzz from the second half of the Lawrence game -- and getting to ride home in the replacement bus, which had comfortable reclining-seats and didn't leak carbon monoxide. Jack was reading Reece Davis's article in *The Maroon* a second time, when Alice Novak and Jan McKay walked up. The women were each holding a copy of *The Maroon*. Jan swatted Tank playfully on the top of his head with the paper. Jack gestured for the women to join them. The four students sat in the sunlight filtered by The Reg's ten foot high bay windows. They chattered happily about the game. Tank declared that the photo of Jack sprawled on the ground with his outstretched arm reaching for the goal line ought to be published in *People Magazine.*

"That's right!" Jan agreed. "And they ought to publish a retraction, because you're not the worst football team ever."

"Ouch!" Jack feigned a pain in his heart. "The article didn't say we were the worst team ever, just currently the worst."

"But you can't be the worst team, if you played so well!" Jan implored.

"Hey! Don't take that away from us. If it wasn't for the *People Magazine* article we'd be nobodies. But we're known around the world. We're the number-one worst team in college football!" Tank said with a laugh.

Jan asked, "Did you read Micah Kleinsmitt's editorial about the team?" The guys nodded. "I really liked the way, let's see, here it is." Jan spread the paper out on the table. "It says, 'Although a significant number of students and faculty opposed the return of football as a varsity sport in 1969 --' Like yours truly! -- 'the tide has completely turned in favor of having the sport back on campus.' He goes on to say, 'Football has become part of our unique U of C culture. From the Kazoo Marching Band to Jim Capps ' zany brand of satirical humor in announcing faux scores at halftime, football has been adopted by the U of C and adapted to the U of C.' I like that!" Jan exclaimed.

"Yeah, I suppose it's true," Jack said. "Football is definitely unique here."

"Exactamundo! Not every team can lose all their games over two seasons and continue that streak into a third year!" Tank bellowed.

"Come on now, Tank. We're not just famous for the *People Magazine* article. What other team has a comedy routine written about it?" Jack asked with a grin.

"You mean that Second City skit -- I love it!" Jan exclaimed.

Alice popped out of her chair and to the surprise of the others declaimed, "Football returns to the University of Chicago! Coach Walter Hass attempts to teach the fundamentals of football to four rookie players with disastrous results. When first confronted with the football, the first player exclaims, 'Why, it's a demi-poly-tetrahedron!' The coach informs the players that he will draw up a play on the blackboard. A rookie asks whether it will be Shakespeare or Eugene O'Neill. Coach Hass, doing his best not to lose patience, reminds his philosophically inclined Maroons that, 'we have a left guard and a right guard — no Kierkegaard here, gentlemen.'" Alice took a bow then sat down to the applause and cheers of her friends and other students in the adjacent bay.

The reference librarian did not, however, appreciate Alice's performance or the resulting commotion. She scooted over to the group of students in her hush puppies wagging her finger and shushing the merry makers.

Alice, Jack, Jan, and Tank decided it was time to exit stage left. They agreed to take a walk over to The Point on Lake Michigan.

The foursome walked across the grass field between The Reg and Bartlett Gym onto University Avenue. They walked north to 55th Street and headed east. They used the underpass north of the Museum of Science and Industry to cross Lake Shore Drive. Promontory Point in Burnham Park juts out into Lake Michigan east of Lake Shore Drive between 54th and 56th Streets six miles south of the Chicago Loop.

It was one of those beautiful Chicago-autumn days in October. The air was crisp and the lake wind was typically chilly, but the sun was warm on their faces and the sky was a deep blue over Lake Michigan. Huge puffy cumulus-clouds drifted above the lake turning the shimmering blue-grey water darker in spots. The view of Chicago's sky line from The Point was magnificent, breath taking. Sun glinted and sparkled off the miniature-looking sky scraping towers six miles north in The Loop.

Promontory Point was constructed from landfill in 1938, which would seem an unlikely stage setting for romance. But, Alfred Caldwell, the landscape designer and a member of the Prairie School of design, added native plants and stone throughout Burnham Park. Caldwell's design featured a raised meadow in the center of the twelve-acre peninsula. Hundreds of flowering trees and shrubs were planted. Caldwell created stone "council rings" near the lake shore. Limestone blocks were arranged in a series of steps leading to a promenade along the lake front.

From the end of Chicago's Big Ten era through the post World War II period, The Point was a favorite place for fraternity boys to pin their best girls and for marriage proposals by graduate students. In the late 60s and into the 70s it was still a favorite romantic rendezvous. However, one would more likely see a young couple skinny dipping or sun-bathing nude and passing a joint than a young man presenting his steady girl with his fraternity lavalier.

[Fun on The Point in 1944; Archival Photographic Files, University of Chicago Library, Special Collections Research Center]

The second week of October 1971 was too cold for nude sun-bathing or skinny dipping. The two couples stood atop the limestone blocks gazing northward across the expanse of lake water at the Chicago skyline. Jack put his arms around Alice. She scrunched her head against his chest feeling its warmth through his sweat-shirt and blue-jeans jacket.

Since fall of 1969, when they first met, the four had been good friends. Tank and Jan were an on-again off-again official couple. They lived together in an off-campus apartment fall and winter quarter during third year, but decided to "take a break" over the summer. They remained good friends. Jan had signaled that she wanted to get back together, but Tank needed to get his grade point up a notch higher to reach his goal of acceptance into an elite law school. He confided to Jack that he missed sleeping with Jan, but she took up too much of his time. He needed to spend more time hitting the books and less time banging Jan.

Alice and Jack were also struggling with the issue of commitment. They were not a formally-declared couple. After their first few get-togethers and a mutual recognition of attraction, Jack and Alice agreed that they didn't have time to commit to an exclusive relationship. They had to focus on making it through the Common Core. They encouraged each other to "date around". But they didn't. By the end of fall quarter their second year, they had fallen into a pattern of going out together on weekends and meeting at least once during the week for tea at the Blue Gargoyle or a beer at Jimmy's or The Eagle.

Their biggest kick together was early in winter quarter second year at the inaugural Lascivious Costume Ball. The "LCB" became an annual February event at U of C commencing in 1970. It replaced the Washington Promenade, which was a formal dance held every winter quarter since 1903. A Miss University of Chicago was crowned at the Promenade. But the times they were a changin'. At the LCB, students either paid two dollars for admission, or they were allowed free entry if they arrived uncloaked in the nude. An appropriately lascivious costume gained admission for one dollar. The Ball was held in Ida Noyes Hall. Popular costumes were made of strategically placed Frisbees and paper cups. A Mr. U of C was crowned based upon the most creative lascivious costume. Reece Davis won for wearing nothing but a jock strap with a huge "Monster of the Midway" pin on his crotch and his body covered in maroon war paint.

Alice and Jack wore nothing but bathrobes and flip flops. They hopped out of Jack's old beater-car parked in front of

Ida Noyes Hall and scampered through the February snow across the sidewalk and up the stairs into the entry way. They let the robes drop off in front of the admissions desk and were allowed to pass. Bathrobes back on, they danced wildly in the ball room to a local band doing its best imitation of Ten Years After and Grand Funk Railroad. They disrobed again and jumped into the swimming pool to skinny dip with a hundred other laughing and squealing students. A net was strung across the pool and the skinny dippers played nude water-volleyball. It was a fantastic night. And it was, Alice, Jack, and their contemporaries believed, unlike anything U of C students would have experienced during the era of The Promenade which culminated with the election of Miss University of Chicago.

[Miss University of Chicago 1949, crowned at the Washington Promenade]

Steven pointed out to Jack during winter break their third year as roommates that Jack's relationship with Alice was clearly taking on the indicia of exclusivity. He asked sarcastically whether Jack was going to give Alice his letter sweater. Jack's reply was a deadpan threat to hang Steven by his ballet tights from Cobb Gate. But Steven's crack inspired Jack to think more deeply about how deep he did want to get into a relationship with Alice. His head clearly told him – confirmed by Tank's temporary shack up with Jan -- that he couldn't afford the time. On the other hand, he was seeing Alice every week as things stood. His heart told him that it quickened whenever he was going to see Allie, and it sank, if she cancelled a date. He'd begun calling her Allie after the LCB.

Now they were into their fourth and last year in the College. She hadn't said anything explicitly, but Jack had the feeling that Alice wanted him to ask her to move in with him or to make some sort of formal declaration that they were a committed couple. Feeling conflicted – or was it ambivalence? Jack carefully ignored anything he interpreted as a hint from Alice in that direction. Best to maintain the status quo he concluded. Anyway, he liked living with Steven. They had been roomies since first year. Other than the intimate parts of his body, Jack was sure that Steven knew and understood him better than Alice did.

Jack's sights were set on Oxford. And then, he wasn't sure where, but he thought he'd probably go on for a doctorate in philosophy or public policy. He hadn't decided yet whether he wanted to stay in academics or enter government service, but he doubted he would come back to Chicago. Stanford and Berkeley had great grad schools, and he'd like to see what it would be like living in California -- the land of opportunity with better weather than the Midwest. It would be unwise to sacrifice his independence for a committed relationship with Alice, Jack told himself.

Alice made it clear that her life was in Chicago. She wanted to go to grad school in U of C's School of Social Service Administration. She planned to get a Masters in social work and run a women's shelter or do some kind of work on social issues, like spousal and child abuse. It sounded very gritty to Jack -- not an appealing life at all --

dealing with abused women and children in roach -infested tenements in Chicago ghettos. Worthy, certainly, but kind of an ugly life, he thought. Part of him missed the hills and creeks of Southern Indiana. He never wanted to live in Indiana again, but, when he'd been a long time in the city without being able to shield his eyes from the sun and look out across his family's farm, well, it made him think he didn't want to live in Chicago forever.

Jack admitted to himself, if not explicitly to Alice, that he felt a very deep affection for her. When he ruminated about it, he thought it could properly be called love. He enjoyed her caustic wit, respected her probing intelligence , and admired her commitment to social justice. He also really dug her soft, little curvaceous-body. At times, he felt guilty for monopolizing her romantic attention. The gender demographics in the College were three men for every two women. There were eight-thousand graduate and professional-school students and only twenty-five hundred students in the College. So, women in the College had plenty of opportunities to hook up with a man. This being a school for brainiacs, most of the women in the College were not exactly centerfolds. Not too many Burt Reynolds among the men either. In Alice's case though, most any other guy on campus would have jumped at the chance to have a steady relationship with her.

Jack knew it was kind of selfish to take Allie out of play for any other guy without making a real commitment to her. But so far, she seemed to accept those terms without complaint. Maybe that was all she really wanted too. Probably best not to rock the boat by talking about it.

The lake breeze was turning colder, so Jan, Tank, Alice, and Jack decided they ought to head back to campus. They carefully stepped around the puddles of urine left by winos and junkies in the 55th Street underpass of Lake Shore Drive. When they emerged into the sunlight, Tank said he had an idea. He asked whether Alice and Jack had ever seen Muhammad Ali's and Elijah Muhammad's mansions on

49th and Woodlawn. Jack said he'd heard Ali lived in the area, but had never seen his house. Alice hadn't either, so it was agreed they'd walk northwest and check out "the Greatest's" digs.

Jack knew a little bit about the Nation of Islam. He'd passed its Mosque Maryam on Stony Island Avenue many times on his way to and from Indiana. Stern looking young black men in black suits, white shirts, black tie s, and sunglasses sometimes stood on the street corner of Hyde Park Avenue and 57th Street selling *The Final Call* newspaper. He knew that Elijah Muhammad had called for the establishment of a separate nation for black Americans. He also knew that the Nation of Islam proclaimed the racial superiority of blacks as the chosen people of Allah. Jack read *The Autobiography of Malcolm X*, co-written by Malcolm X and Alex Haley, when he was in high school.

Jack was a big fan of Muhammad Ali ever since he won gold in the 1960 Olympics as Cassius Clay and then knocked out Sonny Liston to become Heavyweight Champion of the World. Jack followed with interest the legal action and loss of Ali's championship belts in 1967 as a consequence of Ali's claim of conscientious objector status. Jack especially dug Ali's response to the question why he would fight in the ring but not for his country in Viet Nam. "I ain't got no quarrel with them Viet Cong... No Viet Cong ever called me nigger."

Jack whistled in awestruck amazement at the huge brick and stone mansions along the border of Hyde Park and Kenwood neighborhoods. He imagined the least impressive of the houses must cost a quarter-million dollars. When they arrived at the Arabic-looking compound of Elijah Muhammad's house with its sandstone facade, stained-glass windows, and beautiful gardens, Jack's jaw dropped at the sight. "They sure don't make houses like this in Seymour," he intoned in his best Gomer Pyle imitation.

The scrutiny of the Nation of Islam security guards in their black suits, sunglasses, and crossed arms was somewhat unnerving, but Tank said not to worry. The guards were meant to look intimidating.

The two couples strolled south on Woodlawn Avenue gawking admiringly at the three similarly designed houses across the street from Elijah Muhammad's main compound. They stopped in front of a gigantic brick Tudor-mansion at 4944 South Woodlawn Avenue. Tank claimed it was Muhammad Ali's house. Jack's question to Tank of how Tanker knew it was Ali's house was interrupted by a white Lincoln-Mercury limousine turning from 49th Street onto Woodlawn with loudspeakers mounted on its roof blaring , "Muhammad Ali, the greatest fighter of all time! Muhammad Ali, champion of the world! Muhammad Ali, the greatest!"

The limo slowed in front of the mansion and then stopped at the curb right beside the four students. They stood staring open-mouthed at the limo. The passenger window slid down and Muhammad Ali stuck his easily recognizable head out. "What you kids doin' on my property?" he demanded.

Alice and Jan shrank up against their presumed male protectors, who looked to be considering whether or not they should bolt and run for their lives. Tank finally sputtered, "Uh, nothing sir, we were just admiring the real estate."

"Whatch you think of it, then?" Ali asked in a less intimidating tone.

"Uh, great! Spectacular!" Regaining his confidence, Tank added, "We're thinking of buying into the neighborhood." Jan smacked him on the shoulder. Ali laughed.

Now in a friendly tone, Ali asked, "Are you students?"

"We go to the University of Chicago," Jack answered."

"What are you studying?"

Each of the four told the Champ their major concentrations. He asked questions of each of them about the courses they were taking. Then, looking Jack and Tank up and down, he said, "You're pretty big boys, you play any sports?"

Together they answered, "Football! We both play football."

"Football! Whatch you wanna play a sissy sport like football for?" The Greatest let out a deep-throated laugh. "What's your team called? It's somethin' funny, isn't it?"

The four students laughed. Jack said, "We're the Maroons, you know, like 'what a maroon!'"

"That's right, the Maroons. Hey Bundini!" The Champ turned toward the driver, "What's a maroon?"

"A maroon, a maroon?" Drew Bundini Brown looked thoughtful behind the wheel. "That's some kinda cookie, right Champ?" Ali's long time corner man asked expectantly.

"Bundini, you some kinda cookie." Ali turned back toward the students looking triumphant, "It's a color, isn't it?"

"Sure is, Champ!" they chimed back.

"Bundini! You got four tickets for the next fight on you? I wanna give these white kids front row seats," Ali said enthusiastically.

"Champ! We're still tryin' to set up somethin' with that bum Frazier -- maybe in March, Madison Square Garden."

"Yeah, that's right. Too bad for you kids, gonna be the fight of the century. Let's go Bundini. These college students got home work to do. You stay in school and keep your grades up." Ali waved as the tinted window closed. The limo turned into the driveway. An automatic gate opened and the car disappeared behind the security wall. Tank and Jack looked at each other. As one they said, "Did that just happen?"

["The Trials of Muhammad Ali", The Huffington Post
11/08/2013: Ali and Nation of Islam leader Louis Farrakhan
pictured listening to a speaker during the Savior's Day
celebrations at the International Amphitheatre, Chicago,
Illinois, February 27, 1966. Farrakhan's uniform is that of
the "Fruit of Islam", the paramilitary wing of the Nation of
Islam. (Photo by Robert Abbott Sengstacke/Getty Images)]

-20-

Jack knew Coach Rogan had a burr up his ass about Jack coming to three practices per week instead of five. And, there was the confrontation at the preseason practice about Jack not being in uniform. But what the hell? Other members of the team regularly skipped practices. Why did Rogan focus so much of his antipathy about guys' laid back attitude toward football on me, Jack wondered.

Jack tried to ignore any offensive comments the offensive coordinator made. When he felt especially needled by Rogan, he reminded himself of Wally's promise to uphold "scholar" as the first principle in the University's scholar-athlete ethic. He sensed no weakness in Coach Hass's or the University Administration's commitment to the priority of academics over sports. Sure, he knew Wally and Mick wanted him to attend every practice, and Jack realized Wally had the ulterior motive of pressuring him by promoting him as a captain. But Jack had the confidence – he felt with a degree of self-satisfied pride -- that the team needed his talents on the field come game day. So, Rogan might be a pain in the ass, but Jack was willing to put up with it for the other benefits of remaining on the team.

The relationship of Coach Rogan and Number-84, however, took a hairpin turn for the worse as practice was winding down the Friday before the third game of the season.

Rogan whistled his squad of players on offense to circle up after they finished a scrimmage with the defensive unit. He was not a happy camper. Coach Rogan rarely seemed to be in a good mood. His demeanor varied from stoic to irritable. But he was just down right pissed-off and started chewing ass at the players formed up in a semi-circle around him.

Rogan ranted about how they'd practiced "at half speed, when they were supposed to be going full throttle." He asked if their excuse for practicing "so lackadaisical" was because "they still had carbon monoxide poisoning."

Had Donny Dubka, or even Wally or Mick, made a crack like that, it would've been with a smile and been the punch line to a joke at the team's expense. Rogan wasn't joking. He looked around the half circle of unshaven, mustached, and bearded faces. His lips puckered with distaste. Rogan wiped his lips and launched into a diatribe about how the team wasn't hustling and didn't have a winning attitude. He even started bitching about how the players on the sidelines didn't make enough noise. He shouted, "Noise can win a ball game! That's right, gentlemen! And, I use that term loosely. If you're not in the game you ought to be yelling your heads off on the sidelines, clapping and cheering your team on!"

Something snapped in Jack. The hinge which held shut the lid on his self-restraint broke. He burst out, "So Coach, if noise can win a ball game, some of us own our own cars. We could just line them up around the field and lay on the horns. That way, we wouldn't even have to dress out. We'd just beat the other team with noise!" Jack's teammates burst out laughing.

Rogan stiffened and stared at Jack. Then, he ripped off his C-cap and threw it to the ground. He started to charge toward Jack shaking his fist. Moose was standing beside Jack. He stepped in front of Jack as Jack took a step back. Rogan pulled up short in front of the big guard. But then, he drew back his arms and thrust them out smacking Moose in the chest with open palms. Moose let out a thunderous fart.

The other players hooted with laughter. Some fell to the ground laughing and pounding their hands on the turf. Moose looked embarrassed and then started giggling, his big tummy jiggling. Jack put his hand over his mouth trying to hold back, but couldn't restrain his own laughter. Rogan looked around at the players laughing hysterically, rolling on the ground, or bent over holding their knees for support. He turned around, picked up his hat, and stalked off muttering through clenched teeth and shaking his head.

Buck naked guys in the showers after practice were scrubbing off the dirt and grass stains from knees and elbows and shampooing their hair. Members of the offense were telling the guys who played defense about the incident between Coach Rogan and Jack. The players who'd witnessed Rogan smack Moose in the chest and the exclamatory response from Moose's nether region were laughing or making fart noises with their mouths or by pumping an arm with a hand in the armpit. Rick Douglas was narrating the incident while proclaiming he was going to submit a script to Second City for a new comedy sketch.

Without warning Rogan charged into the shower fully dressed in his field shoes. His face was red, nostrils flared, and eyes bulging. He looked maniacal. He shouted at Jack, "Who do you think you are, Blair!?" Naked players clustered around Jack, edging between him and Rogan. The coach blustered, "You're the most talented player on this team and you know it! So what do you do with all that talent?"

Jack said nothing. His mind became very focused and his eyes narrowed. His body, although naked, tensed like a cat ready to spring. Absurdly, he noticed chunks of dirt dislodging from the cleats on Rogan's shoes drifting toward the drain. Jack controlled his breathing. He pushed long blond strands of wet hair behind his ears. He met Rogan's bluster with silence.

The stare down lasted only a couple seconds before Rogan started shouting again. "You don't give a damn about this team, Blair. You don't care whether we win or lose. All you care about is yourself! Getting your picture in the paper, showing up for practice on your own schedule -- not the team's! Some of these men -- take Kovatch here -- they made a commitment to this team! But you!" Rogan shook his head, and then stared at the detritus of chunks of dirt, hair, and discarded band-aids swirling around his shoes and drifting water borne toward the drain. He seemed to deflate. Rogan's chiseled jaw sagged. His shoes, socks, and pants below the knees were soaked from the spraying showers. He started to walk away, then turned back and looked at Jack. "Do you even know how to make a commitment? " Rogan stepped out of the shower and walked out of the locker room leaving a track of wet shoe-prints.

Donny came out of the Coaches' office at the far end of the locker room with a quizzical look on his face. He called out to no one in particular, "Any problem out here?"

Mancusa had already finished showering and was dressing beside the row of lockers nearest the showers during Rogan's outburst. "Coach Dubka!" Mancusa hustled over to Donny and took him by the arm turning him back into the office. "Can we talk inside?"

"Sure, Xavier, what's going on?" Donny asked with a troubled look on his face. The locker room was silent as a tomb.

"It's all right, Coach. Are Coaches Hass and McVale inside?"

"No, they're over in the AD's office in Bartlett."

"Good. Come on, let's talk inside." Mancusa followed Donny back into the office and shut the door behind them.

-21-

Coach Rogan was not on the sidelines with the team the next day. When the team huddled for pregame instructions, Coach Hass informed them, "I'll be directing the offense today. Tom, er, Coach Rogan, called me early this morning. There's a family emergency and he'll have to be out of town for a few days." Wally paused, looked around at the faces of the gathered players, and then added, "I'm sure we'll all keep Coach Rogan and his family in our thoughts and prayers this week." Several helmeted heads nodded. Otherwise, the response to Wally's statement was silence.

Without Rogan directing the offense, the Maroons played erratically when they had the ball. The defense hung tough throughout the first half against the Beloit College Buccaneers. Kovatch and Mancusa, the captains and linebackers, played with more fire than usual. They didn't pull their cars up to the field as Jack had jokingly suggested in practice. But they shouted encouragement, whacked teammates on the helmets and butts, and pounded guys on their shoulder pads after a good hit.

Mancusa and Kovatch ordinarily led by example rather than yelling and shouting at teammates. They were both intense and always played with resolve and determination, but they didn't make a lot of noise. Instead of jumping around and waving their arms and yelling when they lined up their teammates on defense, they normally just barked out the code words for the formation needed to counter whatever the offense was showing. Against Beloit, they seemed almost manic.

It worked. The Buccaneers only scored one touchdown the first half. The Bucs' offense was held to the fewest yards gained by a Chicago opponent in the first half of a game since last season.

Unfortunately, the offense didn't match the defense's effort. They were operating off Rogan's play book. But they weren't executing as well with Wally calling the plays. The problem wasn't that Wally was unfamiliar with the offensive schema. The play book was the joint composition of Wally and Coach Rogan. Wally ran the offense the previous two seasons, but gladly turned that duty over to Rogan hoping the younger coach would be taking the reins after Wally's retirement. But there was a difference in the tactics of the two coaches. While they had the same universe of plays to call, Rogan's choices were more aggressive and bolder than Wally's. Rogan was more willing to risk trick plays and options than the older more conservative head-coach.

At the first preseason-practice, when Rogan took over the offense, he told the squad they were supposed to be more intelligent than their opponents. So, he expected the Maroons to be able to execute a more complex series of plays. He explained that flawless execution of a football play begins with intellectual understanding and is completed through the muscle memory of experience. Coach Rogan emphasized to the players who attended preseason practices that creation of muscle memory requires a base of experience, i.e., practice and more practice. Learning football plays in a play book is one thing, executing on the field is quite another. Rogan pointedly told the players that no matter a player's score on an IQ-test, perfection of execution of the playbook would require practice, drilling, and more practice. Of course, Jack and a third of the team was not present for those preseason lectures of Tom Rogan's.

Rogan's dictum proved to be true. The Maroons were a team made up of intellectually gifted players , but with a significant percentage regularly missing practices. The evidence was that they were at a disadvantage against teams of dimmer bulbs who practiced every day. Increasing the sophistication and complexity of the play book had so far not lessened the disadvantage.

Coach Hass learned during the first season he coached the Maroons that smarts are one thing, mastering football plays another. But, he wanted to give the younger coach freedom to implement his own style and hoped Rogan might instill something in the team he and Mick had failed to do the first two seasons. Rogan's bolder and more sophisticated strategy had yet to produce results in the win column for Chicago. A return to Wally's more conservative play-calling, which had not yielded a win the two previous seasons, wasn't working against Beloit.

Wally assumed a strategy of straight forward runs from the I-formation and standard pass routes from the spread would make it easier for the offense to click. But the team's rhythm was off. The tackles, Kim and Dax, missed blocking assignments they'd executed perfectly in practice on Friday. Heinz and Moose once again were playing slow at their guard positions and they weren't hitting crisply. Backs and receivers screwed up routes. They didn't drop or fumble balls, but the timing between QB Cauley and the skill players was off. Receivers cut out, when Cauley expected them to cut in. Or, they broke off their routes when Cauley was looking for them to go long. On one play from the T-formation, Jonesy and Tank actually ran into each other. They were each expecting the hand-off from their quarterback. Cauley had to eat the ball for a loss.

Chicago did have one successful drive in the half. It started with less than four minutes on the clock. Waters returned a Buccaneers' punt to the Maroons' 43-yard line. The drive stalled, but on third and long Wally finally decided to risk throwing a bomb. He called for Jack to run a deep post with Denny Murphy running a quick out from slot and Johnny Jones leaking out in the backfield as a safety valve. Jack out ran the secondary in his deep route but Cauley threw short. Jack had to break stride and then dive back to the ball to make the catch.

The chain gang hustled down to the Beloit fifteen where Jack made the diving catch. Wally called for Jones to run off tackle between Kimson and Douglas. Beloit anticipated the play. Their outside linebacker plugged the hole between tackle and end and the strong safety came up to support the line. Jonesy met a wall of defenders for no gain.

In the huddle Cauley begged and pleaded with his linemen to hold the pocket on the next play. They all knew Wally would call for a pass. Sure enough, Opey pushed into the huddle with Coach's instructions for a screen pass to Tank. The Buccaneers once again anticipated Wally's play call. The safety blitzed between Brockton and Moose to throw off Cauley's timing. He was forced to throw early and the middle linebacker swatted the ball down.

On third down the Maroons were able to advance the ball five yards on a quick pitch to Murphy at flanker. But that left the Home Team five yards short of a first down at the Beloit ten with just over a minute to play in the half.

Wally called timeout to confer with Mick and Donny. Wally said, "We can go for it and try to end the half tied or send in Chefski to try for three. Mick?"

Coach McVale didn't hesitate. "Let's make sure we put some points on the board now and give the guys something to feel good about. They'll need the confidence for the second half. We come up empty now -- not sure how much they're gonna have left in the tank."

Wally turned to Coach Dubka. "Donny, your defense has played tough all half. Worst case if we go for it and fail, Beloit's got a long way to go in a minute. Chefski makes the kick -- they're going to have the ball a lot closer to our goal. Will the defense hold one more time?"

Donny didn't hesitate. "Our guys will hold no matter where they start, Coach. Your call."

Wally called Mike Chefski over. He took hold of the kicker's face guard and said, "Okay son, we need one of your aesthetically pleasing parabolas to split the uprights. It's in your range." He let go, lightly slapped Chefski's helmet and said, "Make it count." And he did. Mike's kick bisected the uprights in a perfect parabolic arc.

Wally was so delighted with Chefski's kick, he doubled down and sent him back on the field for the kickoff. The kick was another beautiful parabolic arc, but way too short for comfort. The Bucs started with good field position on their own thirty-nine. But Dubka's defense held.

The half ended, Beloit-7, Chicago-3.

Jim Capps announced, "These scores just in, Princeton zero, Harvard. Brown, four score and seven years ago." The Lower Brass Conspiracy led kazoo-blowing students and neighborhood kids through the Brownian Motion anti - routine. The calliope piped "Wave the Flag for Old Chicago". Jack's roommate, Steven Schwartz, capered about in front of the stands and held up placards with the words of a new cheer he'd penned:

Logarithm, biorhythm,
Entropy, kinetics,
MPC, GNP, bioenergetics!
Maximize and integrate,
Titrate and Equilibrate--
GO, MAROONS!

The second half started with Karchuk blasting the kickoff into the end zone. McVale had threatened Wally with loss of his Quad Club membership if he let Chefski kick off again. The ball was placed on the 20-yard stripe for Beloit to begin its second half campaign. It fizzled under the pressure of Chicago's smothering defense. The Maroons took over after the Beloit punt on their own thirty-three. But Chicago's offensive woes continued and the Maroons were forced to punt.

The first possessions of the half were typical for both teams through the third quarter and deep into the fourth. The Maroons' defense bent but did not break. Beloit pounded the interior line with their two big running backs . Each weighed over 220 pounds. The Maroons' defenders were outweighed by their opposite numbers in most cases by at least 20 pounds. The Buccaneers' running backs were as big, or bigger, than the Maroons' linemen. The Bucs' linemen bigger yet.

But Kovatch and Mancusa played like berserkers. Their manic enthusiasm inspired their teammates to a similar recklessness. The defenders threw their smaller bodies against the bigger blockers with wild abandon. Little Jerry Mansueto wriggled between the Bucs' bulky center and hulking right guard for two solo tackles and a sack of the quarterback. Rick Douglas twice executed a perfect spin move from his defensive-end position to beat his man and catch Beloit's QB in the backfield for losses. Zack Stubblefield belted the tailback for a loss when he blitzed from safety between the right tackle and tight end. Whenever the Buccaneers managed to push the ball downfield, the Maroons eventually thwarted the drive. Beloit got within field goal distance only once. The kick was wide left.

But Chicago's offense remained flaccid. They went three and out series after series. Dennis Maroni punted so many times his right foot was getting sore and swollen. But finally, with less than four minutes left in the game, Denny Murphy ran a hitch route and fooled the defender. Denny ran out two yards, appeared to be giving up on the route, but then took Cauley's lightening bolt pass over his left shoulder and streaked up field. The cornerback was left behind grabbing air. Had Murphy been taller than five foot eight with longer legs, he would have run for a touchdown. He was caught on the 19-yard line by the Buccaneers' free safety. An option lateral to Jonesy on the next play brought the Maroons to the eleven. Wally sent in a play with Jack as primary receiver running a curl to the goal line.

The ball was on the right hash mark. Jack trotted out to take his wide-out position near the left hash. He looked to his right automatically visualizing the theoretical line of scrimmage vectoring from the ball to the sideline on the plane of the field. He toed the invisible line with his left foot. His hands were at his sides, his legs spread shoulder wide in a slight crouch. Jack kept his eyes focused on the ball watching for the snap by Shooks. He did not look down field. He would give the secondary no clue to his planned route. Jack heard the shrill tweet from the ref's whistle to start the clock. The sonic wave of Cauley's snap count penetrated the ear holes of his helmet. "Blue thirty two! Blue thirty two! Hut! Hut! Hut!"

Jack burst off the line head down arms and legs driving forward as hard and fast as he could. On the 1-yard line he rotated his shoulders and head left as if he was running a post to the deep left corner of the goal. But then he twisted his torso right so the momentum carried him just over the goal line. Jack looked back at his QB with arms outstretched and hands ready for the ball. Cauley threw high. Jack leaped. The cornerback had lost a step to Jack on the fake move. He launched himself at Jack smashing his left shoulder pad into Jack's right side and lashed out with his right hand trying to knock the ball away. But the pass was high and Jack was three inches taller than the Buccaneer defender. Jack brought the ball down and twisted to his left sticking the ball out to make sure it broke the plane of the goal line.

Chefski kicked the point after and it was Maroons-10, Beloit-7.

Karchuk tried to blast another kickoff into the end zone, but he shanked it. The ball skittered into the hands of Beloit's middle back. He ran the short kick back to the Buccaneers' thirty-eight. The Bucs started their last drive with just under three minutes on the time clock.

With so little time left to score, Beloit's coach changed tactics. The Buccaneers gave up trying to batter the Maroons' line and ran quick-out pass patterns, button hooks, and short slants. They moved the ball steadily up field. The Beloit receivers caught short passes, protected the ball, and got out of bounds conserving time on the play clock. By the time the Bucs reached the Maroons ' 22-yard line there was only fourteen seconds left in the game.

Jack had rotated in and out on defense throughout the game. The Maroons only had seven players qualified to play the four positions in the secondary. Carl Lipscomb was one of the seven and saw little playing time. Opey and Dickey played on all special teams and spelled Murphy, Jones, and Jack on offense. Vendel also played on the punt and kick receiving teams. Only Dalrymple and Stubblefield had the luxury of concentrating solely on their safety positions. Few opposing teams had players "going both ways" on offense and defense. Most of the other teams dressed out at least sixty players, often more than twice as many as on the Chicago roster.

One of the reasons the Maroons had a hard time winning games was that they tended to tire out in the second half, because 1) several of their best players were playing both offense and defense, and 2) some of the Maroons were not in superb condition because they did not attend all practices. Wally and Mick had built the roster up to thirty four players for the 1971 season. The team carried more players than the first two years of "new era" football. But the Maroons were still smaller in number and size than their opponents. Beloit brought sixty five players in their private coach to meet the Maroons on Stagg Field.

Jack was no longer required to play both offense and defense the entire game as he had the previous two seasons. The first game he rotated with Greg Vendel at cornerback. Greg had proved to be an excellent cornerback, so Coach Dubka made him the regular wide-side cornerback. Jack's defensive assignment was down sized to come in at free safety on obvious passing downs, especially if a long pass was anticipated. The coaches wanted Jack's speed, vertical leaping ability, and long reach protecting the end zone, if the opponent was likely throwing deep.

Jack ran onto the field and slapped Dalrymple 's hand as Chuck ran off. Jack lined up inside Greg Vendel's left shoulder at safety. Beloit broke its huddle. Every player and fan on the Chicago's side knew the Bucs had one or two more shots at a touchdown. If the Maroons kept them out of the end zone, Beloit would have to settle for a field goal attempt and, at best, a tie game. For Chicago, a tie game would be the closest they'd come to a win in the new era.

A receiver split wide on Jack and Greg's side of the field. Another was in the slot position. Jack called out to Greg, "Sky! Sky!"

Greg's helmeted head whipped around. He gave Jack a questioning look and shouted back, "Sky? What--"

Jack waved Greg away. The Bucs' QB had started calling out signals from the shotgun. The ball was hiked. In his ready position Jack began to back pedal watching the slot man with eagle eyes tracking his hips, shoulder pads , and eyes to anticipate his route and make a play on the ball if the pass was thrown to the slot receiver. Jack also shot quick glances back at the Bucs' QB to be ready when he released the ball, or to break and run down the quarterback if the play turned into a run.

The QB rolled right to Jack's side of the field. He threw. Jack realized the pass wasn't to his man. The ball was thrown wider and deeper. On the run he turned and looked expecting to see Vendel running stride for stride with the wide out. To Jack's horror he saw that Greg had apparently released his man and was now giving chase trying to catch up. Jack's teammate was three yards behind. The ball was thrown short behind the receiver. Greg threw his arms up in the air as the ball sailed over him and then dove toward the receiver. Too late. The Buccaneer end caught the ball and fell backwards across the end zone just before Vendel bowled into him. The score was thirteen to ten with four seconds on the clock.

Beloit made the point after. The kickoff was a line drive. The ball bounced once then Waters fielded it and took off up field. He stiff-armed and got past the gunner, was hit by the next tackler but lateraled to Denny Murphy streaking up behind him. Three other tacklers converged on Murph. There was no escape. The first Buc hit him. Denny desperately struggled to free himself. Just as he broke the tackler's grip he was buried by the other two.

Game over: Beloit-14, Chicago-10.

After the Buccaneer wide-out made the catch for the winning touchdown over Greg Vendel's flailing arms, Jack ran up to Greg with his arms spread out in a questioning gesture and mouthing, "What happened?!"

Greg pulled himself up. His shoulders drooped in defeat. He took off his helmet and started toward the sideline shaking his head but ignoring Jack.

Jack grabbed Greg's shoulder pad and spun him around. "Greg, what happened? Why'd you let him go?"

Greg shoved Jack's hand away and jogged off the field with Jack following. When they got to the sideline, Greg turned on Jack, "Why did you call Sky? What the hell, Jack? He was split out. I needed to cover him man on, but you called Sky! So, I released when he cut inside to your zone, but you weren't there!"

It hit Jack like a ton of bricks. His face must have given it away, because Greg turned on his heel and started to walk away shaking his head in disgust. Donny Dubka came running up to them with his hands out demanding, "Blair, Vendel, what happened out there!? How did you manage to blow the coverage?"

Jack dropped his helmet to the ground, put his hands on his knees, shook his head and muttered, "Oh shit. Oh shit. It's my fault, Coach. It's my fault." He wanted to cry.

Greg walked away. He wanted to cry too.

Donny put his arm around Jack's shoulders. Other guys started to drift over toward them, but Donny waved the other players away.

Jack finally looked up at Coach Dubka and explained, "I got mixed up. I don't know why." He ran his dirt stained hands through his sweat-streaked hair. "I called Sky instead of Cloud."

"You what?!"

"Yeah, I blew it. Shit! I got the signals mixed up. I thought Sky was man and Cloud was zone."

"Jack, how could you--"

"I don't know--"

"We went over the coverage calls every day this week and again in the defense skull session on Friday!"

"Donny! I was getting yelled at by Rogan when you were going over coverage calls with the D- guys. I didn't practice with you guys all week! Remember, Wally told me to work with the offense all week!"

"Shit, Jack." Donny shook his head. Before he walked back down the line to where Wally and Mick were waiting expectantly, he said, "You know, if you came to practice Tuesdays and Thursdays, we'd have enough time for you to work offense and defense."

[Pep rally 1901; Archival Photographic Files, University of Chicago Library, Special Collections Research Center]

-22-

Professor Blackford opened his Tuesday four o'clock class on Plato's *Symposium* with a question, several statements, and a question. "So, what is love? We've heard from Phaedrus, Pausanias, Eryximachus, and Aristophanes in our reading so far. We have yet to hear from the host of the symposium, Agathon. Nor have we heard from the gadfly Socrates, or that most interesting Athenian, Alcibiades. Thus far in the text, what have we learned of love as it was understood in Fourth Century Athens among privileged free-male citizens?"

Without further prompting, the seven students in the upper-level Classics class launched into an excited, even explosive, discussion and debate. Hairston Swift questioned the claim of Phaedrus that Eros is the oldest of the gods and had no parents. Argument ensued among the students as to whether Phaedrus was correct in his claim and whether there was textual evidence in Greek mythology to support the claim. Blackford settled the question by reminding the students that the purpose of the class was not to review Greek mythology but to understand what Plato, or rather Plato's text, could teach us. "We have to accept what the different speakers say as sincerely believed, unless we have textual evidence to the contrary. Phaedrus was presenting one of several versions of divine genealogy. His recitation presents a minority view, which was not widely accepted as authentic."

Blackford turned to Jack, who had yet to contribute to the discussion, "Mr. Blair, you are the closest thing we have to a warrior among the members of this symposium. What did you think of Phaedrus's statement that for a lover to earn the admiration of his beloved he must show bravery on the battlefield? Do you agree that nothing shames a man more than to be seen by his beloved committing an inglorious act?" Several students snickered.

Jack was usually one of the more vocal members of the class, but had been uncharacteristically silent through the opening round of the discussion. Jack looked thoughtfully out the window onto Harper Quad before he answered. The other six students turned their attention to Jack waiting for his answer. He finally said, "'A handful of men who love each other, fighting side by side, will defeat any opponent. Because, lovers are willing to sacrifice their lives for their beloved.' That's what Phaedrus says anyway."

"And do you agree with that, Mr. Blair, given your experience on the football team?" Mr. Blackford asked.

"You mean, if the guys on the team really loved each other we'd be winning games instead of losing?" The other students snickered again.

Mr. Blackford held up his hand to quell the laughter. "Phaedrus concludes his speech making the point that sacrificing one's self for love will result in rewards from the gods. But I must make a greater effort to stay apprised of sporting events on campus. I didn't realize your team was not winning games. But let's not dwell on the particulars of our own community. What we are interested in here is the community of early Fourth Century Athens. So, how did the other members of the characters Plato assembled for the Symposium in Agathon's house respond to Phaedrus's exposition on Eros?"

There wasn't sufficient time in the ninety minutes allowed for the class to cover Pausanias, Eryximachus, and Aristophanes. The discussion got hung up on Pausanias's legalistic distinctions between "Heavenly Aphrodite" and "Common Aphrodite" and Athenian law on pederasty. Professor Blackford said that in the next class meeting he hoped the group would be able to consider what Aristophanes really meant by claiming that people in love feel "whole" when they have found their love partner. "And please note," Blackford concluded, "Aristophanes includes in his list of loving couples all possible permutations of gender coupling. On Thursday then! Uh, Mr. Blair, a moment of your time?"

Jack hung back waiting for the other students to shuffle out of the classroom. Mr. Blackford cleared his throat, "Uh, Mr. Blair, I hope you understand I did not intend to hold you or our football team up to ridicule. I am no fan of football, but I certainly endorse our University's ideal of the scholar-athlete, and, if there are students who wish to play football, then I am pleased that they are able to pursue their interest as part of the college experience."

Jack was surprised the subject had come up in class. As Blackford was Jack's favorite professor he had tried, and succeeded, in taking at least one Blackford class each of his four years in the College. His relationship with Professor Blackford preceded his relationship with the football team. Blackford had never asked him about playing football, and Jack could not remember the subject having ever been raised between them. He assured Mr. Blackford that he took no offense.

Professor Blackford went on, "I certainly don't mean to pry, but you seemed somewhat out of sorts in class, distracted, I would have to say."

Jack sighed dolefully and then replied, "Yeah, I suppose I am. It actually relates to football."

"How so?" Blackford asked with interest.

"Mr. Blackford, do you really want to talk about football?" Jack gave his academic mentor a skeptical look.

"Yes certainly, but certainly not football per se, but football as to how it is affecting you in our classroom."

"Okay," Jack said hesitantly. "Well, I lost the game on Saturday for the team." He shook his head. "It was so stupid. I blew a coverage call."

"A coverage call?" Blackford asked with a look of interested incomprehension.

Jack started to explain, but then broke off as it was clear that Blackford had no idea what he was talking about with respect to man coverage versus zone and that in the particular passing situation only a fool would call for zone coverage, but he was the greater fool for having called for zone coverage and then played man coverage leaving Greg Vendel to twist in the wind. So he summed it up by saying, "I made a mental error which cost us the game. I let the team down."

"Ah, I see." Blackford looked at Jack with sympathy. "Mr. Blair, if I might ask, why do you think you made the mental error?"

"I've been asking myself that question for the last three days. And it hit me in class today. It's in Plato's *Symposium*."

"Yes?"

"I don't love my teammates and coaches enough."

The coaching staff demanded it and funds were approved for the football team to ride in style to their next game against the Milton College Wildcats in Milton, Wisconsin. Their private coach had individual reclining-seats, storage space above the seats for helmets, shoulder pads, and duffel bags. It even had a toilet in the back. After his third trip from the front of the bus back to the toilet, Coach McVale remained in the back of the bus. That had the unfortunate, or fortunate, effect of squelching the plan of the team's contingent of potheads for toking up on the ride to southeastern Wisconsin.

Wally had fought hard to get Milton College on the 1971 schedule. The teams had not played before. Milton had tied one game during the 1970 season and lost all the others. So, Wally thought this game was one that Chicago definitely had a chance to win. However, Milton's second-year coach, Rudy Gaddini, had completely turned the program around after his first miserable season. They won four games and only lost one so far in the 1971 season. Instead of looking like the marshmallow Wally had expected, the Wildcats now appeared to be one of the strongest teams the Maroons would face in 1971.

What really brought Wally down in the dumps was the depleted Maroons' roster. Only twenty two players were on the bus. It hadn't occurred to Wally in scheduling the game with Milton on the fourth Saturday in October that that was the same Saturday the LSAT and the GRE would be offered for Chicago students. The team lost twelve of its players to the tests. After Mick abandoned Wally to sit near the toilet, Wally turned to the other coaches for a sympathetic ear to listen to his grousing about players choosing to take graduate exams rather than play football.

Donny Dubka joined Wally in the bitch session. But Donny blamed the problem on the dumb asses that would schedule exams on a fall Saturday. "Jesus Christ! Don't they know it's football season?! All over the god damn country fans are loading up their cars with hot dogs and beer to go see their favorite college team play. Students are tail gating in stadium parking lots on every damn campus. Did those a-holes at ETS give that any consideration?" Dubka looked from Wally to Rogan, but didn't wait for a response. "Oh no, they don't give a damn about the position they put a student athlete in." Wally grunted an affirmation. Donny continued his rant, "Sure, most players will wait until the season's over to take the dang test, but what about the players graduating in December? Huh?" Wally grunted affirmatively again. "And what about players who have to get their test scores in before the season's over?" Wally nodded in agreement. "Damn it to hell!" Donny concluded, "We had a real shot at this one." He shook his head in disgust.

Coach Rogan was sitting in the window seat beside Donny and behind Wally. Wally was in the front seat immediately behind the driver. Rogan looked out the window during Donny's voluble rant against the insensitivity of the ETS administrators. Rogan nodded agreement when appropriate, but added zilch to the conversation and didn't take up the thread when Donny broke off. He seemed to be more interested in watching the passing scenery of the Chicago suburbs and then the rolling dairy land of southern Wisconsin than joining in the bitch session.

Tom Rogan had missed the entire week of practice. Not much was said by the coaches to the players about Rogan's absence during the week. Wally reiterated midweek what he'd told the team before the Beloit game. Coach Rogan was still out of town due to "a family situation". During breaks in practice and in the locker room while getting dressed or undressed, players spoke in low tones about their speculations. Early in the week the consensus was that Rogan had some sort of break down after the confrontation with Jack in the showers. By midweek the prevailing rumor was that his wife had filed for divorce and he needed time off to deal with it. At Friday practice the guys were sure that Rogan was in alcohol rehab. And the whispered speculation on the bus ride to Milton College was that nobody knew what the hell was going on with their offensive coordinator.

The Maroons did indeed take a pounding by the Wildcats. All the progress the team had made that season vanished in the game against Milton. The defense, which had played so stoutly against Beloit, was a sieve. Kovatch was missing. He had to take the LSAT. Mancusa did his best to rally his troops and Donny was as fiery on the sideline as ever. But Chicago was outgunned and manhandled by the well-disciplined Wildcats. By the middle of the third quarter the defensive players were dragging ass so bad, Coach Dubka started rotating guys off the bench, like Carl Lipscomb, who normally only played special teams.

Jimmy Blackmon played on the other end of the line from Rick Douglas on both offense and defense. He was so dog tired by the start of the fourth quarter he looked like he needed oxygen. On one play he missed a tackle when the Wildcats ran a sweep around his end. Jimmy sort of waved his arms at the halfback who took the pitch and then cut inside blazing past Jimmy. Jimmy lowered his head in defeat and started to put his hands on his hips when the Wildcats' fullback blasted him with a body block. Jimmy went air borne. His body flew ten feet out of bounds, where he landed on his back, flopped and rolled until he ended up supine under the Visitors' bench. He lay still. Players ran over to him. Donny pushed through, undid Jimmy's chin strap and asked if he was okay. Jimmy winced and then slowly opened his eyes. "Is the game over yet?" he asked.

The offense fared no better. Tank was missing. He was also taking the LSAT. His ability to batter the defense with bucks and blasts from his fullback position was sorely missed. Rogan adjusted his play calling strategy to rely on Murphy's and Jonesy's speed on running plays. He altered strategy in the air as well. He rarely called a deep route. Jack racked up the most catches he'd made in a game so far that season on quick outs, little button hook routes, and flags in the short flats. The offense did manage to move the ball up and down the field, just not across the opposing goal line.

Gassed out blockers could not hold off rushing defenders. Cauley rarely had sufficient time and protection for his receivers to get down field before opponents were piling on him. The Maroons didn't even try to run a route deeper than fifteen yards in the second half. The short passes pushed Jack's stats to twelve catches for ninety-two yards. Had the running game been up to par a twelve-catch-ninety-plus game by a receiver surely would have meant points on the board. But, without the threat of the long ball and the defense playing like Swiss cheese, the Maroons just couldn't maintain a drive to push the ball across the goal line.

They did reach field goal range once in the third quarter. But, being down by three touchdowns, trying for a field goal just seemed too pathetic. So, Wally kept the field-goal kicking team on the side line and signaled Cauley to play on and try to put six points on the board. On the next play Cauley was leveled when he released the ball for a pass intended for Jimmy Blackmon. The pass turned into a floating duck, which was intercepted ending the threat of a Chicago score.

With four and a half minutes left in the game and the Wildcats' bench warmers giving ground to the nearly exhausted but desperate to score Maroons, th e Visitors reached their opponents' 32-yard line. Once again the drive stalled. It was fourth and long. Wally dearly wanted to avoid a shut out. He and Mick had a private, but spirited little tactical colloquy. The only words the nearest players were able to make out was Mick saying "Chefski kicks with a limp dick."

Mel Karchuk had hit forty-five yard field goals in practice, but missed more than he hit. He had tremendous leg strength, but lacked Chefski's smooth technique. Karchuk threw the javelin on the track team. It seems counter-intuitive, but the power generated in a javelin throw comes more from the legs than the throwing arm. Karchuk's leg was a cannon; Chefski's a very accurate pea shooter.

Since goalposts in the college game are at the back of the end zone and the holder is seven or eight yards behind the line of scrimmage, the field goal attempt would be almost fifty yards.

Wally took his old friend's advice and sent in Karchuk with the field goal team. Better to leave the field with three points than zero. Shooksie was taking the GRE, so his backup, Curtis Miller, was the long snapper. Curt's hike was a beautiful spiral. Cauley caught it with both hands, brought the ball down, and spun it into perfect position with laces in line with the goalposts. Karchuk timed his approach to contact the ball just before a Wildcat came flying in from left end. Whump! The kick had the sound of a perfect strike. And then, whang! The ball hit the upright and bounced back onto the field. No good.

The one moral victory the Maroons could claim was to deny Milton the point after on the Wildcats ' seventh touchdown. Opey O'Byrne and Dickey Roudebush had continued practicing their stunt rush which had almost worked against Lake Forest. The special-teams specialists had honed their execution to such a level of precision they could have filed a patent. Opey would line up across from the end on the left side of the defense. Dickey took the inside linebacker position just inside Opey's right shoulder eyeing the offensive tackle. Kovatch would normally line up as the outside linebacker. When the ball was snapped, instead of hitting the end Opey would slam into the tackle. The offensive end would, hopefully, shoot forward at Opey, who had just vanished by throwing himself into the tackle. Kovatch would step in to block the end. Instead of hitting the tackle, Dickey would shoot through the gap between the tackle and end. If there was the slightest delay by the holder in positioning the ball, Dickey had a chance of throwing himself at the holder to block the kick. It hadn't worked yet in a game, but in theory it was perfect.

Maybe it was due to the Wildcats having second stringers in on their point after team, but the holder was a split second slow in bringing the ball down. With Kovatch sweating out the LSAT instead of sweating on the field with his teammates, Dax Brockton filled in. A nanosecond after the brain of the Wildcat's center sent a signal to his hands to hike the ball, Opey smashed into the tackle. Dickey lunged forward the moment Opey moved. The cleats on the shoe of Dickey's lead foot combed the hair on Opey's calf muscle as he bolted over his teammate their timing was so precisely attuned. The Wildcat end threw his forearms out where Opey had been but only found air. Dax stepped in and delivered a resounding forearm shiver to the confused end. Dickey launched himself and swiped at the ball just as the kicker made contact. The pigskin went angling off to the right and Chicago had denied the home team their forty ninth point of the game.

When the referee blew his whistle for the final time signaling the end of the game, the Maroons staggered off the field on wobbly legs their faces hanging down to their knees. Eyes were glazed and tongues lolled out of mouths. Jack's head was bowed as he shuffled along at the back of the line of players weaving toward their bus. His helmet almost dragged on the ground, the face guard hooked in the fingers of his right hand. It felt heavy as a bowling ball. He muttered to Mancusa that the team looked like the scene in "Lawrence of Arabia" when the soldiers were lost in the desert. Mancusa shook his head throwing off sweat in an arc like a lawn sprinkler. "No," replied the future Catholic seminarian, "they look like medieval paintings of ecstatic saints."

Jack was too tired to laugh or cry. "Yeah, but saints get to go to heaven after their sacrifice and death. We have to ride back to Chicago with Coach Rogan."

Final score: Chicago-0, Milton-48.

-23-

Professor Blackford asked for a volunteer to describe Aristophanes' fable about the origin of romantic attraction. After a few ribald remarks among the students in the class on Plato's *Symposium*, Ellen Deshane summarized the speech.

"Aristophanes described spherical creatures that wheeled around like clowns doing cartwheels. There were three sexes, male, female, and androgynous – a half male and half female creature, er, person. These – should I call them proto-humans?" Blackford assented, and Ms. Deshane continued. "Okay, so these proto-humans started to climb up Mt. Olympus to attack the gods. So, Zeus chopped them in half separating each into two bodies. Ever since then people search for their other half trying to recover their primal nature. So the women who were separated from women are lesbians. The men split from other men are gay. Heterosexuals come from the bisected androgynous male-female proto-humans."

Blackford nodded approvingly when Ms. Deshane completed her summation. "And what did you make of Aristophanes' statement that, while some people think homosexuals are shameless, in his opinion they are the bravest and manliest of all?" Blackford asked the class.

"Aristophanes certainly didn't hold heterosexual marriage in high regard, did he?" Hairston Swift asked rhetorically. "He seems to think most married men are adulterous and most wives are unfaithful."

"But does Aristophanes condemn the institution of marriage qua institution, or is his criticism the lax way in which it was being practiced in Fourth Century Athens? " Blackford asked. The question led to disagreement, strife, and discord among the students. Resolution was not reached by the time class had to end at five-thirty. Professor Blackford smiled with satisfaction. He dismissed the class with a final comment on the text, "Aristophanes warns that men, now, we would of course include women, should fear the gods and not neglect to worship them. Zeus might wield the axe again and this time split us at the nose. However, if humans honor Eros, they will escape this fate and instead find wholeness."

After the other students departed, Professor Blackford said to Jack, who had remained seated, "Mr. Blair, you seem distracted once again. I cannot comment on your relationship to the football team, but your classmates are not receiving the benefit of your love either." Blackford gave Jack a penetrating look. "Prior to last week your participation in this class was a joy to your teacher and classmates. We miss you, Mr. Blair. Come back to us."

Jack studied his hands. He looked around the room avoiding Blackford's eyes. He finally responded ruefully, "That's the problem. I signed up for this class so I could skip football practice on Tuesdays and Thursdays. Now, I'm feeling guilty for being here instead of at practice with the rest of the team."

"I had no idea. Hmm. This is a dilemma. I would wield Zeus's axe to create a double for you, but the Administration frowns on axe wielding by faculty. Hmm. I'm afraid it's too late in the quarter to drop the class--"

"Oh no, Mr. Blackford, I wouldn't do that."

"No, I expect not. But there may be another solution."

"Another solution?" Jack asked in surprise.

"If one of my best students is going to sit in my seminar class looking like he's come from his grandfather's funeral, instead of participating as his teacher and classmates had come to expect of him, then perhaps we should consider transforming the class for him into an independent study."

Jack's face lit up. "We could do that?"

"Mr. Blair, you surely remember Max Weber's description of bureaucracy from your social science sequence."

"Uh, yeah."

"Well then, you know that every such system is human no matter how rationalized the bureaucracy. That applies to our college as well. And it shouldn't surprise you that I have a little influence with the humans involved in this particular system."

"So, what do we do?"

"Mr. Blair, would you mind walking with me? I need to pick up some bagels in Harper Court. If recollection serves, that would not be a great distance out of your way, would it?"

Walking north through the Main Quad and then along tree-lined Woodlawn Avenue, Professor Blackford explained how they could turn the course into an independent study for Jack. As Jack had two years of Attic Greek, he would be expected to translate selected passages of *The Symposium* from the Greek into contemporary English as well as write a mid-term and final paper. Blackford would meet with Jack for a tutorial session once each week. Jack agreed enthusiastically.

Then, Blackford told Jack he had a favor to ask. "Mr. Blair, I am quite aware that you are able to move your arms and legs in a coordinated fashion, which does not come natural to most of the faculty or students on this campus. "

"You mean, I'm an athlete?"

"Precisely. I recall our discussion when you asked for my recommendation letter for your Rhodes application. And I told you how I had so enjoyed Oxford when I was there on a Marshall Scholarship. I recall telling you that, if you win the Rhodes, given the well-developed musculature of your upper arms, you should enter the crewing competitio n for the Old Blues. They could use your skills in the annual boat race against their arch rivals from Cambridge."

Jack laughed. "I remember. And I told you that the only boat I'd ever rowed was my uncle's john boat on the White River."

"Well, that aside. The favor I have to ask you is to perform as -- I think the term is 'ringer' -- on the Social

Thought team in the annual softball competition against the players for Ideas and Methods." Blackford went on to explain that faculty and graduate students in the Committee on Social Thought and Ideas and Methods programs held an annual sixteen-inch softball game, known as the Daffodils versus the Turkeys. While Jack would not be eligible to play for the Social Thought Daffodils as an undergraduate, it was within Blackford's power to cross list the independent study course on Plato's *Symposium* as an undergraduate course in Classics and a graduate course in Social Thought. Jack would thus qualify to play as a Daffodil being a one-course graduate student.

Jack gladly agreed. He found it highly amusing that one of the most ivory-tower professors at U of C was such a schemer. He told Blackford that he looked forward to trying to help the Social Thought Daffodils best their foes, the Ideas and Methods Turkeys, in a softball game.

When Jack arrived in the locker room to dress out for practice on Thursday, there was much hooting, bellowing, and ribbing of him by his teammates. Xavier Mancusa had not missed a practice or game since football resumed as a varsity sport. He smiled wryly and said, "Mr. Blair, you do know it's Thursday." Mancusa held up his hand for a single high five.

Jack gave him skin and joked, "You know, I didn't realize how different the locker room smells on Thursdays. Ah, the sweet bouquet! So much more pleasant than Wednesdays and Fridays."

"That's because Moose only farts on Wednesdays and Fridays," Tank cracked.

Rogan did not mention his confrontations with Jack at the Milton game nor at practice on Monday or Wednesday. The players' favorite line of any of the coaches to imitate was still Coach McVale's rant about how the Russians would never beat America, because Americans play football. But jokes with punch lines involving honking horns and wearing shoes in the shower were added to the team's repertoire of in-jokes. All told discretely out of the hearing of the coaching staff, of course.

Rogan had never been chatty with players, but after his time-off for "family reasons" the coach was even more laconic. He seemed down-right subdued following his extended absence from practice. His voice lacked the biting authority it had previously carried when he put the offense through drills. Before, he would blow his whistle shrilly to call the squad to order and would bark out commands at the players. Now, he spoke quietly. Several times during the Thursday practice, guys had to say, "Sorry Coach, could you repeat that," because his voice had trailed off so softly it was hard to make out what he was saying over the crack of pads, players calling signals, and other coaches blowing their whistles.

Jack was happy that Rogan was in no mood to butt heads with him or anybody else. He was a little surprised there was no comment from the other coaches abou t his unexpected appearance at a Thursday practice. Coach Dubka didn't even razz him when he switched over to work on defensive sets. However, when it was time to take a final lap around the field, Wally patted him on the shoulder pad and asked Jack if he would walk with him over to the AD's office in Bartlett.

Wally settled into his comfortably padded roll-chair behind his battered old oak-desk. Jack dropped his helmet and plopped down into one of the steel and plastic chairs facing Wally's desk. Wally smiled and looked Jack straight in the eye. "Mr. Blair, it was good to see you at practice today."

"Thanks, Coach."

"It was a surprise. Was your class cancelled?"

"No, I've changed my schedule. I should be able to make practice Monday through Friday."

Wally looked surprised and pleased. But then, his expression changed to that of someone trying to tread carefully, like he might be on thin ice and didn't want to break through. "May I ask why?"

Jack looked around the room and paused a long time before he met Wally's gaze and answered, "Coach, I loved playing football when I was a kid. Nothing compared. You know, trying to make the perfect catch, or the perfect tackle. I loved the aesthetics of the game. You know, like how Chefski describes the perfect kick." They both chuckled. "I liked running track and swimming, but it's not the same as being part of a football team. I know you've talked to Kovatch about his theory of how a football team should function like the perfect communist society."

"Yes, I've heard his theory." Wally rolled his eyes.

Jack laughed. "Yeah, okay. Well anyway, the joy of playing football was ruined for me in high school. Our coach took all the fun out of it. To him, it wasn't about the beauty of the game. It was all about proving what a bad ass you were and we were supposed to hate the other team and want to kill them and eviscerate their children."

Wally nodded appreciatively. "I know coaches like that at the college level too."

"So when I quit the team in high school I didn't think I'd ever play again. But then, when you and Coach McVale started up the team here, I thought it would be cool to play when it suited me. You know, come to practice two or three times a week, show up on Saturday for the games. Just play for the fun of it."

"Football should be fun, Jack."

"It is, Coach. But, it's no fun losing every week!"

"Tell me about it," Wally said shaking his head and grimacing.

"Coach, I think it's ridiculous that colleges spend millions of dollars on sports programs and players are treated like employees with no benefits and no pay. I don't want any part of that."

"I agree with you, Jack. But we don't do that here. And no Division III school spends millions on their sports programs. At this level, every athlete is playing because he wants to. There are no scholarships. There's not much glory. But what there is, is the love of the game. And being part of a team. And sacrifice. Sacrifice of time and giving up some of the things other students who don't have to practice can do."

"I, I know that. I just didn't want to risk lowering my GPA or jeopardizing my chance for the Rhodes scholarship."

"And now?"

"Now," Jack studied his hands before he answered. "I guess I've come to the conclusion I owe something more to the team, and to you, the coaches."

"Jack, you don't owe us anything. And I hope you're not trying to make amends for the mistake in the Beloit game--"

"No, it's not that. I felt horribly guilty about blowing the coverage, especially since it made Vendel look bad."

"He's young. He'll get over it." Wally remarked with avuncular complacensy.

"Yeah." They both chuckled again. Jack went on, "The reality is that we'll never achieve excellence on the field if guys don't come to practice. At U of C we're all about trying to achieve excellence within the life of the mind. And I love that! That's why I came here. We're striving to stretch ourselves as students to learn as much as possible. But then some of us -- me -- only give a half-assed effort to the football team. I thought if I tried my best during the game that would be enough. I've realized it's not. Coach, even if we have the best athletes on the field, if we don't know the plays, or we screw up signals, because they're not drilled into our heads, we're gonna get beat every week by teams that practice every day. It's bad enough we start a month behind most of the teams we play."

"Yes, that's a handicap." Wally admitted.

"Anyway, I want to do my part to win some games before the season's over."

"I'm glad you feel that way, Jack. I too would like to finish our last season with some victories."

They smiled at each other. The old coach's face was lined and creased from the worry and weather of thousands of hours of practices and games outdoors. Yet, it seemed to glow like a tempura painting of one of the early Christian martyrs. Wally put his arm around the shoulder of his young player when they walked out of the office together.

"Mr. Blair, I'd like to tell you about this dream I've had. It starts out in this long hallway."

-24-

The team bus of the Loras College Duhawks blocked traffic on 56th Street. Players poured out of the bus and ran through the gate onto Stagg Field. They'd made the long bus ride from Dubuque, Iowa on Friday and spent the night at the Holiday Inn by Midway Airport. The Duhawks were able to sleep in late and eat a steak and eggs brunch before the one o'clock game with Chicago. Sixty-eight players from the little Catholic College, which sits atop a bluff overlooking the Mississippi River, formed up into strict lines. Their team captains barked the command to start and the Duhawks began doing jumping jacks in crisp military order. The Loras College Duhawks looked fresh and ready to play.

Maroons were lazily fielding kicks, practicing special - teams plays, and tossing balls back and forth. They'd already warmed up with calisthenics and run a lap around the field. Players started gathering in little groups to watch their opponents with wary eyes. As usual, the Maroons were out-numbered, but at least there were more Home Team fans in the stands than rooters for the Visitors. In the first few years of new-era football, if Chicago played a nearby school, like Wheaton, Valpo, or Northern Illinois, the visiting team might bring as many supporters as there were fans in the stands to cheer on the home-team Maroons.

Moose sidled up to Jack and asked, "So what the hell is a Duhawk?"

Before he could answer, Kovatch butted in, "It's Donald Duck on steroids! Look at their mascot." In front of the fifty or so parents and girlfriends in the Visitors' stands a gaudy blue and gold feathered figure was strutting back and forth. The bird's crest reached at least seven feet high and its yellow shnozzola protruded a foot out from the white face.

"Shit, I wish they would have brought cheerleaders," Moose complained.

The U of C had no cheerleaders in the early years of new-era football. Although, for a home game in the 1970 season Waters somehow convinced the cheerleaders from his high school in Kenilworth to come to the game and perform as if they were the home-team cheerleaders. It was sweet and pathetic. The cute little gals performed their routines in front of the Home stands. They even adapted their cheers from "Kenilworth" to "Chicago". The jaded fans, who were enjoying the affects of hot chocolate heavily laced with peppermint schnapps, either ignored or laughed at the exuberant display of pom-pom waving, fist pumping, jumps, and cartwheels of the sweater-clad girls in short skirts.

After the game, Jack's roommate Steven urged Jack to petition the Athletic Department to bring in high-school cheerleaders to every home game. He said it was much more exciting to see the cheerleaders' little rumps in panties, when they did their flips and cartwheels, than to watch Jack and the Maroons take another beating on the field.

None of the Chicago players had a biological or etymological answer to the question, "What the hell is a Duhawk?" Had one of them asked Wally or Mick, they would have learned that a *Detroit Free Press* sports writer came up with the unique moniker. In 1924 the team had neither a mascot nor a nickname. When the football team from the little college in Dubuque played the University of Detroit, the local sports writer had to call the visiting team something, so he referred to them as the Dubuque Hawks. Later in the article the writer creatively shortened the name to "Duhawks." The nickname stuck.

When the teams were called off the field to their opposing sidelines prior to the coin flip, the Duhawks formed a circle, thrust their helmets in the air, and burst into song:
Hail Loras Varsity
Cheer them along the way
Onward to victory

We will win this game today
Let's hear a cheer for the varsity
Long may they reign supreme
Fight 'til the echoes ring
For the glory of the team!

Chicago players stopped listening to their own coaches' instructions and turned their attention to the Visitors who were now jumping up and down and roaring menacingly at the Maroons. The Duhawks fight song had turned into the full-throated war cry of sixty-eight young men with their blood up ready for battle.

"Yikes!" Heinz squeaked. When he saw Mick turning a gnarly eye on him, he corrected it to, "I mean, let's get 'em! Ulp."

"Damn mackerel snappers," Shooksie muttered.

"Watch it," Mancusa said and gave Shooks a friendly whack on his shoulder pads.

"Get out their and kick some Duhawk ass," Coach McVale growled.

"He really means we should re-arrange the lower anatomy of these Roman idolaters," Jack whispered to Dickey Roudebush.

The first half was hard fought and literally bloody. For good Catholic boys the Loras players hit hard and mean. Forearm shivers were aimed at Maroons' throats instead of the gut or chest. Cut blocks were thrown at knees and ankles, where they could cripple a player, instead of at the thighs which would just take a would-be tackler out of the play. Clothes-line tackles, bell-ringing blows to the helmets, and helmet-leading spears into the sides or backs of unprotected receivers were repeatedly delivered by the Duhawks.

Murphy had to sit out the second quarter nursing a knee injury. O'Byrne had to have a dislocated shoulder popped back into place. Kovatch ended the half with a bloody lip after the Duhawks left tackle popped him with a fist right under his face guard.

Penalties were called, but in those days it was legal to spear, horse-collar tackle, and cut block anywhere on the field by any player. There was no "in the grasp" rule to protect quarterbacks, and using the helmet like a guided missile to spear a ball carrier or unprotected and unsuspecting receiver was legal. It was a much rougher game back then, gentle reader.

The Maroons were royally pissed off by the manner of play of their less than chivalrous opponents. And, they were frustrated and aggrieved by the few penalties assessed by the referees against the Duhawks. By halftime Wally was furious about the dirty play of the Duhawks and the failure of the refs to control it. He waddled out on the field to confront the referees. Wally had his back to the Chicago side of the field, but the players could see their coach angrily gesticulating at the refs. The team knew Wally's exhortations were not well received by the refs when he threw his clipboard down and stomped on it.

While Wally was arguing with the referees, Coach McVale was pacing the sideline growling and grumbling to no one in particular. Jack, Tank, Mancusa, Kovatch, Moose, and other veteran players always got a kick out of Mick 's rants, so they edged over to listen in. He snarled in his raspy smoker's voice that it was time to give the damn yellow peckers or gold Duhawks, whatever they are, a taste of their own medicine. "When I was coaching the prison team at Joliet we had a dirty ref in one game. God damn if we didn't know the bastard had been paid! You could smell it! We took the son of a bitch out. That's right! And when there was a pile up, we didn't just gouge at eyes and throw elbows, we'd get creative. We tied the other guys' shoe laces together. Ha! The bastards fell flat on their faces when they tried to stand up. Hu chu spitooey..." The old coach suffered an attack of hacking and spitting. He stomped off to the Men's room.

Jack and the other vets looked at each other wide-eyed shaking their heads in amazement. "Holy shit! Did you hear that?! Mick coached the prison team at Joliet!" Rick Douglas hissed.

"I'd never heard that one before," Moose said.

"Me neither, brother ungulate," Tank quipped. "But it gives me an idea."

"This is truly a sign of the apocalypse! Tank Stevens fought his way through cobwebs and pot haze to find an idea in the back of his skull," Kovatch cracked.

Before Tank or the others could respond, Wally beckoned the team onto the field. Donny yelled at the kicking team to tighten their jocks and get out there and hit somebody.

The second half was played as rough and dirty as the first, but the Maroons went back into the fray determined to give as good as they got. The referees must have been irritated by Wally's complaints, because as lax as they were in calling penalties against Loras in the first half, they became equally strict and vigilant in sanctioning Chicago players in the second. Penalty yards began to mount up against Chicago, so the Maroons found it difficult to get within scoring range. Whenever the offense started clicking and moving the ball down field, they'd be stymied by a clipping penalty or a flag for an illegal formation. The drive would stall and Maroni would have to come in to punt. A seven point deficit turned into a twenty-one point hole by the start of the fourth quarter.

The umpire, who positions himself just behind the defensive line, was the ref who seemed to have the prickliest burr up his ass against the Home Team. When the Maroons' offense lined up, if a lineman even twitched an eyebrow, the umpire called illegal motion and issued a five-yard penalty. If a Maroon just touched the face guard of a Duhawk, the ump threw a yellow flag for unnecessary roughness resulting in a fifteen-yard penalty against Chicago.

What really infuriated the Chicago side against the umpire was that he got in Jack's way on a crossing route forcing Jack to alter his line to avoid running into the ref. Cauley threw the ball exactly where Jack would have been but for the ump's interference. It cost the Maroons a first down. Jack ripped off his helmet and threw it to the ground in disgust. He gave the ump a menacing look. The ump said matter-of-factly, "Pick up your helmet Eighty-Four or you'll get a delay of game penalty."

Jack didn't shout but bit off his words, "You were in the way. You're supposed to get out of the way."

The ref replied coolly, "I'm part of the field. It's your responsibility to avoid me. And now we'll assess that penalty." He threw down a yellow flag and blew his whistle. The ump told the head ref to back the Maroons up five yards.

On the sidelines Wally threw his clipboard down. Dubka punched air in the direction of the umpire and roared something that sounded like #^&$+!!! Rogan turned on his heel and walked away from the line of players and coaches. He stood by himself looking away from the field of play. McVale ordered the defense to huddle up around him. He winked and said in a conspiratorial tone, "A milkshake for any of you who come off the field with Duhawk blood on your jersey."

Murphy limped into the huddle for Chicago's first series of downs in the fourth quarter. He reported that Rogan wanted the offense to run one of the complicated flea flicker reverses. "Christ!" Cauley groaned, but started to rasp out the play.

"No, god damn it, you're gonna give the ball to me!" Tank ordered. The younger players in the huddle blanched. Tank was seething. The other players could hear his breath coming hard and fast. Everyone turned their eyes back to QB Cauley to await his instructions.

Bob hesitated, looked around the huddle and saw all the veteran players nodding their heads. "Okay Tank, how do you want it?"

"Shooksie, Heinz, I'm coming your side, give me a hole. Jonesy, you're at tail and I'm fullback in the I. Blast through that hole and take out the linebacker or DB whoever's coming in to plug it. Got it?"

They all nodded. Cauley said, "Okay, on two; ready, break!" As one they clapped their hands and broke the huddle. The Chicago linemen trotted to their positions and dropped into a three-point stance. Receivers toed the scrimmage line hands at their hips. Backs crouched ready to spring. Shooks grasped the ball, fingers notching the laces. Cauley bellowed "Red red!" He cupped his hands under Shooks's posterior, "Three twenty five, sixty four hut hut!"

Shooks hiked the ball and bucked forward throwing his left forearm at the chin of the nose guard. The Duhawk tried to push Shooksie off balance by throwing both hands at his chest. But the Maroons' center belted him a ringing blow to the helmet with his right open palm. They both went down. Heinz roared out of his stance as fast as he'd moved in three seasons. His 295 pounds hit the 240-pound defensive tackle before the Duhawk was out of his stance knocking him backwards. Heinz belly flopped onto the poor guy. Whooft! The wind was knocked out of both ends of the Duhawk. Jones hit the hole gaining speed as his powerful sprinter's legs chewed up turf. The outside linebacker slashed in front of him trying to slip past, but Jonesy lowered his helmet and caught the Duhawk in the midsection knocking him ass over tea kettle.

Tank took Cauley's hand-off and followed Jones through the hole between Shooks and Vandenberg. To his left a safety was driving forward trying to close the gap. The field was open in the right flat. The right corner had started to back pedal to cover Jack on what appeare d to be a fly pattern. When the corner realized it was a run, he started to head back toward the line of scrimmage. Jack lowered his helmet and right shoulder, threw out his left arm and hurled his body into the Duhawk's waist and rolled. The perfectly executed roll block opened the entire right side of the field for Tank.

Instead of running right, Tank charged straight ahead helmet down and nailed the umpire in the chest with his helmet. The ump went down like a sack of potatoes which slowed Tank. The safety closed and made the tackle.

The other refs converged blowing whistles and waving their arms. Tank got up and tossed the ball at the chest of the head ref. The ref was still waving his arms and blowing his whistle. The ball thumped him in the chest. He tried to grab it, but bobbled the ball and accidentally spit his whistle out in mid blow. Bleet!

Tank walked over to the stunned zebra and looked at the field judge who was trying to help the ump up. Tank asked innocently, "Is he gonna be all right?"

Rich Blum, the Maroons' student trainer, brought smelling salts from the team's med kit. He officiously snapped in half a little glass vial of ammonium carbonate inside its protective mesh pocket. Rich held the medicine under the ump's nose. The zebra shook his head, then arched his back and turned violently away from the nasty smell of ammonia. The wounded zebra was helped off the field. He refused the offer of an ambulance to the University Hospital ER. He finished the game sitting on the end of the Home Team bench looking dazed and confused.

The Maroons completed the drive successfully. Cauley threw a high pass to Jack deep in the right corner of the end zone. Jack leaped as high as he could to bring the ball in with his right hand while he pressed down on the shorter Duhawk's helmet with his left hand. He caught the pig skin one-handed and dragged the front of his left shoe on the turf as he fell clutching the ball tightly. The tip of Jack's left shoe took a divot out of the turf just inside the white line of lime dust demarking the back of the end zone. The back judge whistled and signaled touchdown. Chicago was still down by fourteen points.

The final minutes of the game were more a brawl than an orderly match of competitors emulating the ideals of fair play and deference to the rules. Scuffles and shoving matches broke out after every play. Challenges were thrown down amidst name-calling, jawing, and trash talking. There weren't any actual hockey-type fights with players taking off their helmets and throwing punches when the ball was blown dead. But plenty of violence took place while the ball was live.

On Loras running plays, Kovatch, at inside linebacker, usually had to take on a brutish 270 pound tackle. Kovatch was out-weighed by 70 pounds. Mike wrestled varsity and was one of the most physically tough players on Chicago's roster. He was used to battling blockers who out-weighed him by 30 or 40 pounds, but he was enduring the most severe test of his football career wrestling with big Number-72 on the Loras offense.

Every few plays, when the offensive set allow ed it, Mancusa signaled a switch with Kovatch. Mancusa would jump from outside to inside linebacker to spell Kovatch from his battle with Seventy-Two. Mancusa had witnessed the whuppings big Seventy-Two was laying on Kovatch. So, whenever he got the chance, Mancusa execute d a swim move side-stepping the brute and then whacked him on the helmet. This enraged the big Duhawk and he turned his anger from Kovatch to Mancusa. If he was on his feet at the end of a play, Seventy-Two lunged at Mancusa. But Xavier was too light and quick for him. The brute was forced to retreat to his team's huddle snarling and cursing.

When the final whistle blew to end the game, Mancusa took off his helmet and jogged slowly toward the Chicago side of the field. Seventy-Two charged after Xavier from his blind side swinging his helmet. Kovatch yelled a warning and made a running diving-tackle at the Duhawk. He bounced off the big guy's hip pad, but it slowed his advance. Mancusa whirled around, grabbed Seventy-Two's lead forearm, dropped to a knee and pulled down with all his strength. The physics of the big man's 270-pound mass multiplied by his accelerating speed created a tremendous force driving him face first into the ground.

Mancusa jumped up and for good measure delivered one swift kick into the buttocks of the big tackle. The downed Duhawk bleated when he felt the sting of Mancusa's cleated shoe contact his ass. He rolled over to reveal a face caked with dirt. Blood was oozing out of the dirt above his eye brows and ridge of his nose.

Kovatch slapped Mancusa on the shoulder pad and said, "He should've kept his helmet on."

Mancusa winked and reminded his teammates that, "Coach McVale said we should kick some Duhawk ass and draw blood. Guess he owes me a milkshake."

The head zebra ran up to them waving his hands and blowing his whistle. But the game was over. There wasn't really anything he could do.

Still, the ref felt compelled to chastise Mancusa. "I know you. You're the one who's supposed to be studying for the priesthood, aren't you?" Mancusa nodded his head. "Do you think that's any way for a future priest to act?"

Mancusa shrugged his shoulders and replied, "The son-of-a-bitch needed a lesson in righteous indignation. "

Final score: Loras-28, Chicago-14.

-25-

Alice walked with Jack the next day, a clear and crisp Hyde Park Sunday afternoon, to the softball diamond between Crowne Field House and Pierce Tower. As they cut through the lawn behind Pierce dorm, Jack recognized Mr. Blackford's tall, lanky frame stiffly throwing and trying to catch a cantaloupe-size sixteen-inch softball. Blackford was attired in black high-top Converse basketball shoes, baggy grey cotton sweat-pants, a rugby style maroon-colored jersey, and a black White Sox baseball-cap pushed down on the crown of his head so the bill pointed upward at a jaunty angle. He couldn't help himself. Jack burst out laughing at the awkward figure his favorite professor cut. Jack thought Blackford looked like Ichabod Crane trying to play catch with a white cantaloupe.

Alice asked Jack what was so funny. He confessed he'd never seen Blackford in anything but a suit, white shirt, and tie. "When Blackford gets really wound up in class he takes his sport coat off. Sometimes, when the heat is too high in Wieboldt Hall, he rolls up his cuffs. But I've never even seen him loosen his tie."

Alice smiled then hooked her arm around Jack's as they walked onto the ball field.

Blackford hailed Jack when he saw him and motioned him over. Alice recognized a friend among the Ideas and Methods grad students, so she let go of Jack's arm and walked over to chat with her friend on the other side of the diamond.

"Mr. Blair! So glad you could make it," Blackford enthused.

"Happy to be here, Mr. Blackford. Hope you won't be disappointed with my contribution to the team. You know, I'm not a baseball player."

"Yes, I know the difference between baseball and football. In fact, I've researched your football team's oeuvre since our last conversation."

"Hmm. Uh, what'd you learn?"

"Well, I was surprised to discover that you had, indeed, lost every game since football has been, shall we say, resurrected at the University."

"Yeah, tell me about it."

"At first I thought how upsetting that must be for you and the other players.'

"It is. For most of us, anyway."

"But then, Jack, er, Mr. Blair, I thought how utterly courageous!"

"Courageous? How so?"

"Mr. Blair, what you and the other players do each Saturday on the field of play is like Hector facing Achilles. Your opponents are bigger and stronger; probably better equipped. You must know in the back of your minds that the deck is stacked against you each game. Yet, you take to the field week after week to battle the superior team – just as Hector faced Achilles!"

"Huh. Yeah, I see what you mean. Of course, Hector ran away at first, so Achilles had to chase him around the walls of Troy until Athena tricked Hector into thinking he could win."

"Yes, yes, and so you and our Maroons are even more courageous than the hero of Troy. You haven't yet run away before a game started, have you?" Blackford deadpanned.

Jack laughed, "Not yet."

"Nor have you been tricked by a goddess?"

"No, but we could certainly use her help."

"We'll see what we can do about that. But the point is that your football agon is as heroic as the Trojans fighting the Greeks in Homer's *Illiad*. Someday the bards may sing of your exploits and the poets write of it."

Jack laughed again. "Well, be that as it may, Coach Hass and the fourth-years would like to win at least one before we fold our banners and sail for home."

Wayne Booth, Chairman of the Committee on Ideas
and Methods and captain of the Turkeys, walked over to
Blackford and Jack. Professor Booth was taller than Jack
with white hair and a neatly trimmed white-beard. He
looked like an athletic Moses attired in a smart-looking
rayon sweat-suit.

Booth shook hands with opposing captain and Chairman
of the Committee on Social Thought, James Blackford. The
two were close friends and colleagues. They worked together
to create the College's New Collegiate Division. Both were
passionate advocates of cross-disciplinary studies. They
would defend the College's tradition of Common Core
requirements and original sources to the death. But they
were concerned that maintaining the walls of separation
among the traditional divisions of the University over time
encouraged specialization and stultification within the
different disciplines and departments. They believed that by
creating graduate programs like Social Thought and Ideas
and Methods, and the New Collegiate Division, cross
fertilization would breed new ideas on ancient and original
texts and subjects. So, the members of the two graduate
programs and New Collegiate Division came from various
departments, divisions, and the professional schools. The
multi-disciplinary approach resulted in a raft of new and
creative courses, such as Philosophy of Discourse, Anatomy
and Astrophysics, and Rhetoric of Fiction.

"Ah, Blackford, I see you've brought in a ringer," Booth
said smiling and shaking hands with Jack. Booth had
supported the resurrection of football and was one of the
few faculty members who attended at least some of the
team's home games.

"Booth, I'm surprised at your accusation. 'Ringer', I
believe is slang for imposter or one playing for a team under
false pretenses--"

"It also refers to an Australian sheep shearer--"

"Of course it does, but my dear fellow, Blair is neither
an Australian sheep shearer nor an imposter."

"James, I'm surprised you would sink to these depths. Just because we've beaten you two years running--"

"Exactly old friend, time to reinvigorate the old Daffodil gene pool with a little new blood."

"And the genes you chose to graft into the hybrid just happened to be those of one of the best known athletes on campus."

"And one of our best fourth-year students--"

"Indeed, James; while you have lowered the Daffodil standards and invited a college student -- a mere ingénue -- into your iniquitous conspiracy, the Turkeys remain pure-bred faculty and graduate students only."

Blackford and Jack laughed at Booth's bombastic rhetoric. "But you acknowledge that Blair is eligible to play?" Blackford queried.

"Yes, I received the copy of your cross-listed course from Dean Strauss."

"If I may interject," Jack said, "I might not be such a great addition to the Daffodils. I'm not a baseball player and where I grew up we didn't play sixteen-inch softball. I'm really not very experienced with the game."

"Said like a true ringer," Booth replied with a grin. "Next he'll be suggesting a five-dollar bet."

"I was going to suggest twenty, but enough talk. Let us gird up our loins and let the games begin!" Blackford piped confidently. He rounded up the Social Thought players to take the field first. He assigned Jack first base. When Jack looked at him questioningly, Blackford read his thought -- why put your best athlete on first rather than center field or short stop? Blackford said, "Mr. Blair, you'll soon learn that not many balls will be hit out of the infield and there are lots of plays to first. And--"

"Let me guess. Being able to move one's arms and legs in a coordinated fashion might help one to catch balls thrown without the highest degree of accuracy?"

Blackford winked in reply and said, "Exactly."

Sixteen inch softball is played without gloves. Fielding a hard-hit roping line-drive can be a dangerous pursuit without a glove to protect your face. Jack soon learned there was little danger of that from the Ideas and Methods players. One of the rules of this particular competition was that the pitcher was honor bound to slow pitch and to try to let the batter hit the ball. The intent was to avoid strikeouts and to make a game of it. Two women strikingly small in stature on the Turkeys' side, nevertheless, managed to strike out each time they came up to bat despite Blackford's easy arcing pitch over the plate. They each swung the bat in a jerky whipping motion that more resembled a badminton swing than any baseball or softball swing Jack had seen. Most of the hits by the Turkeys were little dribblers into the infield. But the Daffodil defense was porous enough that even a dribbler could result in a base hit. Jack's ability to move his arms and legs in a swift and coordinated fashion was tested. Throws to first came in at all angles, rolling on the ground or ten feet high.

Wayne Booth was the best hitter for the Turkeys and when Blackford gave him a pitch without much a rc to it, Booth smacked the ball hard right back at the pitching mound. The ball was flying two feet directly over Blackford's head. He reached up, got his hands on it, and then toppled over backwards like a tree felled in a forest. The ball rolled out of his hands and Booth dashed around first. Jack ran over, picked the ball up to hold the Turkeys ' captain at second base. Blackford stood up slowly and stiffly. But he smiled, shook his finger reprovingly at Booth, and swatted the dirt off his butt with his Sox cap.

Booth was the only runner to score for the Turkeys, so it was one to nothing when the Daffodils took their first at bat.

While Jack was swinging two bats to loosen up and ready himself for his first try at the plate, he noticed Dean L orna Strauss sitting beside Alice with a gaggle of spectators. Jack waved at Alice and Dean Strauss. Dean Strauss had replaced Warner Wick as Dean of Students and, like her predecessor, was a stalwart supporter of the football team.

She attended every home game even when the freezing-cold and biting Lake winds punished the spectators. Lorna was one of Wally's staunchest allies during the long fight to win approval for the return of football.

Dean Strauss called out, "Hit her outa the park Blair!" Jack gave her the thumbs up sign.

The Daffodils lead-off hitter was a PhD candidate named Wendy Olmsted. She was blond, slim, athletic looking, and made solid contact with Booth's second pitch. The ball went through the legs of the Turkeys' short stop. Ms. Olmsted sprinted down to first base, turned the corner and ran to second while a lumbering heavy-set left fielder picked up the ball.

Blackford was up next. He took a wild cut at the first pitch which nicked the top of the ball. It dropped right in front of the plate. He stood looking at the ball contemplatively, but when he saw Booth charging toward him yelling at the catcher to throw the ball, Blackford took off toward first. The catcher was one of the Turkeys' diminutive women. Instead of picking the ball up and throwing to first base, she two-hand rolled it toward Booth running up to the plate.

Blackford ran toward first. His long arms and legs shot out at awkward angles. Jack thought he'd never seen so much motion resulting in so little forward momentum.

Booth grabbed the ball ten feet in front of the plate and hurled it toward first. The ball struck Blackford in the middle of his back and he went down for the second time in less than one inning of play. This time he fell forward sprawling across first base. Safe.

Jack came up to bat next with Ms. Olmsted on third and Blackford on first. Jack had never played, or heard of, sixteen-inch softball until his first year on the Flint House intramural team. He played plenty of hardball and softball as a kid in Seymour. Throughout high school, and when he was home from college, he played summer league baseball on a team sponsored by the local American Legion. But the first few times he tried to hit a sixteen-inch ball, he had a hell of a time hitting anything but centerfield line drives and smoking hard grounders. Eventually, he mastered the upward arcing swing it took to really blast the ball and make it carry.

Jack took the first couple pitches from Booth to get comfortable in his stance and calculate the drop in Booth's arcing slow pitch. The third pitch came looping down on the outside of the plate. Jack smacked the ball with the bat in the upward angling swing he'd perfected by the end of the first intramural season. The ball took off from the bat with a sweet sounding whack. It flew over the field and hit the arched copper roof of Crowne Field House with a whump!

Booth shaded his eyes with his hands watching the trajectory of the ball rocketing across the sky above him for an out-of-the-park home run. Mr. Blackford was doing some sort of skipping dance that resembled Scottish toe dancing as he rounded the bases. As Jack loped by Alice and Dean Strauss he doffed his C-cap. They pumped their fists and yelled "Whoo hoo!"

The next time Jack got up to bat he cracked what should have been a double down the third base line into left field. But the slow-footed left fielder took so much time getting the ball back to the infield, Jack dashed around the bases for an inside-the-park home run. By the end of the third inning the score was Daffodils seven, Turkeys one.

The Turkeys fared no better as the game progressed. The score was thirteen to three at the end of the sixth inning. Captain Booth threw in the proverbial towel by invoking the ten-run rule and conceded defeat.

It was an unseasonably warm and mild fall day, sunny and sixty-two degrees the first Sunday in November. After the game, players and on-lookers gathered around a keg to fill plastic cups of bitter piss-tasting Hamms Beer. The intensely intellectual members of the Committees on Social Thought and Ideas and Methods let their hair down by dropping 'g's on words that ended in 'ing' and limiting polysyllabic words to every other sentence. Turkeys and Daffodils traded friendly insults and barbed anecdotes under a cobalt sky in the crisp autumn air. Everyone was having a good time.

The convivial state of communal consciousness was altered when David Cohen, who was pursuing a Masters in Ideas and Method, approached Jack beer in hand and blurted at him, "Football is atavistic and retrograde! Why would any civilized person want to risk injury to self or others playing such a game? What possible value is there in crashing into other helmeted brutes?!"

"Now just a minute--" Blackford started to say.

"Cohen! Grace in defeat is the order of the day," Booth remonstrated.

Jack said, "It's okay. I'd like to answer the question." Jack took a moment studying the five foot eight, wire - rimmed curly-haired Cohen, who eyed Jack with beady brows and rictal grimace. "Mr. Cohen, if you haven't played football, you might find it hard to understand that when the game is played well it has a beauty that transcends your image of grunting brutes crashing into each other."

Cohen started to interrupt, but Wayne Booth held up his hand and nodded at Jack, "Please continue, Mr. Blair. I think we're going to find what you have to say quite interesting."

"The aesthetics of every sport are different. Football may be seen by those who haven't played it as more violent or brutal than non-contact sports. And there is a significant element of violence in the game in terms of players trying to physically dominate each other. But developing the unique techniques required to dominate the opponent on the other side of the line requires discipline, practice, and mastery. When two linemen are well matched in size, strength , and skill, their struggle becomes one of will and determination. As they tire, and have tried all the different techniques within their repertoire to win their one-on-one struggle, and all that is left is the will to win or not to give in, one of the most beautiful aspects of human being is revealed. " He stopped. Jack looked around at the circle of faces that had gathered quietly around him.

"Yes, yes, go on Mr. Blair," Blackford encouraged.

Jack shrugged. "What do you call the beauty of the human spirit that refuses to yield?"

Blackford cleared his throat and quoted,

"In the fell clutch of circumstance
I have not winced nor cried aloud.
Under the bludgeonings of chance
My head is bloody, but unbowed.

William Ernest Henley," Blackford concluded and bowed acknowledging the hoots, cheers, and claps from the bystanders.

Jack went on, "To achieve excellence an athlete has to develop a base of experience, which comes through the pain and suffering of practice and training. When it all comes together and he or she is in that special zone where muscle memory takes over and performance is the spontaneous reaction to the situation of the moment -- it is sublime. Willie Mays making an over-the-shoulder basket catch, Oscar Robertson twisting in midair to shoot over a taller defender, or Gale Sayers swiveling his hips and bounding past a tackler -- those are displays of breathtaking genius. It's a different mode or form of intelligence than the intellectual brilliance that we so prize here at the U of C. But it's still sublime."

"Your description reminds me of the work by a colleague in the Psychology Department with the wonderful name of Mihaly Csikszentmihaly," Booth remarked.

"Yes, he's propounded a theory of what he calls 'Flow' or the 'the state of flow'," Blackford added.

"Yeah, I went to an open lecture of his in Kent Hall," Jack said. "The way he describes an athlete being in a state of flow, or in the zone, is part of what I'm talking about. It's like losing yourself when everything is clicking. But another aspect of playing football, like other team sports, is community--"

"You mean a bunch of heavily muscled men sitting around a locker room farting and belching together!?"

Cohen said archly while looking around at other grad students for support.

Jack didn't take offense. He laughed and then responded, "Yeah, that's part of it. Bonds of brotherhood are created through shared suffering, trials , and combat, including suffering the farts and belches of teammates. But what's most essential is commitment and trust. A football team functions like a community during each play. For the play to work, every player has to do his job. A football play is like a snapshot of an organic community that depends on each of its members to make the community work. We need the garbage collector, the teacher, and the doctor for our communities to work. Linemen, backs, and ends all depend on each other for protection and to move the ball forward. We have to trust and depend on each other. The backs depend on the linemen to block and open holes and the linemen trust the backs to run according to the blocking assignments. As a receiver, I depend on the quarterback to throw the ball where I can catch it, and he trusts I'll run my assigned pattern when he throws the ball. We sublimate our own egos into a communal organism and we sacrifice our bodies to protect our teammates. To get kind of spiritual about it, it's like what Jesus was talking about when he said we should love our neighbors as ourselves."

"Well said Mr. Blair, well said!" Blackford gushed triumphantly.

Jack's soliloquy was followed by clapping and cheering. Mr. Cohen nodded tight lipped, then joined the others clapping appreciatively.

"Mr. Blair and the other members of our football Maroons have competed honorably and bravely w ith little support from the wider university-community," Dean Strauss interjected. "These young men understand that athletic participation enhances mind, body, and spirit. I think we all witnessed in Mr. Blair's performance on the softball diamond this afternoon -- and what we just heard from him - - proof that our football team is producing scholar-athletes of the first order."

After the post-game socializing wound down and players and spectators began to depart, Jack asked Alice to take a walk with him along the Midway Plaisance. The sky was just beginning to turn into a dusky-grey evening. The young pair held hands and swung their arms gaily. Jack still felt the warm glow of satisfaction from his dominating performance in the softball game, but even more gratifying was the appreciation -- maybe even adulation, he thought to himself -- he'd received from the revered U of C figures of Booth, Strauss, and Blackford.

At the east end of the Midway, Alice and Jack pranced around the Memorial to Thomas Masaryk, the first President of Czechoslovakia. The Memorial is an equestrian statue by the sculptor Albin Polasek. The mailed horseman is the Knight of Blanik, a legendary Czech figure who emerges from Blanik Mountain in his nation's hour of need.

Alice joked that Jack was to the Social Thought Daffodils what the Knight was to the Czech nation, their savior.

"Savior might be a little too strong, but, okay, I'll accept your syllogism," Jack said sticking his nose skyward and looking side-to-side with supercilious haughtiness.

Alice gave him a punch on the shoulder, "And modest too!"

When they arrived at the west end of the Midway, the pair sat down on the edge of Fountain of Time, a sculpture by Lorado Taft. The sculpture is 127 feet in length. Figures representing all humanity pass before Father Time and a mournful poem by Henry Austin Dobson, "Paradox of Time", is stenciled into the concrete. Jack declaimed in a loud and stilted tone:

"Once in the days of old,
Your locks were curling gold,
And mine had shamed the crow.
Now, in the self-same stage,
We've reached the silver age;
Time goes, you say? - ah no!

How far, how far, O Sweet,
The past behind our feet
Lies in the even-glow!
Now, on the forward way,
Let us fold hands, and pray;
Alas, Time stays, - we go!"

Alice shook her head and guffawed at Jack's performance. They fell silent for a time. Darkness had descended on the campus. Gazing up at the Moon and the stars beginning to twinkle in the night sky, Jack tried to recognize familiar constellations through the diffuse urban light. He broke the silence with a smug tone in his voice, "Well, I'm waiting."

"Waiting for what, Mr. Blair?"

"Waiting for your syllogism, such as, since I'm so much older than you, I'm like old Father Time up there." Jack hooked a thumb at the figure behind them.

"You're less than a year older than me, and that's a metaphor not a syllogism, wise guy."

He tweaked her upturned nose. She cuddled closer to him.

They sat quietly for awhile, until Jack broke the silence again. "You know I had the strangest experience the other night."

"Tell me."

"I was walking home from The Reg, glanced up and saw the Moon. It was a full Moon."

"What's so strange about that?"

"I thought it was a street light."

"You thought it was a street light!?" Alice laughed and gave him a little push.

"Yeah, it was weird. For just a moment I thought the Moon was a street light."

"Jack, you've been in the city too long!"

"That's exactly what I was thinking."

"So the innocent farm-boy from Seymour Indiana has turned into a fully realized city slicker!" They both laughed.

"Well, I guess I'll get to see some of the Indiana countryside again when we ride to Oberlin for the game Saturday."

They stood and leaned against the cool concrete side of the sculpture and gazed back down the Midway. The waning Moon hung over Lake Michigan. Alice laid her head on Jack's shoulder.

Fountain of Time on the Midway

-26-

Blaat! Phuhlooff.

"Jesus, Moose! Did you sit on a ferret?" Kovatch complained.

Moose looked relieved, then sheepish. But before he could reply, Tank said, "Hey, leave him alone. He can't help it if he suffers from annular rectosis."

"Did you conduct a proctological exam to determine your clinical diagnosis, Dr. Stevens?" Jack asked with an arched brow.

"Come on guys, you know peanuts make me fart, " Moose explained as he broke another shelled peanut in half, pulled out the two nuts, popped them into his mouth , and dropped the shell on the floor of the bus.

The guys sitting around Moose shifted in their seats trying to gain a little more distance from their large flatulent teammate.

The Maroons were only down three players from a full roster for an away game against Oberlin College. The bus left Crowne Field House at noon on Friday, which meant any players with Friday afternoon classes had to choose between attending class and playing on Saturday. The core of veteran players all chose to make the trip.

"Hey Waters, do you have any Mothers?" Tank called up to Dave Waters, who was sitting several rows closer to the front of the bus. The upper-class vets had claimed the back section of the tour bus for the day-long ride from Chicago to Oberlin, Ohio. Several first and second-years collected around the center of the bus with Waters and Lipscomb.

"What? Whose mother are you talking about?" Waters yelled back.

Tank started laughing. "The Mothers of Invention, ya dipshit!" He looked around at the third and fourth-years occupying the back rows of the bus with a complacent smile. "Whose mother? Sheesh."

"Oh! Yeah, I've got 'Absolutely Free'."

"Well, pop it in, dude."

Water punched out The Rolling Stones' "Sticky Fingers" and popped into his battery-powered Orrtronic 8-Track tape player Frank Zappa and the Mothers of Invention 's "Absolutely Free". Zappa's weirdly satiric voice accompanied by his psychedelic orchestra blared out of the 8-track player's tinny speaker.

Brown shoes don't make it
Brown shoes don't make it
Quit school, why fake it
Brown shoes don't make it

TV dinner by the pool
Watch your brother grow a beard
Got another year of school
You're okay, he's too weird

Be a plumber
He's a bummer
He's a bummer every summer
Be a loyal plastic robot
For a world that doesn't care
That's right
Smile at every ugly
Shine on your shoes and cut your hair

"Nice to have a rich kid on the team with all the latest gadgets," Mancusa whispered to Jack.

The Mothers provided the sound track as the team bus cruised across Northern Indiana on the Indiana Toll Road. There wasn't much to look at except acres of fallow corn and soy bean fields. So Mancusa, the team's self-appointed historian, decided it was time for a history tutorial on Chicago Football for the benefit of the third and fourth-years relaxing in the luxury of reclining individual seats. Xavier introduced his discourse on relevant Nineteenth Century gridiron history by informing his fellow scholar-athletes that

Oberlin College was one of a few schools that has a rivalry with Chicago dating back to the earliest days of college football.

Oberlin's football program began in 1891. John Heisman, for whom the Heisman Trophy was named, was hired to coach the team the next season. Oberlin won all seven games under Heisman in the 1892 season . They outscored their opponents 262 to 30. 1892 was the year U of C's program began under Coach Stagg. Luckily, the Maroons didn't face Oberlin that year. They did play the following year and the Maroons got pasted 12 to 33.

The other schools both the Stagg-era Maroons played and the new-era Maroons play are Lake Forest, Beloit, and Wheaton. Chicago played Lake Forest each year 1892 through 1897 tying three of the six contests. But the Maroons slaughtered the Foresters the other three years white washing them with scores of 28, 52, and 71 to 0. The Maroons played Beloit in 1894 and thumped them 16 to nothing. Beloit managed to score 6 to the Maroons 39 in 1897, but then went scoreless the next year to the Maroons 21 points. In 1899 the Maroons again blanked Beloit 35-0. Wheaton only played Chicago once in the 1890s and lost 47-0 in 1896.

Stagg's Maroons got their revenge on Oberlin the next time they played in 1896, thrashing the Yeomen 30-0. In 1899 the Maroons really humiliated the Yeomen beating them 58-0. Apparently, Oberlin's administration had had enough of the Maroons as another game between the schools was not scheduled again until the last year of the Monsters of the Midway in 1939. Chicago won only two games in that final season. But the very last victory of the Monsters of the Midway in 1939 was against the Oberlin Yeomen 25-0.

"So let's keep the streak alive," Mancusa said, concluding his tutorial with a self-satisfied smile.

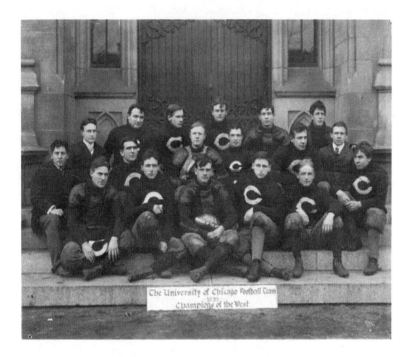

The University of Chicago Football Team
Champions of the West

Guys fell into a reflective silence staring out the tour bus windows at the flat Indiana landscape. When they rolled past the Elkhart-Dowagiac-Goshen Exit on the Indiana Toll Road Kovatch broke the silence. "So Blair, last time we crossed the state line into the hinterlands of Indiana to play Valpo, the question was raised as to the meaning of the term, Hoosier. And I recall there was much equivocation among the Hoosier members of our symposium. Correct me if I'm wrong, but I think you invoked the typical dodge of claiming contextualism."

"Glad you raised the issue again, Vatch, because this time I came prepared." Jack pulled a folded 8.5 x 14 inch paper out of his back pocket. He shook it out and cleared his throat. "From literary obscurity I have rescued the definitive opus on Hoosierism. Maroons! Lend me your ears! 'The Hoosier's Nest', by John Findley." He read:

I'm told, in riding somewhere West,
A stranger found a Hoosier's Nest -

In other words, a buckeye cabin,
Just big enough to hold Queen Mab in;
Its situation, low but airy,
Was on the borders of a prairie;
And fearing he might be benighted,
He hailed the house, and then alighted.

The Hoosier met him at the door -
Their salutations soon were o'er.
He took the stranger's horse aside,
And to a sturdy sapling tied;
Then having stripped the saddle off,
He fed him in a sugar-trough.

The stranger stooped to enter in -
The entranced closing with a pin -
And manifested strong desire
To seat him by the log-heap fire,
Where half-a-dozen Hoosieroons,
With mush-and-milk, tin-cups, and spoons,
White heads, bare feet, and dirty faces,
Seemed much inclined to keep their places.
But Madam, anxious to display
Her rough but undisputed sway,
Her offspring to the ladder led,
And cuffed the youngsters up to bed.

Invited shortly to partake
Of venison, milk, and johnny cake,
The stranger made a hearty meal,
And glances round the room would steal.

One side was lined with diverse garments,
The other spread with skins of varmints;
Dried pumpkins overhead were strung,
Where venison hams in plenty hung; Two
rifles placed above the door;
Three dogs lay stretched upon the floor -

In short, the domicile was rife
With specimens of Hoosier life.

"All right! Yeah! Encore! Encore!" Jack's recital was
followed by shouts of acclamation and a standing ovation by
his teammates in the rear section of the bus.

"Our own Hoosieroon!" Tank bellowed.

"I had suspected he was reared in a buckeye cabin and
raised on johnny cake," Heinz added snidely.

When the cheers died down, Kovatch said, "Okay, nice
performance and recitation -- so does this mean you agree
with the definition of 'Hoosier' as a rustic rube?"

Moose interrupted before Jack could respond. "I
thought it was how rustic rubes from places like Seymour
Indiana, said 'Who's there?' Hu huh!" Blaat! He farted
again. "Oops! Sorry. Maybe I better lay off the peanuts."

"No, you're both wrong," Mancusa interjected. "It
derives from the Hungarian Hussars who fought as
mercenaries for both sides during the Napoleonic Wars in
the Americas. Many of the Hussars settled in the Indiana
Territory." Mancusa folded his arms and scanned the faces
of his pals in satisfactory triumph.

Johnny Jones was playing five-card stud with Curt Miller
and Jimmy Blackmon, the other African-American players
on the team. The three black guys occupied the seats in
between the guys gathered around Jack and the guys
listening to Waters' 8-track tape player.

Jonesy leaned over the back of his seat and said,
"Xavier, man, you're wrong. 'Hoosier' comes from Harry
Hoosier who was an Afro-American itinerant evangelist. He
was a freed slave and ordained Methodist preacher. After
the American Revolution he traveled around the frontier
preaching Methodism and abolition of slavery. He spent
most of his time in the Indiana Territory. Harry Hoosier was
the greatest preacher of his day. Check it out, Mancusa.
You're supposed to be the team historian."

"Hmm, I've never heard of him," Mancusa said with
interest.

"Course not! He's black and they didn't teach Black History at your honky Catholic-school, did they Mancusa!?" Jimmy Blackmon burst out.

"Be cool, Jimmy." Jonesy said calmly. "I wouldn't have known about Harry Hoosier either if I hadn't done a research project on the etymology of 'Hoosier' my senior year in high school."

"Jonesy, you went to Gary Roosevelt, didn't you?" Jack asked.

"Class of sixty-nine."

"Sixty-nine is fine!" Tank shouted irrelevantly.

Jack ignored Tank. "Did your research really determine that the term Hoosier was first used for Harry Hoosier's followers?"

Jonesy smiled slyly. "I got the feeling you had the same assignment down at Seymour High, right Jackie?"

Jack laughed. "So, since we're the two Hoosier experts in this group, do you agree there's no definitive etymological source for the term, but there are a bunch of – shall we say – mythos origin legends?"

Jonesy chuckled. He said slowly, "You might be right about that, my brother, but I like my etymology best."

Curt Miller broke in, "Shee-it! In St. Louis, 'Hoosier' means white trash."

An uncomfortable silence followed, until Tank exclaimed, "Shee-it indeed! We got an expert from Gary, the armpit of Indiana, and Seymour, the rectum. I myself find this whole topic of conversation pretentious, ludicrous, tendentious, and sophistic. In Bridgeport 'Hoosier' means a dude who wears white socks with high water pants. " Tension-relieving laughter rippled through the group. "But who gives a shit anyway. Time to change the subject and the mood." Tank hoisted himself out of the bus seat to rustle around in his duffel bag stashed on the rack above. He pulled out an 8-track tape. "Dudes, I got a treat for us." He walked up the aisle to where Waters and Lipscomb were sitting and handed Dave Waters the tape.

Waters eyed it and then burst out, "Holy shit! Woodstock! Where'd you get this, Tanker?"

"A special friend."

"Damn! It's gotta be pirated, right?"

"Now Dave, that would be illegal." Tank chuckled. "Pop it in, my man."

Pretty soon all the guys in the back half of the bus were grooving to the tunes played at the greatest rock concert of their young lives. The sweet acrid-smell of marijuana was wafting forward from the back of the bus by the time the track of Country Joe's anti-war anthem played. Most of the teammates sang along:

"And it's one, two, three, what are we fighting for?
Don't ask me I don't give a damn,
Next stop is Viet Nam!"

Before the players were allowed off the bus in the parking lot at the Oberlin Inn, Coach Dubka called out room assignments. Dubka's methodology was to group players together in fours by randomly counting off jersey numbers. Jack, Jonesy, Hayes, and Winkler were assigned to room together. Hayes and Winkler were both second-years and good friends. They both played guard on offense behind Moose and Heinz and were on the second string of defensive linemen. When the four guys discovered their room had two double beds, they gave each other pained looks. "Shit!" Wink succinctly expressed their mutual feelings.

Attempting to take charge and resolve an unpleasant dilemma, Jack said, "Well, since I'm the tallest and Wink's the shortest, I guess we should share a bed." Hayes and Winkler looked at each other uncomfortably. Jack noticed the look, but wasn't sure what to make of it.

Jonesy said, "You guys sort it out. I gotta find Blackmon to get my cards back." He dropped his duffel bag on the end of the nearest bed and took off in search of Jimmy Blackmon.

As soon as the door closed behind Jones, Hayes and Winkler rushed over to the other bed and said in unison, "We'll take this one!"

Jack was confused for a moment. Then, an ugly thought began to emerge. His eyes narrowed and he said slowly and carefully, "You guys aren't refusing to share a bed with Jonesy because he's black, are you?"

Hayes and Winkler shot meaningful glances at each other. Then Hayes replied, "There's just no fucking way I can sleep in the same bed with Jonesy."

Winkler nodded his head and muttered, "Me neither."

"You gotta be kidding!" Jack looked from one to the other. "You won't share a bed with your teammate, because he's black!"

Hayes said, "Not saying that. We're, we're..." He glanced nervously at Winkler. "We just think it'd be better for us two to share a bed. Right Wink?"

"Yeah, it's better this way," Winkler said avoiding Jack's glare.

Jonesy walked back in whistling Marvin Gaye's "What's Going On". "So what's the score, dudes? What's with the long faces?"

Hayes cleared his throat. But before he could speak, Jack cut in, "Oh, these two yahoos decided us Hoosiers ought to stick together, but we get dibs on the shower. So don't save any hot water for them." Jack forced a laugh. Hayes and Winkler both laughed nervously.

"That's cool, Jackie." Jonesy eyed the other two quizzically.

Hayes cleared his throat again and said, "Yeah, so that's cool. You guys get the bed closest to the bathroom, so, uh, you can shower first."

The players were supposed to be in their rooms by ten with lights off by eleven o'clock that night. Rogan and Dubka walked the hall of the hotel calling "Lights out!" and rapping on any doors they heard voices coming through.

Ten minutes later Tank Stevens and Rick Douglas surreptitiously pushed opened the door to Jack's room and snuck in. "Who's coming with us?" Tank whispered excitedly.

"We know where there's a dance on campus," Douglas hissed.

Jack poked Jonesy in the side. "You up for it?"

Jonesy didn't answer, he just hopped out of bed and started throwing his clothes on.

"All right, man!" Jack said enthusiastically and jumped out of bed.

"Hayes? Wink?" Tank asked.

"They've got homework to do," Jack said with an edge in his voice.

"Let's go! Kovatch and Waters are waiting outside," Douglas said while pushing Jones and Jack out the door.

Waters and Kovatch emerged from the shadows as Tank, Douglas, Jonesy, and Jack exited out the back door of the hotel. "Where are we going?" Jack whispered excitedly.

"The Student Union -- it's just down the street," Tank answered.

"How'd you find out about it, Tankman?" Jonesy asked.

"One of the busboys working in the hotel restaurant -- I was toking up behind the hotel. We struck up a conversation while we were sharing a roach. Turns out he's an Oberlin student. Said there's a shindig at the Union building with a DJ. They've got a student-run disco, light show, and a great sound system."

Red, blue, and yellow lights rotated across the dance floor washing gyrating bodies in color. A disco ball hanging from the ceiling shot silver flashes of sparkling light from floor to ceiling. "Bang a Gong" by T-Rex was blasting out of a stereo system amplified by stadium-size speakers as the six Maroons entered the club. "Get it on, bang a gong, get it on! Get it on, bang a gong, get it on!"

The teammates formed a single wing and charged onto the dance floor. About half the sixty plus dancers were paired off and the rest were dancing in clumps of fours or fives, except a few individuals with very large pupils moving to a slower, distant rhythm only they could hear. The six guys worked their way into different groups of dancers.

Jonesy wore a wide brimmed purple hat, wide-lapelled lime-green leisure-suit, and white shirt with ruffles. His snappy square-toed boots were light brown naugahyde. With his neatly trimmed pork-chop side burns and goatee he looked cool as Shaft. His smooth, coordinated style of dancing drew chicks like a magnet. Before the DJ spun another disc, three young women were shimmying with Jonesy.

Tank wore a blue jeans jacket over an "Are You Experienced" t-shirt, ripped and patched jeans, and work boots. He joined up with four long-haired head bangers thrashing wildly around the dance floor.

Douglas stood on the edge of the dance floor tapping his foot and bobbing his head with his fringed buckskin-jacket slung over his shoulder. He wore a blue work shirt, blue jean bell-bottoms, and brown cowboy-boots.

Jack had pulled on his pegged Tuffy-jeans, penny loafers, and a Chicago Bears sweat shirt. He slid into a group of two parallel lines of dancers.

Waters paired off with a petite blond. She snuggled her head against his silver-grey-colored rayon Slazenger track-suit. They began bumping and grinding so tight, Douglas yelled across the dance floor, "Hey Waters! Get a room, for Christ sake!"

Kovatch, always the observer, leaned against the bar on the opposite side of the room cradling a green bottle of Pilsner Urquell. He wore an Army-surplus jacket over olive-drab coveralls and black military boots.

Dancing got wilder and crazier as the DJ played through the Doors' "LA Woman" album. The crowd got even more down and dirty when he put "Led Zeppelin IV" on the turn table. The climax came when the DJ played "I Can See for Miles" by The Who.

Tank shouted, "Snake dance! Snake dance!" The head bangers made pretend glasses by curling their fingers into Os in front of their eyes – a sign the cognoscenti within the drug culture gave whenever Roger Daltrey's voice was heard singing, "I can see for miles and miles and miles!" A disjointed, stumbling conga-line began to form behind Tank.

Pete Townshend's whanging staccato guitar, Keith Moon's manically battering drums, John Entwistle's driving bass, and Roger Daltrey's soaring vocals inspired the rest of the dancers to follow Tank's lead. Everyone on the dance floor joined the line, shaking, grooving, and mouthing: "I know you've deceived me, now here's a surprise, I know that you have 'cause there's magic in my eyes. I can see for miles and miles and miles and miles and miles!"

Even Kovatch put his beer down to join the line. He put his hands on the hips of a dark-haired hippie chick at the end of the line and engaged in a flat-footed sort of stomping maneuver that resembled an injured goose.

Coach Donny Dubka entered the disco to witness his six missing players shakin' their things. He stood for a couple minutes just inside the door with his hands on his hips glaring at the dancers. Douglas noticed him first. He clapped Tank on the shoulder and yelled in his ear, "Oh shit!" while pointing at the coach.

Tank shook the cobwebs out of his head, focused on Coach Dubka's lurking form across the smoky room, and shouted, "Hey Coach! Donny, come on in," while waving and gesturing with his hand for Dubka to join the snake dance.

Donny walked to the edge of the dance floor shaking his head and muttering to himself. As Kovatch, at the end of the line, passed him looking sheepish and abashed, Donny said, "Oh what the hell." He grasped Vatch by the shoulders and joined the snake dance just as the DJ dropped the needle on "My Generation". Donny danced with a surprisingly rhythmic and suggestive hip thrusting movement.

People try to put us d-down
Just because we get around

Things they do look awful c-c-cold
I hope I die before I get old ...

The six players, led by their sober assistant coach, stumbled drunkenly and loudly along Main Street back to the Oberlin Inn at 1:30 a.m. When they got to the hotel parking lot, Coach Dubka hushed them with a commandingly loud whisper, "You slip into your rooms quiet as mice, or by God you'll be doing grass drills right here and now!"

"But Coach, there's no grass here, the parking lot's paved," Douglas slurred.

Dubka responded with a swift kick to Rick's ass just hard enough to herd the group forward while he continued hissing at them to be quiet.

-27-

Wally Hass looked upon Dill Field in Savage Stadium at the end of the first half with wild surmise, like Balboa when he first gazed upon the Pacific. The Maroons had not played so poorly since the Milton game, when they were missing a third of their players. They were lucky the score was not worse than 21 to nothing at the half.

Several key players had turned in their worst performances of the season. Tank Stevens, Chicago's big bruising fullback, was not hitting the Yeomen's line like a Sherman tank. Coach McVale rasped that Stevens looked like he was playing in a sorority pillow fight instead of a football game.

Normally fleet-footed Johnny Jones was so slow off the mark, QB Cauley had to eat the ball twice on called hand-offs to Jones. By the time Johnny reacted to the snap from his tailback position, got out of his three point stance and started to move toward the ball, defenders were breaching the Maroons' line. On another play, Cauley audibled at the line to change Jonesy's assignment from a hand-off to an option-lateral. The synapses in Jonesy's brain were not operating optimally and the signal failed to register. He ran right into Cauley knocking his own quarterback down for a loss.

Rick Douglas, usually a stalwart blocker at tight end and a stout defender on the other side of the line, moved like he was wading through molasses. He was manhandled by Yeomen defenders on blocking assignments and was bowled over on pitch outs and sweeps when he was on defense.

Kovatch's reaction time was so slow, Oberlin was blowing big holes in the Maroons' defensive line that Mike typically filled. Dubka yelled at him to cut loose the piano he was pulling. On several plays when it was his responsibility to call the defense's formation, Kovatch stood like a potted plant and didn't call out the adjustment before the ball was snapped.

Of the six Maroons partying into the wee hours before the game, only Waters and Jack played with any intensity and skill. Waters batted a ball down to frustrate a Yeomen scoring drive. His punt return of eighteen yards was the longest ground gain of the half for Chicago.

Jack continued to rack up record-setting reception statistics. He caught seven passes from Cauley for fifty-six yards. He even completed a pass to Murphy on an end - around pitch-pass. Jack lined up wide right. Cauley took the hike from the shot gun, ran right pitching to Jack on a reverse. Murphy ran a crossing pattern from slot left. Jack rotated his torso right and threw the ball with all the strength in his right arm across the field to Murph. He was off balance but put enough stuff on the ball to launch it right into Denny's out-stretched hands. Murphy made the catch for a gain of twelve yards and a first down.

Despite having broken curfew to go out dancing, and downing a couple beers, Jack played with as much passion and reckless abandon as he had in his three seasons with the Maroons. On defense he threw his body at blockers and ball carriers desperately trying to hold back the tide of Yeomen racking up yards against the retreating Chicago defenders. He stopped one drive and forced a punt when the Yeomen had third down and needed only a yard and a half for a first. Jack blitzed from strong safety and launched his body over the Yeomen's left guard crashing helmet to helmet into Oberlin's tailback as he charged through the line. The ball carrier outweighed Jack by 10 pounds, but as Jack bounced off the runner he grasped the Oberlin jersey with the fingers of both hands and pulled with all his strength as he fell. The running back landed on top of Jack just short of a first down.

Mancusa also played like a man possessed on defense. He did his best to cover for Kovatch's uncharacteristic slow-footed play. Mancusa screamed and yelled encouragement to his teammates on the defensive line and hurled his body at Yeomen blockers like a berserker. Jack tried to rally the secondary to match Xavier's intensity. But the defense was handicapped by the Maroons inability to sustain drives on offense. Time after time Chicago punted and Oberlin got the ball with good field position. The Maroons' defense played with their backs to the wall the entire first half. Chicago gave up two touchdowns because Douglas failed to hold his end of the line. He was over run on sweeps around his end for two Yeomen scores. The other touchdown was a draw play run up the middle. Kovatch should have read the draw and plugged the hole. He was slow getting into position and was knocked on his ass by the Oberlin left tackle.

The Maroons' passing game was respectable the first half. Neither Jack nor Murphy dropped any balls throw n to them. But to call Chicago's running game anemic would have been generous. Instead of cracking jokes and bucking up his teammates like he usually did, Tank slouched into the huddle and leaned against Jones looking dog-faced tired. He gained a total of two yards on five carries. He ran -- using the term liberally -- like he had a ball and chain attached to both legs. Jonesy normally exuded a serene confidence in the huddle and was always cool under pressure. The Maroons' leading rusher acted dazed and confused. He was so drained of energy he had to counterbalance against Tank to stay upright in the huddle. Jones gained six yards on seven carries. Cauley was sacked five times, because Tank and Jones didn't execute blocking assignments to protect their quarterback. Cauley's run stats were a painful negative nineteen yards.

Grimy players slumped on the floor or sat on a bench resting their heads in their hands in the Visitors' locker room. Sweat trickled down foreheads, gathered in reservoirs at eye brows, then ran down cheeks, dripped off chins and pooled on the floor. Elbows and knees were raw and gritty from the natural grass of Dill Field. Players sucked on bruised knuckles and tried to straighten jammed fingers. The white jerseys of the visiting Maroons were streaked with dirt and grass stains.

Just as Wally stepped forward to address the team, a
WGN-Channel Nine cameraman and reporter walked in
with camera rolling and microphone on. Channel Nine is
owned by the *Chicago Tribune*, whose banner proclaimed
"the Trib" to be the "World's Greatest Newspaper". So,
maintaining that level of modesty the call letters chosen for
its TV station were WGN.

Mick McVale growled at the intruders and stood up
from a bench as quickly as his creaky old bones allowed. He
started to head off the reporter and cameraman, but the
reporter said in a crisp voice looking at Coach Hass, "We
were invited by the Athletic Department to film in the locker
room as well as the game for our piece on the restoration of
Maroons' football. Right, Coach Hass?"

Wally grimaced but nodded his head. "That's right." He
looked around at his team. Only one player was missing.
Jack Blair was on the other side of a double row of metal
lockers. His forehead was pressed against a locker door. He
was sobbing quietly.

Jack was overcome with grief and rage. What was the
point!? He'd given up a class he loved. He'd come to
practice every day. He'd poured himself into the role of
team captain. But then, he and the other team leaders had
blown it by breaking curfew and getting drunk. He wanted to
smash his head through the locker door. Instead, Jack
sobbed like a little boy who'd lost a toy.

The camera panned around the locker room sweeping
over the figures of dejected, beat up, dirty players. It was
deathly quiet, except sniffling sounds coming from behind
the first row of lockers.

"Follow me!" the reporter commanded his cameraman.
As they rounded the row of lockers with camera rolling, the
reporter spoke into his mike, "Will George in the Oberlin
College locker room halftime in the game between the
visiting University of Chicago Maroons and Oberlin
Yeomen. With the Maroons down by three touchdowns at
half it appears the losing streak of the team once known as
the Monsters of the Midway will continue." He covered the

microphone with one hand and pointed and mouthed at the cameraman to film Jack.

Jack tried to fight back tears while he slowly and methodically banged his head lightly against the closed door of a gun-metal grey locker. He wasn't hitting his head against the door with any real force, just making contact while he sniffled and tried to choke back sobs. Jack didn't notice the camera pointed in his direction.

Wally began to speak and the reporter motioned the camera operator to redirect the eye of the camera in Coach Hass's direction. The reporter held his mike out toward Wally.

"We've dug a pretty deep hole. You can hang your heads and keep looking at the floor. Or, you can look up. You can look your teammates in the eyes. You can look your coaches in the eyes. And you can make a commitment. You can make a commitment to go out the second half and play your very best. You can commit to playing with all your heart, and all your mind, and all your body. You can fill yourselves with determination. Forget about the score. It doesn't matter. What matters is your decision. Are you going to make that commitment to play your best, to play for your teammates, to play for your coaches? You can sit here and feel sorry for yourselves, or you can go out on that field and show yourselves and show your teammates who you really are."

Wally paused and looked around the room. He fixed his gaze for a couple seconds on each of the five captains. Jack had come around from the other side of the lockers when he heard Wally start speaking. He leaned against the end of the row of lockers with his shoulder pad.

Wally resumed, "I don't want any cheering when we leave this locker room. I want you to walk together as a team. I don't want you to run through any warm-ups before the half starts. Just stand on our side in a line. I want you to stand in a line and hold hands with your teammates. Men can do that. Just stand there. Look at the field and decide whether you're going to make the commitment I asked you to make. Let's go."

The Maroons finished taping jammed and dislocated fingers, adjusted straps and tightened hasps on shoulder pads, pulled on forearm pads, picked up their helmets , and walked quietly out of the locker room. The only noise was their cleats clacking on the concrete floor. Wally whispered to Mick, "God knows they don't need to spend anymore energy on warm-up drills. Let's see if they wake up this half." A guttural noise rumbled up from Mick's throat.

The Maroons did as their head coach instructed. When they emerged from the locker room, instead of running onto the field, they walked across the field to their side in silence. They stood in a line holding hands staring ahead. When the ref blew his whistle to signal the kicking and receiving teams should take the field, Jack yelled for Kovatch, Tank, Douglas, and Jonesy to huddle with him. Tears welled in his eyes as he said, "Guys, we owe it to Wally and Mick. Come on! I don't give a damn if you're hung over. Okay?" He looked into each pair of eyes. They all nodded.

"Let's do it!" Tank yelled

"Right now, right here!" Douglas shouted.

"Kick some Yeomen ass!" Jones bellowed jumping up and down.

Only Kovatch was silent as the teammates pounded each other on the shoulder pads and head bumped each others ' helmets. But his narrowed eyes burned with an angry intensity as he ran onto the field.

The Maroons were a different team the second half. The first play from scrimmage Tank and Jones lined up in a T-formation. Cauley faked a hand-off to Tank who charged through the hole opened between Shooks and Heinz. Jones took the hand-off and followed his fullback. Tank blasted the middle linebacker and Jones juked past the safety. He was tackled on the Oberlin twenty-two. Three plays later Cauley lofted the ball to Jack on a skinny post for the touchdown.

Oberlin went nowhere on their next possession and gave the ball back to Chicago on a short punt out of bounds at the Chicago forty-six. Then, Jonesy took over. He demanded the ball from Cauley. First he took it around end on a pitch for a first down. Then he battered the Yeomen's defensive line running bucks and draws up the gut three plays in a row for another first down. The next touchdown was set up by a screen pass to Tank who dragged three Yeomen with him to the Oberlin seven. On the next play, Johnny ran the ball in untouched for six points through a hole Moose opened from his left-guard position.

The Yeomen took Karchuk's kickoff and moved the ball steadily down field. But Chicago's defense stiffened as Oberlin crossed the line into the Visitors' territory. Oberlin's coaching staff had good reason to believe they would be successful running around left end, given the weak defense Douglas had put up the first half. On third and four on the Chicago forty-seven the Yeomen's coach called for an option around Rick's end.

The flanker lined up left and dashed forward on the snap driving helmet down and hands up at Douglas. Rick's feet were moving, chop chop, hands in the ready position. When the flankerback lunged at him, Douglas turned the left side of his body with a swim move, then smashed his left hand into the flanker's helmet and shoved the Yeoman's left shoulder pad with his right hand. The flanker ate dirt. Still moving his feet up and down holding his ground, Rick saw the QB closing on him with the ball. Would he pitch to the trailing tailback or lower his head and try to drive through Douglas? The QB did both. A yard away from Douglas he pitched the ball left. Then he lowered his helmet and drove at Rick's numbers. Rick slammed his left forearm into the side of the QB's neck felling him with a groan. Rick pivoted and threw himself at the ball carrier. The back was surprised by the QB's last second lateral. He bobbled the ball. As Rick's shoulder pads slammed into the Yeoman's chest Rick threw his arms around the ball carrier and twisted as the two went down. The ball popped out of the Yeoman's hands.

Vendel dashed from his corner position in the flat and dove on the ball. Fumble recovery and first down for Chicago.

When the Maroons' offense took to the field it was running on all eleven cylinders in high gear. Rogan's play calling took advantage of the fired up Maroons by alternating running plays with Jones and Tank slamming into the defensive line and then quick out-passes to Murphy and Jack. They didn't need to try anything fancy. "Big Mo" had totally shifted. The Yeomen were knocked back on their heels. The momentum which propelled Oberlin the first half had, by some psychological or spiritual osmosis, seeped over to the Chicago side of the field.

Rogan had not called a pass play with Douglas as the primary receiver at tight end all season. Rick was a good blocker but had club hands, so he was only used as a decoy when sent out on a passing route. When the Maroons pushed the ball down to the Oberlin six, Wally edged over to Rogan and whispered in his ear. Rogan shook his head and started to argue. Wally held his hand up cutting off his assistant's objections. He stood close-by listening in as Rogan sent Murphy in with the next play.

In the huddle Murphy said, "You're gonna love this. Douglas on the hook and ladder."

"What the fuck!" Cauley exploded at Murphy.

Douglas looked dumbstruck. But Jack cut in, "No, it's the right call. Rick started this drive. He deserves to end it. We've practiced it. I'm wide on Rick's side. I run a curl four yards deep in the end zone. Rick's gonna fake to the flat, then cut under me. Sell the route Rick, then make your cut and just watch my hands. Don't even look at Cauley. Bob, throw it high."

"Okay; on two, break!" Cauley barked.

The Maroons QB lofted the ball high toward Jack's up-stretched hands. The Yeoman safety blasted Jack in the back as the ball slapped into his hands. Jack's feet went out from under him, as he pushed the ball up and away from him like a volley ball setter.

The Oberlin coaching staff had scouted Chicago well enough to know that they would never throw a ball to Douglas within the red zone on a potential scoring play. The cornerback didn't even make a pretense of covering Rick. He back pedaled to double-cover Jack with the safety. Murphy ran a flag to clear out the linebacker. The linebacker stayed with Murph, which left an open space in the middle of the field in between Jack's arching body and the linemen grappling in the trenches.

Douglas kept his eyes glued on Jack's hands when he made his cut. He ran hell bent for leather toward the little opening in the middle of the goal line. Luckily no defender stepped in his way, because his lumbering 215-pounds was totally concentrated on Jack's hands batting the ball toward him. Rick stretched out his big hands and the ball fell right into them. Even though he was across the goal line when he made his first catch of the year and his first touchdown as a college player, and the field judge immediately whistled a touchdown, Douglas kept running around inside the end zone as if someone was chasing him. No one was chasing him. The ref finally caught Rick by the arm and yelled in the ear hole of his helmet "Touchdown! You can let go of the ball now."

Rick's senses returned to him. He let out a whoop and threw the ball up in the air. Chefski's kick was good and the score was tied, 21-21.

Unfortunately, a five-yard penalty for delay of game was assessed due to Douglas's temporary loss of touch with reality in the end zone. Kicking from the 25-yard line, instead of the 30, should not have made much difference, given Karchuk's cannon-leg. But he topped the ball on the kickoff. The Yeomen returned the ball to their own forty-four. Oberlin's offense was in good field-position with five minutes and thirty-six seconds left in the game.

The Yeomen guarded the ball well and used the clock wisely. It was apparent they intended to work the ball close enough to attempt a field goal. Three points would probably win the game. Time was of the essence.

Chicago's defense bent but it didn't break. Oberlin's drive was stopped on the Visitors' 24-yard line. It was fourth down. The Yeomen needed eight yards for a first down. One minute and twenty-five seconds was left on the game clock. They had not tried a field goal in the game, but it was the sensible call. As tough as the Maroons' defense was playing they were unlikely to give up eight yards on a running play. The Yeomen had not completed a pass over eight yards in the second half. The field goal would be a forty-one yard try -- a real challenge for a Division III kicker, but possible.

Wally called a timeout when he saw Oberlin's field goal unit trot onto the field. He huddled with the defense on the side line. "O'Byrne, Roudebush, this is your play! Run your stunt. Do it right and we get the ball back with a chance to win." Opey's and Dicky's eyes lit up. Eleven pairs of hands raised and eleven voices shouted in unison, "Go Maroons!"

Chin straps were tightened and snapped on. Guys took their positions and dug in. Big bodies in the middle of the line were snorting, chuffing, and pawing the turf like bulls getting ready to charge. The speedsters on the ends were flexing their arms and shaking out their fingers. The DBs jumped up and down off their toes testing thei r reach for a low kick. Kovatch hopped out of his linebacker position and barked into Dickey's ear hole, "I'm right behind you!"

The instant the ball was snapped Opey blasted from the right end into the left tackle who also took a forearm shiver from Curt Miller. With a groan he toppled right. The Yeomen end lunged forward to block Opey but pulled up when Opey veered left into the tackle. He must have realized it was a stunt. But, that split second before he swiveled his helmet and shoulder pads, Dickey was flying past him. The end threw out an arm which glanced off Dickey's hip. The slight blow caused Roudebush to stutter step. That little hitch would have been enough to doom Dickey's mission to block the kick except Kovatch slammed into Dickey's back and hurled him forward. The extra force was enough to propel Dickey sprawling onto the holder just as he was spinning the ball to line up the laces. Instead of the ball, the kicker whacked Dickey in the shoulder pad with his foot. The ball spit out of the holder's hands. Jimmy Blackmon, coming from the other end, jumped on the loose ball. Chicago ball on their own thirty with a minute sixteen left on the clock.

It seemed destiny had finally arrived. The worst they could do was leave Savage Stadium with a tie. But Wally's blood was up. He could taste victory. He shouted at Rogan he wanted him to go for it. "Get them down the field in Chefski's range!"

The football muses are capricious gods. The momentum which had buoyed the Maroons to play the best half of their season leaked out of them. Whether it was fear of success or all their adrenaline was spent, whatever the cause, the offense regressed to playing like slow-witted shambling oxen.

The first two plays Rogan sent in were conservative side-line pass plays with Jack and Murphy as primary and secondary targets. They ran standard routes designed to get the ball down the field but out of bounds to save precious time on the clock. Similar plays had worked successfully even in the first half. But the Yeomen rushers overwhelmed the Maroons' interior line both times. Cauley was hurried, had to throw off balance on the run, and missed his target on both plays.

In desperation on third down, Rogan called for a trick play. It was the reverse flea-flicker which should have tied the game against Lake Forest but was called back by the ref. This time the play seemed destined to fail as soon as the ball was snapped. As the ball left Shooksie's hands on the hike to Cauley, Oberlin's nose guard smashed his forearm under Shooksie's chin strap. His head snapped back and he fell backwards. Cauley was slow to break into his running bootleg. Shooks's helmet nicked Cauley's shoe as Bob was trying to back pedal and avoid getting sacked by the onrushing nose guard. That little jarring contact caused Cauley to lose his balance. Before he was mauled by the nose guard, Cauley two-hand pitched the ball toward Murphy who was sprinting toward him expecting a hand-off. Murphy dove for the ball but it was out of his reach and he went sliding chest first on the grass flailing ineffectually in the direction of the ball. Jones had started his break back to take the reverse hand-off from Murphy. He made a running dive for the ball the same time the defensive end came flying in. They smacked helmets and pads and tussled with each other trying to corral the pigskin. The only thing that went right on the play was Jonesy out-wrestled the Yeoman for the ball.

It was fourth down on the Chicago 19-yard line. The result of three plays was a loss of eleven yards. The Maroons had to punt, because there were twenty-eight seconds left to play.

Wally called his last timeout. The punting team huddled around him. "Okay, a tie is as good as a win. We'll take it. You know what you have to do. Just execute and we walk off this field with a tie." He looked at Shooksie. "You got your bell rung pretty good. You okay, Shooks?"

Shooksie nodded his head and wiped snot from his nose with a grimy knuckle. "I'm okay," he mumbled.

"All right then. Hands in," Wally commanded. The punting team let out a half-hearted "Go Chicago", then trotted onto the field.

They formed up. Maroni called for the ball. Shooksie hiked it. The ball sailed so far over the punter's head that when Maroni leaped to try to catch it, the ball was several inches above his fingers at the apex of his jump.

Maroni spun and sprinted for all he was worth. Two lanky Yeomen ends were closing fast. The ball contacted mother earth at the five and bounced. Maroni dove for it. Just as his reaching right hand closed on the ball, the first Yeoman landed on Maroni's back. That drove Maroni's body forward. Instead of pulling the ball in Maroni's arm slammed into the turf and his grasping fingers pushed the ball toward the goal line. He heaved his body up with all his strength but all he could do was swat at the ball because of the crushing weight of the Yeoman. The ball dribbled to the goal line. The second speeding Yeoman threw himself on the ball as it crossed the goal line. Touchdown Oberlin.

Final score: Chicago-21, Oberlin-27.

Team picture of the 1975 Maroons; Coach Hass's and the author's last team photo

-28-

It was very quiet on the bus ride back to Chicago that evening. Little round shafts of light pierced the darkness every few rows of seats, where athletes were attending to the scholarship of their reading assignments. Otherwise, darkness enveloped the interior of the tour bus. Only the periodic lights of interchanges and exit ramps broke through the wall of darkness outside the bus windows as it cruised across northern Ohio. Maroons were either trying to snooze or had their eyes glued to books under the reading lights. They felt like shit but they still had Econ and Organic Chemistry tests coming up, or Lit and Poli Sci papers due.

Jack had claimed the entire back row of the bus for himself. He raised all the arm rests of the individual seats, stretched his long legs out, and scrunched his back against the naugahyde-covered side of the bus. He turned away from the other passengers intending to send the clear message that he didn't want to talk to his teammates.

Nevertheless, when the bus passed by the exit-ramp lights for US-6, Sandusky-Fremont, Rick Douglas plopped down on the seat beside Jack's feet. He gave Jack a playful slap on the side of his leg. Rick said, "We were close."

Jack ignored him.

"Hey, thanks for getting the ball to me on the hook and ladder." Douglas paused to see if that got any reaction from Jack. It didn't; so he went on. "I know it's not a big deal for you to score a touchdown, but this is the first one since high school for me." He looked at Jack, but got no response. "Anyway, that's the coolest thing that's happened to me all season."

Jack turned his head slowly toward his friend. In a strained voice he said, "Cauley delivered the pass. I just batted it in your direction."

"Yeah, but Cauley didn't even want to call the play. If you hadn't butted in, he probably would've checked signals at the line and audibled something else."

"It was the right call. Wally wanted you to have that touchdown." Jack turned his head away.

"Jack, I know you feel like we ought to stick a hose on the exhaust pipe and fill the bus with carbon monoxide. We all feel the same. But, we'll win the next one. It's against Marquette. Before you showed up for preseason the coaches were talking about the schedule. It was pretty clear they think Marquette is definitely vulnerable," Rick said hopefully.

"Not if we play the way we did against Oberlin," Jack muttered.

"Hey, it's the fourth-years' last game, right?" Douglas asked rhetorically.

Jack shrugged.

"And it's probably Wally and Mick's last game, right?"

"So?" Jack answered in a pained tone of voice.

"We'll play like we did the second half today. But for the whole game, and not--"

"Not blow it at the end! Like we did today!" Jack replied angrily. He turned away again.

Rick sat quietly for a minute. Then said, "Hey, I won't hassle you anymore, but I wanted to tell you what my Econ prof said to me last week."

Jack mumbled, "Go ahead."

"Well, he asked me to stay after class. It was the damnedest thing!" Douglas laughed, then went on, "So he says, 'Mr. Douglas, you've gotten As on every paper and test in this class, and I checked your record and you have over a 3.5 GPA.' I'm nodding along, like yeah, but so what. Then he says, 'I wanted to ask you whether you'd like to apply for the Econ honors scholarship this year, but there's something bothering me.' I ask him, what's the problem? He says, 'Well, you must be smart, but you look dumb.'" Douglas laughed uncontrollably for a minute.

Jack turned toward Rick when he said the prof had a problem. Jack started to smile, then couldn't hold back and started laughing. "He actually said, 'You look dumb?'"

"Yeah!" They both laughed hysterically. "But that's not all--"

"He added more insult and injury on top of that!" Jack said trying to stifle more laughter.

After Douglas was able to control his own laughter, he went on, "He said he'd checked on my record and noticed I was a football player, so that explains why I look stupid!" They both roared with laughter and kept laughing until tears came.

"Oh shit!" Jack spluttered. "Which prof is it?"

"It's that wing nut, Ted Pointer. Needless to say, I declined his generous offer!" They both burst out laughing again.

Their laughter had roused a group of curious players. Tank, Jonesy, Kovatch, Mancusa, and Moose had made their way to the back of the bus. "So, who said you look stupid?" Moose asked.

Jack and Douglas went into paroxysms of laughter again. It was contagious and the others all started laughing even though they didn't know what the hell was so funny. It was a relief to let out pent up emotion and to let go of the grief and pain over another loss.

"Hey Waters!" Tank shouted. "Bring the 8-track back here. Let's crank up some tunes dudes!"

That was too much for Coach Rogan. He jumped out of his seat near the front of the bus and started to charge down the aisle toward the expanding group of players in the back of the bus. Donny jumped up and started after him. Rogan snarled, "After the way you played! The way you finished--"

Wally stood up and called out, "Coach! Tom! Come here."

Rogan stopped and spun around almost hitting Donny. He glared at Donny and then at Wally.

Donny said, "It's alright, Coach. We'll take care of it Monday." He put his hand on his colleague's shoulder.

Rogan shrugged off Donny's hand. Staring fiercely at Wally, he demanded, "You're just going to let it go!? You're going to let them sit back there laughing and playing music after the way they gave up on the field?"

Wally said quietly, "Not now, Tom. We'll address it on Monday."

The players had fallen silent to witness the altercation between their coaches. They looked at each other waiting for someone to break the silence. Finally, Tank said, "Waters, put in Joni Mitchell's 'Blue'. It's mellow."

"Naw, I'm tired of Joni Mitchell. Steven's been playing her all week, and it's depressing," Jack said with a defiant edge to his voice. He looked at Rogan's retreating back. "Play Lennon's 'Imagine'. It's got a good message." Waters punched in "Imagine".

> Imagine there's no heaven
> It's easy if you try
> No hell below us
> Above us only sky
> Imagine all the people
> Living for today
>
> Imagine there's no countries
> It isn't hard to do
> Nothing to kill or die for
> And no religion too
> Imagine all the people living life in peace
>
> You, you may say
> I'm a dreamer, but I'm not the only one
> I hope some day you'll join us
> And the world will be as one...

Coach McVale took charge of the offense at practice on Monday. Coach Dubka ran the defense as usual. Coaches Hass and Rogan were behind the closed door of Wally's office in Bartlett. The players were subdued and went through their drills and set plays mechanically. There were whispers among them speculating about what Rogan and Wally were talking about. Otherwise, just the blast of coaches' whistles, QB Bob barking signals, the crack of pads, linemen's grunts, and the pop of the ball into backs' and receivers' hands were the only sounds on the practice field.

McVale and Dubka whistled the team in, when Wally and Rogan walked onto the field. The twenty-four players in attendance formed a semi-circle. The four coaches faced the players. Wally cleared his throat. "I want to let you all know that Coach Rogan will be leaving us." He stopped and looked around at the faces of young men in padded uniforms holding their helmets at their sides. No one said anything. Wally cleared his throat again and went on. "It is truly with deep regret that I have to make this announcement. Coach is going to pursue some other options. But he wanted to address the team, so, Coach Rogan, go ahead."

Rogan studied the churned-up gritty turf of the practice field by his field shoes for a moment. When he spoke, his voice, at first, was so soft the players at the ends of the semi-circle had to step in closer to make out his words.

"I'd like to say it's been a privilege to work with the coaching staff here. I want to thank Coach Hass for giving me the opportunity to coach at the University of Chicago. " He cleared his throat and looked around at the players. "I know some of you think I've been too hard on you, or maybe you think my expectations didn't fit with the University's attitude toward athletics." He paused again, shook his head and continued. "If you thought that, I guess you were right. When Coach Hass hired me, we agreed part of my job would be to instill a higher level of discipline in the team. He warned me that I'd have to figure how to do that within the culture that exists on this campus and on this team. And I have to admit that I have failed. We haven't turned things around as far as winning on the field and, as far as I'm concerned, there is still not a winning attitude on this team." Rogan shot a glance at Wally.

A low muttering of disagreeable sounds made its way around the group of players. But no identifiable voice actually challenged the statement.

Rogan continued, "I'm not blaming anybody but myself. A coach takes his players as they come, and it 's up to the coach to figure out how to inspire his players and to get t he best out of them." Coach Rogan choked up. He sniffled and wiped his eyes before he proceeded. "Whether you believe it or not, everything I did for this team was meant to try to develop a winning attitude." He let out a painful strangled sort-of-laugh, looked directly at Jack and then said, "Even confronting a player in the shower."

Another rumble of negativity rolled around the semi - circle of players.

"Maybe I was wrong. It was inappropriate. But I wanted to challenge Mr. Blair to get his hackles up, to bring out his competitive spirit." He looked at the ground and shook his head again. "Anyway, I just wanted to say to all of you, I feel like I let you down, and I don't have anything more to offer to this team. So, I wish you all the best. Thank you for letting me be your coach--"

Jack stepped forward, "Coach, why can't you stick it out for the last game?" His voice was strained with emotion.

Rogan stared at Jack for a moment before he answered. "Mr. Blair, if I thought my continued presence could benefit this team, I would. But, it's clear to me -- and Coach Hass and I have talked through it -- that I'm no longer an asset to the program. Again, I wish you all well." He nodded at Wally, who nodded his acknowledgement, and Coach Rogan walked away.

Wally looked around at the team and said, "I want all of you to know that I did ask Coach Rogan to stay on through our last game. It's his feeling that the team will perform better without him."

"I'll be right back!" Jack blurted out and broke into a run after Coach Rogan. He caught up to him and said, "Coach, I want you to know that you did inspire me to try to play better."

Rogan stopped and turned to face Jack. "Mr. Blair, you and I both know you're the most talented player on this team. You could play on any Division I team. And yes, I acknowledge that you've been coming to practice every day. And I recognize that your commitment to win during the game has increased. But you still don't love the game with all your heart and all your soul."

Jack started to speak, but stopped himself.

Rogan went on, "When I took the job here, I thought I could handle coaching players who put football down a few pegs on their priority list. But I learned that I can't. Jack, you are a scholar-athlete. And I've come to realize that at the U of C 'scholar' will always come before 'athlete'. And that's how it should be here. It's me that's not right for this place. I just don't belong here." He paused, then smiled and clapped Jack on the shoulder pads. "I think you know that as well as I do."

Jack stuck his hand out to shake, then remembering what a bone crushing handshake he'd suffered when Wally introduced them, he stiffened and sort of winced in anticipation.

Rogan grinned, took Jack's hand and once again crunched his phalanges. "Keep your grades up, Mr. Blair. And, good luck with the Rhodes." He walked back to Crowne Field House to clear out his desk and locker.

A bunch of players, friends, and girlfriends gathered at Jimmy's Woodlawn Tap on Wednesday evening to watch the Sports Extra show on Channel-Nine TV. Wally told the team at the end of the practice on Tuesday that he'd gotten the word that a ten minute piece would be aired during the show on the resurrection of football at the U of C. He made the announcement with a bit of trepidation in his voice. Wally had suffered *in extremis* when *People Magazine* published its story the previous season about "the worst team in college ball". Wally no longer believed in the adage that any publicity is good publicity.

WGN Television began broadcasting on April 5, 1948 on Channel 9 in Chicago from a studio in the Tribune Tower. Colonel Robert McCormick ran the Tribune

Company in 1948 and was still in control in 1971. When he decided to expand operations into television broadcast, he announced that the Company was entering the new field because, "In television we have embarked upon another of America's adventures." WGN proved the Colonel right by producing one of the most popular shows of the 1950s, "Bozo's Circus". In 1970 WGN once again created television history with "Donahue". Phil Donahue hosted the first successful all-talk show with a format which combined political and social commentary with celebrity guests. Serious discourse was blended with superficiality as guests yakked about anything and everything. The strategy was to stimulate, or titillate, the audience up to the limits allowed by censors. WGN also became the on-air source for local sports news, where Bulls, Bears, Cubs, White Sox, Blackhawks, and Notre Dame fans tuned in to follow the exploits of their favorite teams. Northwestern University even got a little coverage. Mention of a University of Chicago athletic team, however, would be as rare as the Cubs making the playoffs.

Kovatch and Mancusa anchored the end stools of the bar in Jimmy's with a dozen of their teammates and a few friends, including Alice Novak, Jan McKay, and Steven Schwartz crammed in between them. Moose was given a little extra space in case of an outbreak of flatulence. Maroni was squeezing a tennis ball. He said he needed to strengthen his hands so he could clamp down on any fumbled balls in the upcoming game against Marquette. Tank was slamming down beers like a man just back from an expedition in the desert. Jan leaned on his shoulder. Steven kept trying to get Jerry Mansueto's attention for a critique of the new cheer he'd composed. But Jerry's attention was focused on Leyla, the dark-haired willowy bartender. They were engaged in a debate about whether the new Broadway musical, "Grease", was a commercial rip-off of working class youth-culture or a meaningful commentary on the tendency of pop culture to emphasize narcissism and superficiality. Bob Cauley was declaiming on the subject of which team, the Cubs or the

White Sox, was a more truly authentic representative of Chicago's character as a city. Alice sat on Jack's lap.

The black-and-white TV-set on a ledge up above the bar was tuned to Channel Nine at the students' request. The piece about the resurrection of football at the U of C began with a brief history of the Monsters of the Midway. Old photos of Stagg, Berwanger, and Stagg Field Stadium were shown while Will George's voice-over gave bullet points about the team's dominance of the Big Ten during the first third of the Century. The commentary transitioned to a description of the new-era Maroons. "... After a 30-year hiatus football returned to the University of Chicago in 1969. But the team has yet to earn back their former nickname. Monsters they are not as they have yet to win a game by the Midway or anywhere else." The image of Jack leaning against a locker in the Oberlin locker room, his body wracked with sobs, filled the screen.

The happy chatter of the gathered players and their friends died. "And once again the Maroons lost in a heart breaker to the Oberlin Yeomen. But football may be taken more seriously by some players at the intellectual bastion than you might suppose if you've seen the Second City routine about the return of Maroons football. Number-84, Jack Blair, turned in a performance including eleven catches for 120 yards, but the game was lost on a bad hike over the punter's head resulting in a touchdown ..." Shooksie's beer glass came rocketing down the bar coincident with an expletive about reporters. The glass hit the end of the bar. Mancusa snatched it out of the air with a one-handed reception.

Throughout the rest of the segment Shooks and Maroni muttered to themselves. Everyone else remained silent.

When he saw the video of his sobbing image on the TV screen, Jack involuntarily inhaled. He immediately heard and felt a buzzing inside his skull. For a full sixty seconds he experienced a strange tingling-sensation throughout his body. His consciousness receded to a small point somewhere at the very back of his head. He finally noticed Alice was squeezing both of his thighs with her hands. If she said anything, he was unaware of it. He didn't hear anything outside his buzzing skull. A voice emerged from the buzzing that might have been his high school football coach's. It kept repeating, "Cry baby, cry baby."

Jack felt the blood pulsing in his temples and his face redden as awareness of his surroundings returned. Except the low muttering tones of Maroni and Shooks , no one among Jack's friends said anything. They were all staring fixedly at the TV. But Jack neither saw nor heard the rest of the program.

Eventually, members of their group started moving and talking again. Guys shifted their weight on bar stools. People cleared their throats and coughed. Alice hopped off Jack's lap, pressed herself against his side, and asked, "Well, what'd you think?"

"I think I need some fresh air. It's kind of smoky in here," he replied in a choked voice. He stood up and started unsteadily for the door. Alice followed.

Steven called out, "Hey roomie! Where you going?" He stood up to follow, but Mancusa grabbed his arm. "Give him some time," Xavier whispered to Steven. With a worried look on his face Steven watched Jack's tall form straighten and then stride out the front door of Jimmy's with Alice hurrying after.

Jack walked half a block west on 55th Street, stopped and bent over with his hands on his knees . Alice put her hand gently on his shoulder and asked if he was alright. It took a moment before he could respond, but he shook his head, straightened up and said, "Yeah, I'm okay. I just felt a little sick. I ... I just needed to clear my head. I'm okay now."

"Would you like to take a walk?" Alice asked.

"I don't think so. Do you want to come back to the apartment for awhile?"

Alice took Jack's hand. They walked slowly up 55th Street toward Greenwood Avenue hand-in-hand. As they walked under the street light at the intersection with University Avenue, Alice pointed at the light and said, "Look, it's a full Moon."

Jack brought Alice a warm cup of tea. She was sitting on the edge of his bed. After accepting her thanks, Jack s at down on the bed beside her, and began caressing her thigh. Alice took hold of his hand with her free hand to stop him, and said, "Jack, you know we haven't talked about our relationship for a long time."

Jack sighed, but then met her eyes with his. "Yeah, I know. It just seems like things have been so good between us, I didn't want to rock the boat."

"I know. Me too. But this is our last year in college. Jack, I don't want to lose you." Alice put the tea cup down and squeezed his hand with both of hers.

"I don't want to lose you, Allie." He lifted her hands to his lips and kissed her finger tips.

"So what are we going to do about it?"

He grinned and said, "How about if we spend the night together, and talk about it tomorrow. We've got all winter and spring quarter to figure it out."

"Not if you win the Rhodes!" Alice pulled her hands away. "And what about applying for grad school? We have to narrow down schools and send in applications in the next month or two. Jack, we have to start making choices!"

Jack sighed again, lifted his chin, but looked away from Alice. "Yeah, you're right. I, uh, I just don't want to close off any options." But then he grabbed both her hands again and held them tightly. "Could we really stay together if I went to Oxford and you stayed at the U of C? Or, if, say, I got in to grad school at Stanford?"

Alice threw her head back and shook the hair from her eyes, but didn't take her hands away. "Who says I'm staying at U of C?"

"You did, silly!"

"Well, maybe I'll change my mind and enroll in Cambridge," she said with a fake haughty-English accent.

Jack snickered and then bussed both her cheeks trying to imitate some sophisticated Englishman he remembered seeing in the movie "Chariot of the Gods'. "So now, who's trying to avoid the subject?" he asked.

"Which is?"

"Commitment."

"Hmm ... commitment."

"Jack!" Alice pushed Jack's arm off of her naked shoulder and sat up. He rolled drowsily onto his side, rubbed his eyes, then propped himself up on his elbow to face her.

"What? I'm sorry. Did I fall asleep---?"

"Yes, but I have something to say."

"Okay. Sorry. I'm listening."

"Do you really want to stay together no matter what happens and where we go after graduation?"

"Allie, do you really want a definitive answer right now?"

"I do."

"Okay, I do."

"What do you mean, 'I do'?"

"I mean I really want to be with you, to be in your life – to, uh, you know, be, uh, like married or something."

Alice burst out laughing. She grabbed Jack by his broad shoulders with her little hands and shook him. "Is that a proposal, Mr. Blair?"

"Uh, well, yeah. I guess it is."

"You modern men are such romantics!"

Jack threw his arms around her, wrestled her naked body off of him, and gently pinned her arms to the mattress. "You prefer a macho-football-player-cave-man? Grrr-owwlll!"

Alice giggled, pulled her arms out of his loose grasp, and encircled Jack in a tight embrace. He kissed her tenderly on the top of the head, then on each cheek, then their lips found each other, and their tongues began to explore.

Moonlight dimly filtered through the lone window of Jack's bedroom in the Greenwood Avenue apartment. Had a light been on, the tall figure of a man and the much shorter one of a woman could have been seen by passers -by. The two naked figures gazed out at the dark and starry sky holding hands.

-29-

Wally had not seen Maroons' players so amped up before a game since the resurrection of football at U of C. Guys were whacking each other on the helmet, slamming fists on each others' shoulder pads, and banging on locker doors. Tank, Douglas, and Moose had each stuck unpeeled oranges in their mouths and were chomping on the oranges while hooting and bellowing with juice streaming down their chins. Heinz ordinarily sat quietly meditating by his locker for his pre-game prep. Instead of meditating he was stomping around with nothing on but a jock strap in his 295 pounds of glory while growling what he claimed was a Sumerian war chant. The line backing corps, led by Kovatch and Mancusa, formed a circle around a bench and were taking turns jumping up onto and off the bench while the others roared, whooped, and beat their chests. Opey and Dickey, two of the taller players, hoisted Jerry Mansueto, the shortest player on the team, onto their shoulders. He stood balancing with one foot on Opey's shoulder and the other on Dickey's while he pumped his fist and shouted "Go Maroons! Go Chicago!"

Rather than join the Dionysian frenzy of his teammates, Jack stepped into the coaches' office at the back of the locker room. Wally, Mick, and Donny stood in the office with the door open looking out at the bacchanalia frenzy. Dubka smiled broadly seeming to thoroughly enjoy the mayhem. Mick's face was contorted into an expression which was as close to a smile as possible with his wattles and jowls. Wally looked a little taken aback by the tumult. He might have been calculating whether the Athletic Department budget could afford the repair or replacement costs of a bench and a couple lockers. But he didn't interrupt the players' manic mayhem.

Wally turned to Jack and said, "I hope you're feeling okay about what aired on the television now that you've had a couple days to let it sink in."

Jack grinned and said, "I hadn't planned on making my acting debut crying on TV, but it's okay."

"At least we know you're not a rock or an island," Dubka said with a mischievous smile.

Wally and Mick looked at Donny uncomprehending.

Jack chortled. "I get it, 'a rock feels no pain and an island never cries.'"

Mick and Wally shared another look of incomprehension as Jack and Donny high fived.

"Anyway, Jack," Wally resumed. "That TV program really affected a lot of people. There's going to be a ceremony at halftime and a special guest called me and said he wants to meet you."

"Who's that, Coach?"

"Let's leave it as a surprise for now," Wally said cagily. "We've got other things on our plate, like the Marquette Warriors, to worry about for now."

"Yeah, okay. Last game, huh?"

"Yes it is -- for you and all the fourth-years, and for Mick and me. Let's go out with our heads held high. What do you say, Mr. Blair?"

Jack drew in his breath and gulped. "Coach Hass, I want to thank you for all you've done for me." Jack turned to Mick, "I want to thank you too, Coach McVale." Before he could thank Coach Dubka, Donny put his arm around Jack's neck and pulled him close.

Donny said, "Blair, the pleasure is all ours. Now, why don't you get out there with your teammates. It's time to call the team to order. Your coaches may have a few things to say." He released Jack and gave him a butt slap on the way out of the office.

The coaches followed Jack into the uproar of the locker room. Donny yelled at the players to "Listen up!" The hooting, bellowing, snorting, and roaring subsided like an old motor puttering out. Wally asked the guys to gather round. Players in varying levels of dress, from only a jock strap and socks to full uniform, closed in around the three coaches.

Wally looked around wistfully at his motley crew of players. They were so different in appearance than the young men he had coached a generation ago, with their shaggy hair and head bands. Yet, they were football players, each one of them. He loved this team. He tried to speak, but was too choked up. He patted Mick on the shoulder.

A low rumble started somewhere down in Mick's lower intestine and worked its way up through his gullet. What came out of his mouth was at first unintelligible but resolved into, "Grrawak-uh ... This is your last chance this season. For you fourth-years it's probably the last time you'll wear a helmet and pads. Coach Hass, Coach Dubka, and me -- we're proud of the effort this team has given this season. We've made real progress this year. Let's see if we can put it all together for four quarters. Leave it all on the field today, fellas. Coach Dubka?"

Donny had a big shit-eating grin on his face. "I just want to say that coaching you guys has been the greatest challenge of my long coaching career." The players sniggered, noting this being Donny's first coaching job. "I know you guys all want to end the season with a win. So, how about it? Can we get this one for the seniors!?" His exclamatory question was met with shouts of agreement. He resumed, "Let's win this one for Coaches Hass and McVale! How about it!?" The players stomped their feet and cacophonous acclamations burst out, "For the Coaches! Yeah! Go Chicago!"

Donny asked for quiet. His voice took on a somber tone. "We haven't had the success on the field we hoped for at the beginning of the season. But, we're making strides. Let's end the season having fun, but let's make it memorable. What d'ya say, guys?" Heads nodded and several guys responded, "You got it, Coach."

Coach McVale stepped forward again. He looked around at the now silent players. He said, "Some of you are speed merchants and some of you are stickers, right?"

Players shook their heads hesitantly with an uncomprehending-blank glaze in their eyes. "Well, you speed merchants gotta use your speed today! " Mick rumbled. "And you stickers gotta stick 'em!" Players began to nod. "Today, there's no mercy on the field of battle!" It was apparent Mick was working himself into one of his oratorical flights of fancy, understandable possibly only to himself. "This one's for your mothers, and for your fathers!"

Tank whispered in Jack's ear, "Don't forget America."

"And for all those boys in uniform fighting the Communist Chinese," Mick concluded.

A moment of vacuous silence followed during which players exchanged sidelong glances. Until, Jack stepped forward with an ear-to-ear smile, pumped his fist, and yelled, "For the mothers!" All the other players yelled with crazy enthusiasm, "Yeah! For the mothers!"

Wally shook his head, then smiled and said, "Okay, finish dressing and let's go out there and win one for the mothers."

Thirty-two pairs of cleats clacked along the sidewalk on 56th Street.

"Last time we make this walk in uniform, huh Bob?" Jack commented wistfully.

Bob Cauley looked thoughtful for a moment before replying. "Not to be excessively literal, but we do have to walk back to the Field House after the game. So technically, this will be our penultimate walk in uniform. Although, it will be the last time we walk west on 56th Street in our uniforms, this being the last game of our careers as college football players. That is, assuming we are not stripped naked before our return to the locker room."

Jack chuckled, then replied, "Cauley, you sentimental fool. Your analytical exactitude has truly plucked at my heart strings."

Mancusa and Kovatch, Opey and Dickey, Heinz and Moose, Jonesy and Murphy, Brockton and Kimson, Douglas and Blackmon, Waters and Lipscomb , the

Maroons walked two-by-two toward Stagg Field. Cratch, the manager, and Blum, the trainer, brought up the rear of the double line. The players had come down off the high of their locker room blow out. They walked in silence or quiet conversation with a teammate.

Jack dropped back to walk beside Tank. The Maroons' fullback ignored Jack for a moment. He held a Japanese transistor-radio pressed to his ear tuned to Larry Lujack's Top-40s show on WLS. "Brown Sugar" by the Rolling Stones crackled through the miniature speaker. When the song finished, Tank pressed the little red and white radio to Jack's ear. "It's your theme song, country boy." John Denver's voice was barely discernible through the pop and crackle of static interference.

...I hear her voice in the morning hour she calls me
Radio reminds me of my home far away
Driving down the road I get a feeling
That I should have been home yesterday, yesterday
Country Roads, take me home
To the place I belong ...

"You do know there's a difference between West Virginia and Indiana, don't you? Like, uh, Ohio and Pennsylvania," Jack added sarcastically.

"Yeah, they actually teach U.S. geography in Chicago Public Schools. The real difference is hillbillies like Winkler come from West Virginia and Hoosier hicks come from Seymour, Indiana."

"Jeez Tank, I don't know who's more into the moment, you or Cauley," Jack said shaking his head in mock disgust.

"Hey that reminds me, Blair, have you read that book, 'Under the Bleachers'?"

"Yeah, by Seymour Butts -- did you really think I haven't heard that one?"

"Just trying to get you properly psyched for the game, Jackie dude." Tank slung his arm around Jack's shoulders and Jack put his around Tank's. They walked into Stagg Field for the last time as Chicago Maroons. Their final opponent was the club team of Marquette University, the Warriors.

Marquette University, located in Milwaukee, has a history with the sport of football which, in some respects, is similar to that of the University of Chicago. Marquette had a power-house football program in the 1920s and 30s. They were called the Golden Avalanche and they had undefeated seasons in 1922, 1923, and 1930. In the 1922 and 1923 seasons Marquette won seventeen games without a loss and only one tie. They outscored their opponents 374 to 15. The 1930 team shut out its opposition every game except one and ended the season with an amazing 155 to 7 scoring advantage. In 1937 the Golden Avalanche played in the very first Cotton Bowl Classic against Texas Christian University. The Golden Avalanche's long-time coach, Frank Murray, was later elected to the College Football Hall of Fame.

However, just like at Chicago, the cost of maintaining a first-class football program at an urban university began to take a heavy toll on the University's budget. The program ran a budgetary deficit throughout the 1940s and 50s. The decline in revenue from football went hand-in-hand with a decline in the quality of play. In 1956 and 1957 Marquette did not win a single game. Football was terminated as a varsity sport in 1960. Marquette Stadium, the football team's proud home since 1924, was demolished in 1978.

Marquette, however, took a different approach than Chicago to the elimination of its football program. Rather than waiting 30 years to bring the sport back, it sanctioned a club team in 1967 and joined the National Collegiate Football Association, as distinguished from the National Collegiate Athletic Association (NCAA). As interest in football declined, basketball replaced it on the Marquette campus as the fans' sport of choice. Marquette maintained its Division I status in basketball with the NCAA. By the mid 1950s Marquette routinely qualified for the NCAA Men's Basketball Championship Tournament. Under the garrulous

Al McGuire, Marquette won the NCAA championship in 1977.

Another difference with the Chicago Maroons is that Marquette has been quite fickle about its team name. They were the Warriors from 1954 to 1994. Prior to that, they were called the Golden Avalanche, but they were also called the Blue and Gold and the Hilltoppers. In 1995 they finally settled on Golden Eagles. But then, in 2004 the university planned to change the name back to Warriors. A poll revealed that 92 percent of alumni and 62 percent of students wanted to change the name back to Warriors. However, the Board of Trustees overruled the Athletic Department on the grounds that 'Warriors' is disrespectful to Native Americans. The Trustees decreed that the nickname would be 'Gold'. A fan revolt ensued and in 2006 'Golden Eagles' was restored as the team name, at least for the time being.

But, in 1971 the Maroons played the Marquette University Warriors.

Jay Berwanger, pictured here in 1972 with the first Heisman Trophy, which he won in 1935. (AP)

-30-

Waters took the kickoff on the run at the Maroons' 18-yard line. A thunderous body block by Carl Lipscomb on Marquette's gunner sprung Waters loose for a 20-yard return to the thirty- eight. Wally's initial strategy for the offense was to start out conservatively. He ran a series of bucks and draw plays with Jones and Tank hitting the middle of Marquette's line behind Shooks, Heinz, and Moose. He wanted to make the most of the Maroons ' superior size before the two big guys, Heinz and Moose, tired out. Jonesy and Tank managed to gain three or four yards on each play. Chicago's bigger linemen pushed the opposing Warriors off the line. The Home Team racked up two consecutive first downs running at the interior line .

After the second first down Wally started to step on the gas in his choice of plays. He called some runs off tackle behind Kimson and Brockton and sweeps around end with Douglas or Blackmon as lead blockers. More yards piled up for the Maroons. The longest ground gain came on a lateral option from Cauley to Murphy around Blackmon 's end. Jimmy pushed the defensive end inside while Dax Brockton pulled out from tackle and leveled the Warriors' 150-pound cornerback. Starting from tailback Jones cut down the outside linebacker. Murphy skittered through the hole. He was brought down on Marquette's 6-yard line by the safety.

Chicago struck pay dirt on the next play. Jack ran his familiar curl route into the end zone and out leaped the shorter strong-side safety. Chefski was able to admire the aesthetically pleasing parabolic arc of his point-after kick as it bisected the parallel lines of the goalposts. With less than five minutes played in the first quarter the Maroons led seven to nothing.

Karchuk blasted the kickoff into the Warriors' end zone. Instead of cautiously taking the touch back, the deep back made an unwise decision to run the ball out. The Maroons speed merchants lanced through the Marquette return team.

Opey, Dickey, and Lipscomb gang tackled the ball carrier on the Marquette 12-yard line.

The Warriors' tried to catch the Chicago's secondary sleeping on the first play from scrimmage. A speedy wide-out ran a deep post, but Vendel and Jack sandwiched him in double coverage. The Warriors' QB decided to take the risk and threw the ball into coverage. Vendel timed his tackle perfectly and nailed the receiver just as his fingers closed on the ball. It squirted out of the receiver's hands. Jack dove for the ball and cradled it in for the interception. Chicago ball on the Marquette 40-yard line.

Wally sent Dickey in to spell Jack on offense.

There would later be sharp but affable debate during halftime as to whether Wally actually called the play or Dickey just decided to call his own number. Whatever the truth, when he showed up in the huddle the play Dickey reported to Cauley sent Dickey on a fly pattern as primary receiver. He out ran the Warriors' cornerback and free safety. QB Bob delivered and Dickey fielded the ball over his right shoulder without breaking stride. Chefski notched another extra point.

The Maroons were ahead fourteen to zero less than eight minutes into the first quarter.

When the Warriors filed into Stagg Field under the wary eye of Chicago players, it was apparent that, except for Moose and Heinz, the teams would be evenly matched in size. The Maroons actually outnumbered their opponents for the first time in the 1971 season. The Warriors dressed out twenty-six players to Chicago's thirty-two.

In many respects Marquette's club team approach to football was similar to that of Chicago's. Whatever the coaches might have preferred, the universities provided little financial support for the teams and the fan base was modest. Players on both teams played, not because they received scholarships, and not for adulation of adoring fans. They played because they enjoyed playing football.

"For the love of the game" is the standard phrase used to describe the reason Division III and college club -athletes play their sports. When they are running up and down bleachers at the end of practice, scrambling o n all fours doing bear crawls, or getting crushed by a tackler that is heavier by 50 pounds, the question may be raised as to what sort of masochistic love this "for the game" is.

It is the same sort of love that has inspired men, and women, to test their physical limits and to represent their communities in athletic and military commitment from the dawn of human civilization. Even on the Athenian-like campuses of universities like Chicago and Marquette, there are men and women willing to undergo the Spartan rigors of college-level athletic competition. Likewise, some young people volunteer for the military to test themselves and join a band of brothers. Of course, there are many other reasons enlisted men and women join the military, but there aren 't many other excuses why a student at an expensive and academically challenging college would choose to spend a significant amount of time playing a sport; except, for the love of the game.

The amount of time non-scholarship athletes at academically challenging colleges are willing to commit might vary widely within the team. With Marquette as their opponent, the Maroons were finally facing an adversary with some players that had not made absolutely consistent commitments to attend football practice. In that sense, there was parity between Marquette's club team and Chicago's varsity squad.

Perhaps it was the pent up frustration of three losing seasons. In the first half of that last game of the 1971 season, every player on the Maroons' roster saw action. And, every one of those players committed fully to hard-nosed disciplined play. Chicago outplayed the Warriors in every aspect of the game in the first thirty minutes on the field. The Maroons' offense overpowered and out ran the Warriors. The Maroons' defense was like the Berlin Wall.

If a Marquette ball carrier managed to find a way around the wall, the "stickers" in the Maroons' secondary stuck him.

Marquette only managed two first downs in the half and no scoring plays. Chicago scored a third touchdown midway through the second quarter on a skinny-post pass from Cauley to Jack. Halftime festivities began with the score 21 to 0.

The stands in Stagg Field were packed to standing-room-only for the first time ever since the commencement of "new era" football in 1969. And, there weren't any protesters to inflate the attendance figures. The fans on the Home-field side were in good cheer rooting for the team to end the season with a win. It was an unusually clear and crisp "Indian-summer" November day with a blue sky and a couple fluffy cumulus-clouds floating majestically above Lake Michigan. The temperature was a pleasant fifty-nine Fahrenheit. The lake breeze was minimal, so there was no need to bundle up in blankets or pass around hot toddies to stay warm. Cokes spiked with 151-rum and coffee laced with peppermint schnapps were passed around among the students nonetheless.

It was a grand day to root for the home team at a football game. And the way Chicago played in the first half, perhaps the weary spirit of Amos Alonzo Stagg would finally be able to rest easy.

Halftime festivities began with the usual hijinks of The Lower Brass Conspiracy, Big Ed and the Kazoo Marching Band, the anonymous calliope player, and the satiric announcements by Jim Capps of faux scores. Steven introduced his new cheer:

e to the y, dy/dx
e to the x, dx
cosine, secant, tangent, sine
3 point 14159
square root, cube root, btu
sequence, series, limits, too.
Rah!

But the high light of halftime was the introduction of University of Chicago greats from the Big Ten era. Jay Berwanger and several survivors of Chicago's last Big Ten championship team of 1924, known as "the men who stopped Red Grange" were on hand. The quarterback of the 1922 Big Ten champions, Milton "Mitt" Romney, and a few of his surviving teammates, also took to the field once more. (Romney was the cousin of George W. Romney, Governor of Michigan from 1963 to 1969 and the U.S. Secretary of Housing and Urban Development from 1969 to 1973. George so admired his football-star cousin that he named his son Milton "Mitt" Romney. Mitt's namesake would grow up to become Governor of Massachusetts and run for President as the 2012 Republican nominee.) The old fellas paraded to the center of the field where they were each respectfully introduced by student-announcer Jim Capps. University President Ed Levi presented each of the old Maroons with a C-blanket and cap.

When the teams jogged onto the field to stretch and warm up for the second half, Wally called Jack back to the Maroons' bench. He said there was someone who wanted to meet Jack.

George Halas, "Papa Bear", was standing on the running track behind the Chicago bench wearing a trench coat and holding a cigar in his right hand. Two very large men, big enough to be linemen for the Bears, stood on each side of Mr. Halas. Wally said, "Jack, I'd like you to meet George Halas Senior. George, this is Jack Blair."

Halas shifted the cigar to his left hand, stuck out his right hand, and said, "Jack Blair, I wanted to meet you after I saw that Channel Nine program about the Maroons."

Jack's face flushed, but his voice didn't betray any discomfort. "It's very nice to meet you, Mr. Halas."

"Coach Hass told me you were a little embarrassed about being seen crying on television."

Jack laughed nervously but replied lightly, "Yeah, it probably didn't enhance my reputation on campus as a tough guy." Laughter rippled around the little group of men.

Halas said, "Jack, let me tell you. What I saw was a kid who really cared about football, who really cared about his team. An athlete who wasn't afraid to let himself go and give his all to the game. What I saw was what college football should be."

"Uh, well, gee, thanks Mr. Halas. I, uh, don't know what to say."

"Well, I do. Listen, if you want a tryout with the Bears, here's my card. My secretary will put you through. I'm not the coach anymore, but I still own the damn team. If I tell 'em to give you a shot at making the team, by God, they'll give you a tryout."

"Wow! Uh, thank you, sir. Thanks, Mr. Halas. I really don't deserve it just for letting my emotions show. "

"It's not just that. I looked up your stats, young man. You've put up very impressive numbers. I've known Coach Hass a long time, and he tells me you're a quality player and a quality human being. If you played Division I, we'd be looking at you in the draft. But you don't, so we can probably get you on the cheap. Heh Heh!"

Everyone laughed at the joke. Of course, Halas's tightness was no joke. It flickered through Jack's mind that he could ask whether Mr. Halas regretted being so tight - fisted he failed to sign Jay Berwanger for the Bears. He thought better of it. "Well, I sure appreciate the offer. I, uh-- "

"You get on out there with your team. You've got another half to play. I'm afraid we'll have to leave now, but I'm glad to meet you, Mr. Blair."

"Thanks again," Jack said as he turned toward the field, strapped on his helmet, and ran to join his teammates for warm ups. He'd never felt so light on his feet.

"Seems like a good kid, just like you said," Halas remarked to Wally as he extended his hand.

The two old coaches shook hands. "He is, George. Did I mention he's in the running for a Rhodes scholarship?"

"Yes, you said something about it. So the kid might have to choose between a tryout with the Bears or going to Oxford, huh! Shouldn't be a tough decision."

Wally watched Papa Bear and his over-sized body guards walk toward the gate. He gave in to the urge to turn inwardly reflective for a moment. They're all tough decisions when you're that young and standing in the hallway looking at all the doors to choose from. But at least you have choices when you're young. Wally turned his attention back to the field. He watched his players stretching out, running short wind sprints, and chucking the ball around. His leathery face broke into a smile. A tear trickled out of the corner of his eye.

[George "Papa Bear" Halas]

Karchuk booted another kickoff into the end zone to start the second half. This time Marquette's deep back made the wise decision to take the touch back. Starting on the 20-

yard line did not, however, markedly improve Marquette's ability to move the ball down field. The Chicago defense was smothering. On the third play of the second half, Wally sent in Opey and Dickey with instructions to try their patented stunt on what was a likely passing situation. The Warriors needed twelve yards for a first down. It worked just like it was drawn up. Dickey shot through the gap and took a flying leap at the quarterback. The Warriors QB was back pedaling for all he was worth, but Dickey slapped the ball out of his hands. There was a mad scramble of twenty-two players diving, fighting, scratching, and clawing to come up with the ball. After repeated and frantic blasts from the ref's whistle, players started to untangle and roll off the pile of bodies. The zebras had to pry the last few players apart. At the very bottom of the heap was little Tony Mansueto wrapped around the ball.

The Chicago offense took over and moved the ball inexorably toward the goal line. When they were inside the ten, Opey pushed into the huddle and reported Wally's instructions to run the hook and ladder play to Douglas. The play worked as well as it did against Oberlin. This time, Rick managed to keep his wits about him after making the catch and did not run around the end zone like a chicken with its head cut off. He casually tossed the ball to the ref as if catching a touchdown pass was as routine as coffee in the morning.

Up by four touchdowns Wally called an unexpected timeout. While the ball was cleaned off and the chain gang repositioned, Wally and Mick engaged in animated conversation. They faced their team with broad smiles and twinkling eyes. Wally said, "Coach McVale and I have decided to have some fun. The guys who came to the Friday spring practices are going to get a chance to demonstrate they were paying attention. Heh heh! I hope you guys remember the historic plays and formations Coach McVale and I taught you. We're going to give those old Maroons in the stands a real treat."

"A trip down memory lane," Mick interjected.

"We're going to run some of the plays Coach Stagg taught those guys. Can you handle it?" Wally asked looking around the circle of helmeted players.

His question was met with uncertain looks and tentatively nodding heads. But then Jack piped up, "Sure Coach, we can handle it. Just tell us what you want us to do."

"Okay then, we're going to start out simple. When we get the ball back, we'll start out with a single-wing formation and then build on. Blocking assignments will be simple and we won't be throwing the ball much. We're going to have some fun and put on a show those guys in the stands will really appreciate. Are you with me?"

"With you Coach!" the team responded as one.

"Okay Maroons, go out there and make some memories!"

Pop Warner, not Stagg, is credited with developing the single-wing offense for his Carlisle Indians team captained by Jim Thorpe. But Stagg used it and refined it by integrating the forward pass into the strategy. The classic single-wing features only two blockers on the weak side of the center and four on the strong side with a wingback just off the outside shoulder of the end. The other three backs are arranged in a diagonal from the wingback with the quarterback behind a tackle, fullback behind a guard, and the tailback behind the center. The center can hike the ball to any of the backs except the wingback. The wing formation can be modified by placing the backs in various alignments, such as the double-wing with wingbacks at each end of the line. Using a wingback as an extra blocker, receiver, or decoy was the first step toward modern formations with multiple receivers spreading out from the line as opposed to all four backs bunched closely together.

Marquette finally sustained a drive into Chicago territory, but had to settle for a punt into the coffin corner. Chicago took possession on its own 9-yard line. The Maroons' line-up changed to reflect the guys who regularly attended the

optional Friday practices in the spring. Curtis Miller
centered the ball. Hayes and Winkler came in at guards,
which gave the line more speed if less weight. Two strapping
third-years and reliable linemen on offense or defense, Mike
Strauss and Nick Dunway, were inserted into the line as the
tackles. They'd attended the Friday spring practices and
knew that in the single-wing tackles lined up on the same
side of the ball. Another vet who normally played defensive
tackle, Jim Doyle, took the weak-side end. The line was
completed with Rex Twitchell at the strong side end. Rex
was a lanky second-year with real promise to take over for
Blackmon or Douglas after they graduated. Second-year
speedster Marco Ramero took the wingback position.
Cauley remained at QB. Jack replaced Tank at fullback,
since Tank hadn't attended any of the optional Friday
practices. Dan O'Shea replaced Jones at tailback. Dan was a
stalwart Irish-Catholic and fourth-year who was a team
manager for two years before deciding he 'd rather wear a
uniform than wash them.

When Chicago lined up in the classic wing set, there was
a rumble of recognition from the center of the stands where
the grand old men from the Stagg era were seated. The first
play Wally called was a simple off-tackle run by the tailback.
The Warriors were utterly befuddled by a formation they
had never seen before. Their coach was yelling from the
sidelines, "Single wing! Single wing!" But the captain of the
Warriors defense had no clue as to what formation to call to
counter Chicago's off-balanced line. When the ball was
hiked to the tailback running behind three blocking backs as
well as the linemen, the confusion helped O'Shea to run for
a first down. It was the first time he handled a ball in a varsity
football game.

Wally signaled from the sideline to run a fullback wedge.
Jack knew the play was intended for him. But he'd seen the
joy in O'Shea's eyes when he got to run with the ball for the
first time in his last game as a Maroon. After the team broke
the huddle and the players were about to dig in to their
positions, Jack grabbed O'Shea's arm and pulled him over

to the fullback position. Cauley didn't even notice the switch, so when he signaled for the hike, Miller flipped the ball between his legs to O'Shea. Strauss, Dunner, Twitch, and Doyle, playing with the excited energy of second-stringers, bolted out of their positions on the line. Jack, Cauley, and Ramero formed a wedge in front of O'Shea, who followed the two lines of blockers pushing the Warriors off the line of scrimmage. The fired-up Maroons opened a running lane and O'Shea burst through it. If he had Jonesy's speed O'Shea would have run for a touchdown. He was caught from behind by the safety and brought down at the Chicago 40-yard line.

When Jack pulled himself up off the ground he shot a glance over at Wally fearing he might be in trouble for switching positions with O'Shea. Wally smiled and gave him the thumbs up sign.

The next play was one that Wally told the guys Coach Stagg used regularly in the 1922 season when Mitt Romney quarterbacked the team to a Big Ten championship. Touchdowns were scored against Illinois, Ohio State , and Indiana on the play. Instead of a wing set the team lined up in a standard seven man line, but the wingback lined up as a third tight end on the strong side and the other three backs dropped into a T-formation. When the old guys in the stands saw the line up they eased up onto their feet and let out appreciative huzzahs.

The guys decided in the huddle it was Ramero's turn to carry the ball so they traded positions moving O'Shea out to the wide side. Cauley took the snap at right half. All three backs ran left in a sweep as if the intention was a run around the strong side. The whole line ran left and then crack-back blocked to open up the left side of the field for Cauley. Dunner and Strauss each took out a linebacker and Doyle rolled up the defensive end. Jack rounded the corner and laid out the Warriors cornerback. It looked like the field was clear for Cauley to sweep around end for an easy five or ten yard gain. Instead, he threw the ball to Ramero who had drifted way out by the sideline. Had Bob not thrown the ball

behind Marco, it would have been another Maroons '
touchdown scored on the play that sealed the 1922 Big Ten
Championship. But Ramero had to stop and come back for
the ball. The Marquette safety was able to recover and make
a diving tackle. He dragged Marco down at the Warriors' 38-
yard line. The old lettermen in the stands clapped, cheered ,
and waved their C-caps in acknowledgement.

Opey ran in from the sideline to replace Ramero. In the
huddle he reported that Wally said the next play was the one
that beat Ohio State in 1922 and sealed a tie with the great
Illinois team captained by Red Grange in 1924. "Coach said
you guys should remember it, because it was the last play we
ran in the spring. Jack and I were the receivers. Here's what
we do." Opey drew it out with his finger in a spot of dirt in
the middle of the huddle.

It was elegantly simple. The backs line up in the "four
horsemen" formation with the quarterback on center and
the other three creating a wide T behind him. Stagg used it
to create the original play action, which is still the most
common set up for a pass play. After the quarterback takes
the snap he pivots and fakes a hand-off to the fullback. The
two halfbacks block any defenders that blitz or break
through the line, as does the fullback after the fake hand-off.
The two ends streak down field and execute a crossing
pattern. As soon as they cross, one or the other should be
open because, if they run the cross very tight, it 's almost
impossible for the defensive backs to maintain their coverage
without running into each other or interfering with the
receivers.

Opey re-assigned positions as he scratched out the play.
Twitch was required to drop back into left half, since Jack
was taking the left end position. Doyle took right half since
Opey had the other end. O'Shea moved to fullback. When
he finished, Opey looked around the circle of helmeted
faces for any questions. Jack made the only comment, "Bob,
if Opey's open, you throw it to him, okay?" Cauley nodded.

When the ball was hiked, Jack and Opey took off pell
melling down field at full speed. The defensive ends

opposite Jack and Opey charged into the Maroons' backfield unblocked, but Twitchell and O'Shea doubled on the right end to cut him off. When the left end came tearing ass toward Cauley hoping to sack him, instead of meeting a smaller running back, he met up with big Jim Doyle. Jim lowered his shoulder and gave the smaller player a lick which drove the Warrior back into the maul of players grappling and scrapping at the line of scrimmage.

Bob took a four step drop, set up and watched Opey and Jack cross thirty yards down field. He drew back and let it fly. The ball dropped into Opey's hands on the 6-yard line. He loped into the end zone to put Chicago up by five touchdowns.

The Home Team fans went nuts in the stands. Bernie DelGiorno waved a maroon Monsters of the Midway pennant. General Whiting pumped both fists until he had a coughing attack and had to calm down. Berwanger, Romney, and the surviving teammates from the 1922 and 1924 teams rose slowly from their seats, many using canes, and sang , "Wave the Flag of Old Chicago".

Wave the flag of old Chicago,
Maroon the color grand.
Ever shall her team be victors...

Wally had one more trick up his sleeve to entertain Stagg's surviving disciples. He'd seen Karchuk practicing drop kicks for fun between drills. Wally called the long kicker off the bench and asked if he'd like to try a drop kick for the extra point. Mel literally jumped with joy at the prospect. Mick tried to bring down Mel's adrenalin level by reminding him he'd never tried a drop kick with opposing rushers charging at him. "No worries Coach! Miller will give me a good snap and I'll put it through!" Karchuk enthused. Coach McVale sent him in with a sharp slap on the butt.

Mick turned to Wally, "Walter, do you know the last time a drop kick was made by a Chicago player?"

"Can't say that I do, Mick, if you mean a University of Chicago player. The last time that other Chicago team, the Bears, used it was in the 1941 championship game when they beat the Giants 37 to 9. I think it was Scooter McLean who kicked it."

Mel Karchuk lined up twelve yards behind Curtis Miller in what appeared to be punt formation. The Marquette Warriors looked across the line at their opponents like the Maroons had gone bonkers. Friendly jibes were thrown, "These Chicago geniuses think it's fourth down. Yeah, go ahead and punt the ball!"

The ref blew his whistle signaling the play clock to start. No holder knelt behind center, so the Warriors just stood on their side of the line chuckling, pointing, and poking fun at their egg-head opponents who seemed to have forgotten they needed a holder to kick the point after. But their coach started screaming, "Drop kick! Drop kick!" Too late. Miller sent a spiraling hike back to Karchuk. Mel caught it with both hands. He dropped the ball point downward. As the nose of the ball touched the turf, Karchuk gave it a short chopping kick with a more acute follow through than a punt. The ball went end-over-end through the uprights.

After the fifth score, Wally dialed the offense down. He cleared the Chicago bench and put all the reserves in. Coach Dubka did the same on defense. The guys who rarely got to play other than on special teams played both ways the entire fourth quarter. They played with heart, if not with great skill or consistency. Marquette was finally able to move the ball and managed to score two touchdowns. Wally did not respond by trying to run the Maroons' score up any higher. He nixed any long pass-plays. He mandated that the second string offense stick to simple run-plays and short passes. Guys like Lipscomb and Robertson got their first chance to run the ball. Twitchell and Strauss each caught passes – a first for each of them in a college football game.

Final score of the final game: Chicago-35, Marquette-14.

Jeff Raseley grapples for the football in the Chicago secondary. (Photo by David Jaffe)

[Photo from *Chicago Maroon* archive supplied by Richard Rubesch, Maroons defensive back, UChicago Class of 1977: Maroons break losing streak in final game of 1975 season by beating Marquette University. It was the last game the team was coached by Walter Hass.]

When the game-ending whistle was blown elated students poured out of the stands onto the field. They attacked the south goalpost with delighted malicious-intent to tear it down. The old Maroons did not join in the fray on the field, but they hugged each other and yelled encouragement to the exuberant students.

Dean Lorna Strauss stood on the sidelines with her arms crossed watching the assault launched against University property. Wally breathed a sigh of relief when he saw the Dean was smiling.

After sharing hugs with all of his teammates, Jack stood arm-in-arm with his co-captains, Kovatch, Mancusa, Cauley, and Shooks in the middle of Stagg Field. He watched Alice and Jan McKay run onto the field and throw themselves into the melee of student-fans pushing and pulling on the goalposts. Steven hung from the crossbar. Jack smiled with amusement watching Steven's efforts to pull the steel crossbar down. It was probably the most athletic effort Steven had attempted since he took ballet to fulfill his Phys Ed requirement.

It was an effort, but with over a hundred revved up college students pushing and pulling on the hollow steel-posts, they managed to bend the west pole out of alignment. Steven fell off the crossbar like a piece of plucked fruit, but he hopped up unhurt. As the pole yawed out of its parallel alignment, the crossbar broke loose.

Kovatch tapped Jack on the shoulder, nodded toward Alice, and asked with a sly smile, "Would you call that irony?" Alice was alternately jumping up and down cheering on the others and then throwing herself headlong into the scrum of fans attacking the goalposts.

Jack felt something stir deep in his chest watching Alice. It kind of hurt but then the stab of pain filled his chest with a warmth that spread out into his shoulders and arms. He wanted to wrap his arms around her and hold on for dear life.

But he laughed and brushed a strand of hair out of his eyes. "Yeah, I remember Alice with the protestors, when they tried to prevent the start of our first game." Jack pictured Allie with her small fist thrust defiantly in the air." He muttered, "The Chicago Phoenix has arisen indeed."

The guys didn't want the moment to end, but Mancusa finally said, "I wish we could hold onto this, but I've got a Systematic Theology paper due on Monday."

The five co-captains shared one more group hug. Shooks said, "Hey, party at my apartment tonight."

Cauley asked, "Aren't you coming to Bernie's?"

"Yeah, come on guys, let's shower, head over to Bernie's, get some grub, and then party at Shooksie's," Jack urged.

"I'll try to catch up with you guys later, but I gotta put in some research time at The Reg for my paper," Mancusa said as they started to shuffle toward the gate out of Stagg Field.

Jack stopped and yelled at Alice. She was in a group of students parading around with the crossbar of the goalpost in tow as if it was a prized treasure they'd captured. "Come over to Shooksie's! We're going to party!"

Alice waved both hands and then threw a kiss at Jack across the field. She pumped her fist in the air – a victory salute, not a defiant protest.

The guys started toward the locker room again, but Jack noticed Wally and Mick sitting together on the Home Team bench. He whacked Kovatch on the shoulder pad and said, "I'll catch up in a few minutes." He jogged over and plopped down beside Wally. "That makes number-100, right Coach?" Wally patted Jack on the knee.

Mick hoisted himself up off the bench. "I better get down to the locker room. Make sure the kids don't tear it up like the fans did the goalpost."

"Coach Dubka's already there, he'll take care of things," Wally said placidly.

"Hell, he'd be dancing naked while the Vandals sacked Rome," Mick growled his wattles jiggling happily. "Good game, Blair. You played like a real speed merchant and a sticker out there. You've made some memories on this field, huh?"

Jack stood and extended his hand. "Thanks Coach." Mick shook Jack's hand, then took hold of Jack's hand with both his hands and squeezed Jack's hand warmly. He sniffled, looked away, and then shuffled off toward the locker room in Crowne Field House.

Wally stood. His twinkling blue-eyes fixed on Jack. "Well son, er Jack, any thoughts about Mr. Halas's offer for a try out with the Bears?"

Jack looked past Coach Hass at the stands. Litter covered the steps where the joyful fans and old Maroons had been sitting. He looked at the remains of the south goalpost. "Yeah, I couldn't help thinking about it when I wasn't in the game."

Wally waited.

"Coach, I wouldn't want to play for anybody but you. You made it possible for me and the rest of the guys to play football again. I didn't think I'd ever play the game again. And I'm so grateful to you. But now, I'm really done with football. I hope I'm chosen for the Rhodes, but even if I don't get it, I want to go to graduate school. I've been thinking about applying to the Committee on Social Thought. If I stay in Chicago, maybe I can help out the next coach with the team."

Wally smiled. "Maybe that will be the next door that opens for you, Mr. Blair."

They walked arm-in-arm across Stagg Field.

Author's Note & Disclaimer

The book is in part a "truthy" fictional-memoir based on my experience playing football at UChicago. But, all player-characters are fictional. If any of my teammates from the 1974 and 75 teams, or our predecessors from the 1969 team, think they recognize themselves in the fictional characters, don't flatter your selves! Any resemblance to actual persons is pure coincidence or your imagination.

Jack Blair is fictional. He bears little resemblance to the author, who was much less talented as an athlete , being smaller and slower than the fictional Jack. The author stipulates that he knows nothing about Seymour High School, except that's where a real Hoosier legend, John Mellencamp, graduated. The Owls' coach in the mid 1960s might have been a liberal tree-hugger for all the author knows.

Many of Jack's experiences at U of C were inspired by those of the author's and his friends. However, the author graduated from the University of Chicago in December 1975 and was not on campus during the time period of the fictional narrative, 1968-71. Some of the incidents in the book were inspired by stories related to the author by players on the 1964 club team, the 1969-71 teams, and some are conflated with the author's own experiences at UChicago.

The time-line and record of the Maroons' 1969-71 teams is not historically accurate as Chicago actually won seven of the twenty games played in their first three seasons. In 1973 the Maroons tied one game and lost all of the others. When I played, 1974-75, we lost every game for two seasons until the final game of the 1975 season, which was Coach Hass's final game and 100th victory as a college coach.

The description of the first game of the 1969 season is actually a depiction of what happened when football was introduced as a club sport in 1964.

The *People Magazine* article describing the team as "the worst team in college ball" was published November 1974, and referenced the 1974 team, not the 1969 team.

Illinois drinking age was 21 in 1969-71, so there were probably not many first and second-year undergraduates drinking in Jimmy's during that time period. The drinking age was lowered to 19 for beer and wine in 1973, so when I was at UChicago there were regular gatherings of undergrads at Jimmy's.

Apologies to the Loras Duhawks are owed. They were tough, but not dirty players. The Foresters were the dirty players according to my sources on the 1969-71 teams.

The TV program described as broadcast on WGN is fictional but similar to a program broadcast at halftime of a Bears game on Chicago's CBS affiliate, Channel 2, in 1975.

Portrayals of living and deceased faculty and staff of UChicago, including Wally Hass, as well as Chicago characters, such as Muhammad Ali, George Halas, and others, within the 1968-71 narrative, were inspired by the author's experiences but are otherwise imaginary.

The violence of the game of football and crudeness of young men in locker rooms as depicted herein may be offensive to some current readers. The potential harm to football players has been reduced to some extent by rule changes and equipment improvements, but it remains a dangerous sport. Young men in groups often have a tendency toward crude behavior. The vulgar behavior of the characters in this book should be judged (I hope) by the standards of the time. (But I can affirm that the "locker-room talk" I experienced as a high school and college athlete never reached the level of misogyny of Donald Trump's in the infamous 2005 video released by *The Washington Post* during the 2016 Presidential Campaign.)

The UChicago Maroons have become a very respectable NCAA Division III football team. They have, in fact, established a winning tradition. The team has won conference titles in 1998, 2000, 2005, 2010, and 2014 in the

University Athletic Association. The UAA includes other universities with rigorous colleges, Brandeis Univers ity, Carnegie Mellon University, Case Western Reserve University, Emory University, New York University, the University of Rochester, and Washington University in St. Louis.

The author hopes that the guys who played for the Maroons during the resurrection era enjoy the story. It is romanticized, satirized, and exaggerated in some respects for narrative or humorous purposes. In other respects the story of the courageous guys who played on those early teams far exceeds the story told in the book. Had it not been for them, and the perseverance and dedication of Coach Walter Hass, the return of the Monsters of the Midway would remain but a dream haunting the campus along with the ghost of the great Stagg.

Jeff Rasley, UChicago 1975

If you enjoyed this book, please consider other books by Jeff Rasley, such as *False Prophet, a Legal Thriller.*

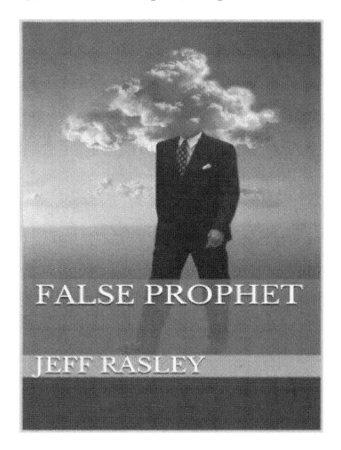

Excerpt from *False Prophet*:

Just then, Reverend Brown walked into the courtroom and up to the counsel table. He stood beside Jack with his hands humbly crossed behind his back.

Jack's mouth dropped open, but then he collected himself. He took hold of Rev's shoulder and gave it a warm squeeze. Jack looked at Judge Hole for direction.

Judge Hole squinted at Rev over his half-glasses and said, "I assume you're Reverend Brown?"

"I am," Rev replied.

The two men quietly regarded each other for a few seconds. Then a little smile played around the corners of the Judge's grizzled lips. "You're a pretty brave man, suin' the biggest newspaper in the state."

Rev continued to meet the Judge's eyes impassively. Finally, Judge Hole rested his chin on his liver-spotted hand and asked, "Are you standin' in front of me cause you got somethin' to say?"

"Yes, your Honor, I got something to say," Rev replied. He proceeded to tell the Judge about his vision. But he explained that now it couldn't be fulfilled because the remaining property owners in the four-block area won't sell to him. Rev said that the vision had been stained by the false accusations in *The Bulletin* article.

"Your Honor, sir, I got to be given the opportunity to prove that I'm no slumlord or tax cheat. If I don't get to do that, well then, I got nothin' to live for. But your Honor, if you let me show that I been doin' the Lord's work all along, then me and the church, we can get back to doin' what we're supposed to do – workin' to fulfill the vision God gave me. We been entrusted to build a holy tabernacle in the middle of what some call a slum. But Judge, there's good people in that neighborhood in Brighton. And there's sinners too. But all them people need to hear the gospel and to be served. When the tabernacle is built, it will serve all the people in need in that poor area. But Judge, sir, without the rest of the properties the church needs, that tabernacle's just a vision."

During Rev's exposition Ted Schweibel tried to object. The first time he stood up he shouted that this was highly irregular and without notice and plaintiffs were not allowed to present oral testimony at a hearing on defendant's 12(B)(6) motion. The Judge said, "Yeah, yeah, yeah," and asked him to sit down, because he wanted to hear what Reverend Brown had to say. The second time, Ted pounded his fist on the counsel table as he stood up, but before he got further than "I strenuously object!" Judge Hole cut him off and told him to keep his seat. Schweibel started to rise a third time, but Ed Johnson restrained him by grabbing Ted's right arm with both hands and pulling Ted back into his seat.

Ted had invited two associates, one law clerk, and two interns to come to the motion hearing to witness his expected evisceration of Jack's case. They were biting their knuckles in the gallery to keep from bursting out laughing at their boss's exasperation.

When Rev finished speaking, the preacher and the judge looked deeply into each other's eyes. The Rev's were so dark brown the pupils and irises couldn't be distinguished. The Judge's were a dim and bleary gray-blue with deep circles under them. The Judge finally broke what almost looked to Jack like a stare-down contest. He nodded respectfully at Rev, slowly picked up his gavel and rapped it once with surprising force. "Defendant's motion is taken under advisement," the Judge said sharply. Then he stood up and walked out of his courtroom.

Other books by Jeff Rasley:

- **Polarized! The Case for Civility in the Time of Trump**
- **Bringing Progress to Paradise -- What I Got From Giving to a Village in Nepal**
- **Island Adventures**
- **Pilgrimage -- Sturgis to Wounded Knee and Back Home Again, a Memoir**
- **Light in the Mountains -- Namaste, Rakshi, and Electricity in a Himalayan Village**
- **India-Nepal Himalayas in the Moment**
- **GODLESS -- Living a Valuable Life Beyond Beliefs**
- **Hero's Journey**

Made in the USA
Lexington, KY
15 August 2019